THE WASHINGTON PROPHECY

ROBERT RAPOZA

THE
WASHINGTON
PROPHECY

ROBERT RAPOZA

virgil
BOOKS

By Robert Rapoza

The Nick Randall Series

The Lost Tribe
The Bermuda Connection
The Devil's Heart
The Washington Prophecy

Vinci Books

vinci-books.com

Published by Vinci Books Ltd in 2025

1

Copyright © Robert Rapoza 2022

The author has asserted their moral right to be identified as the author of this work in accordance with the Copyright, Designs and Patents Act 1988. This work is a work of fiction. Names, characters, places and incidents are the product of the author's imagination or are used fictitiously. Any resemblance to actual persons, living or dead, places and incidents is entirely coincidental.

All rights reserved. No part of this publication may be copied, reproduced, distributed, stored in any retrieval system, or transmitted in any form or by any means, including photocopying, recording, or other electronic or mechanical methods, nor used as a source for any form of machine learning including AI datasets, without the prior written permission of the publisher.

The publisher and the author have made every effort to obtain permissions for any third party material used in this book and to comply with copyright law. Any queries in this respect should be brought to the attention of the publisher and any omissions will be corrected in future editions.

A CIP catalogue record for this book is available from the British Library.

Paperback ISBN: 9781036702847

Printed and bound in Great Britain by Clays Ltd, Elcograf S.p.A.

Prologue

Valley Forge Pennsylvania

February 2, 1777

So, this is how freedom dies?

General Washington rode his trusty mount, slowly traversing the snow-covered ground while surveying his troops. Ragged faces stared back. Tired, hungry, and beaten. The stench of defeat permeated the encampment, filling the air with anguish and despair. Everywhere his eyes fell, he captured the sight of men struggling against the bitter cold, some wearing threadbare uniforms, clinging to blankets thrown about their shoulders in a last-ditch attempt to fend off the brutal winter cold.

The general had repeatedly pled his case to the Continental Congress, begging them for supplies for his men. His pleas fell upon deaf ears. Aside from fighting the British, he had been forced to defend himself against a cabal of unfriendly political rivals, led by Horatio Gates, bent on removing him from his post. What he surveyed in front of them had been the result.

The bloody bandaged remains of the wounded littered the pristine snow, transforming an otherwise beautiful winter landscape into a nightmarish carnage. War is hell and nowhere better than this place showed this simple fact. As the sunken eyes of his troops looked back at him, the general, a deeply pious man, wondered if the creator had abandoned their cause.

Finally arriving at his headquarters, the general dismounted his horse, handing the reins to his orderly. He wandered into a nearby thicket alone. Finding a bare spot on the earth, he knelt and prayed to God for guidance and support. He rose to his feet and plodded back to his quarters, informing his orderly that he didn't wish to be disturbed. He entered the stone structure serving as his headquarters, seeking refuge from the dreary prospects facing the future of the Revolution. Following his general's instructions, the orderly escorted the horse back to the stable.

Hours passed as afternoon gave way to twilight, and the orderly returned to check on his general.

"Sir, is there something I can get you?"

"Bring me General Greene immediately. We must make plans!"

The confused orderly scrambled about the camp, finally finding General Nathanael Greene, taking stock of the army's meager supplies. "General Greene, General Washington requests your presence."

Greene quickly finished his count, recording it in a journal, then gazed up at the orderly. "Did the General state the nature of this meeting?"

"No sir. He simply said he needed to speak with you immediately."

The two men hurried through the snow, their breath producing small wisps of steam as warm air mingled with cold. As they crested a hill, through the fading sunlight, the camp headquarters came into view. Pacing the ground in front of the stone building was the tall figure of Washington, his hands clasped behind his back. Upon seeing Greene, his eyes grew wide as he strode directly toward his Major General.

Washington grasped Greene under his arm, steering him towards the steps of the headquarters. "Nathanael, we shall emerge victorious from this struggle!"

"That's wonderful General," Greene replied, turning nearly backwards as Washington pulled him towards the steps of the building. Glimpsing the orderly, Greene noted a broad smile on the man's face.

"To what do we owe this cheerful news?"

Washington stopped, turning to face Greene. Taking his shoulders in his large hands, he peered into his friend's eyes. "Do you believe in spirits?"

Chapter One

Mt. Vernon, Virginia

May 8, 5:27 p.m.

Five men in black fatigues, toting weapons, fanned out around the library. Three turned over bookcases and ripped paintings from the wall, while a fourth stood guard by the door. The final gunman stood next to a docent who was dressed in colonial garb and near tears.

"Please, I told you I don't know where the book is. I've never even heard of it before!" The kneeling docent pleaded with the gunman, who towered over him.

The gunman struck the docent in the face with the butt of his weapon. "Did that help jog your memory?"

His teeth bloodied and his lip split open the docent spit out blood and rubbed his injured face. "You have to believe me. I don't know what you're talking about?"

Another strike.

"Please stop!" A woman, also dressed in a colonial costume, sobbed.

The lead gunman racked his semi-automatic pistol, chambering a round. "If you don't tell me where I can find the book by the count of three, you're dead. One."

"I don't know about any book!" the docent pleaded.

"Two."

"Please don't shoot him!" the woman cried.

"Three."

The gunman discharged his weapon; the bullet piercing the front of his skull, then exiting out the back, bits of pink brain matter and skull fragments spraying from the back. His limp body slumped to the ground.

The woman wept openly, covering her mouth with her shivering hand as her gaze moved between her dead colleague and the lead gunman, who now turned to face her. "I hope you learned something from your friend. I want to know where Washington's book about the device is located. If you tell me, there'll be no further bloodshed today."

The woman nearly collapsed, but one of the gunman's associates caught her before she fell to the ground, propping her back up on her feet.

"The book?"

The woman looked up at the gunman, eyes wide, shaking her head from side to side as if afraid to tell the gunman she couldn't help him.

The man grunted, then cocked his gun again, placing the steel barrel against the woman's temple. "I strongly suggest you start talking."

Chapter Two

George Washington University, Washington D.C.

May 9, 6:51 a.m.

Professor Nick Randall thumbed through the thesis paper on his desk. Though he didn't have class or office hours today, he had arrived at his office at 5:00 this morning, coffee cup in hand, ready to finish reviewing the draft document as a favor to one of his former students. Nohel Gomez had asked for his help in preparation of submitting his final draft and, though it was a big task, Randall couldn't refuse him. Besides being one of his best students, Nohel's backstory was truly inspiring. His parents had been forced to hastily seek asylum in the United States after his father, a member of the Policía Federal Ministerial, had nearly been assassinated in a cartel hit after testifying at a criminal hearing of a cartel boss. Their family had to abandon their extended family and friends to escape certain death. Nohel had been sixteen at the time and had to finish high school in a new country while learning a new language.

After nearly two hours of uninterrupted reading, Randall glanced at his silenced phone and noticed he had missed a call. It was a local number, but one he didn't recognize. Whoever had called had also left a message. Randall dialed his voicemail and discovered the call had come from a familiar voice from his past, General James Flores. The General's message was vague, only stating he had urgent business to discuss with Randall and asking if he was free to meet at the Pentagon this morning.

Given his ties to the Department of Defense, it was no surprise Flores was at the Pentagon, although, based on experience, it wasn't a surprise to find the General anywhere. It also wasn't a surprise to get a call from Flores, but Randall was hesitant to call him back. Given what had transpired last year in Germany, the General trusted him, but Randall had little interest in another adventure like that one. His Army Ranger days were well in his past and, although they had successfully stopped a madman from detonating a nuclear device at the G-20 forum, Randall had nearly lost his daughter Sam and had taken a bullet to the leg for good measure.

Randall checked the remaining pages of Nohel's thesis paper and estimated he needed an additional two hours to finish. Though surely important, Flores would have to wait. He had promised Nohel he'd finish his review this morning, and he wasn't about to break that promise. Taking another sip of coffee, he dove back into his work.

Shortly before 9:00 a.m. Randall finished his review, added his final comments and placed the thesis paper in a manila envelope, then dropped it off at the department office for Nohel to pick up. He walked to his truck, fired up the engine and dialed the number, putting the call through the vehicle's Bluetooth connection, as he pulled out of the lot. A Pentagon switchboard operator answered.

"This is Dr. Nick Randall. I'm returning a call from—"

"Yes, the General was expecting your call. He's not available at the moment, but wanted to see if you could confirm the meeting for later this morning."

"I'm free the rest of this morning and can come over any time."

"Now would be fine."

"Are you sure you don't need to check his calendar or try to contact him?"

"No, Dr. Randall, he's almost finished and will be waiting for you. Are you on your way?"

"Yes, I should be there in 15 minutes."

"Very good, I'll notify the General."

Randall hung up the phone, perplexed by the situation. Pushing the question from his mind, he made his way to the Pentagon, arriving a short time later. Just as with the receptionist, the guard at the front gate was expecting him and gave him brief directions on where to park and which entrance to use to find General Flores. He then handed him a visitor's badge and instructed him to clip it onto his jacket before trying to enter the building. Less than half an hour after being at the college, Pentagon staff escorted Randall to a familiar meeting room.

Painted a muted taupe color with a checker patterned brown and navy carpet, the room looked like it could have been in the business center of any standard hotel chain. Randall took a seat at the top left corner of a u-shaped wooden table, facing a projector screen mounted to the far wall. He strummed his fingers on the tabletop, wondering about the General's call. He didn't wait long. Randall pivoted his head as he heard the door opening. Entering alone was General Flores.

"Nick, good to see you."

Randall rose to greet Flores, "Thanks, same here."

The two men shook hands, then took their seats.

"What did you want to see me about?" Randall assumed Flores wanted an answer to a question posed several months back about Randall joining his team. Though flattered, Randall had purposely not responded to the general.

"There's has been an incident, and I'd like to get your opinion on it."

"Okay, shoot."

"There was a break-in and murder at Mt. Vernon yesterday. It happened right after the library closed for the day."

"Jesus, who was killed?"

"The intruders killed one docent and beat a second one severely, putting her in the hospital."

"That's horrible! Did they catch the guys who did this?"

Flores shook his head.

"How can I help?" Randall asked, feeling sheepish about assuming the nature of the meeting.

Flores took a deep breath, removing his hat and scratching his head. Randall had seen this before, and it usually presaged the disclosure of something significant. The General was a noble soldier and leader, but would make a lousy poker player. "It's the nature of the item the intruders were looking for that caused me to call you. What do you know about the history of George Washington?"

"President Washington? Well, I know he was the first President of the United States and was the Commander of the Colonial military during the Revolutionary war. I also know that many of the state representatives at the time wanted to make him the de facto king of the United States because he was so well trusted, but he turned them down. Why?"

"The intruders were searching for an artifact, a book, which was alleged to contain correspondence, written by Washington himself, predicting future events. Based on my conversations with several historians who are experts on Washington, we believe this book to be nothing more than a fabricated tale, but…"

"If it's a fairy tale, why is an armed group searching for it?"

"Precisely."

Randall rocked back in his seat. "You say this happened yesterday?"

"Yes."

"I didn't hear about it in the news."

"We're keeping a lid on the situation and feel going public would be counterproductive."

"Okay, but I still don't see how I can help. I'm not an expert on Washington. My son John is a big Washington buff, but I only know the basics."

"Are you familiar with Dr. Elizabeth Williams?"

Randall shook his head.

"She has extensive experience with the American Revolution and President Washington specifically. In fact, she's recognized as one of the premier experts in Washington lore. She was just invited to serve as an Associate Professor in American History at George Washington University. I believe she just started teaching today."

"What did you want me to do?"

"I'd like for you to speak with her and see if she might have any thoughts on the matter of the book. Since you're both university professors, I thought you might relate to her as a peer and see if she can shed some light on the matter."

Randall took a deep breath. Aside from the incident in Germany, his only other experience with the General involved a situation with a faction of the People's Liberation Army who were trying to steal a mind-altering compound that Randall's son John had developed. Randall first had faced off against a murderous band of mercenaries who had tried to kill him, before going up against the PLA team. Although they had defeated the Chinese, both it had nearly killed him and John. Randall's former Special Forces training had undoubtedly helped him, but the thought of another episode like the past two was less than enticing.

"The last couple of times we worked together didn't go very well. Even though everything turned out fine, it nearly cost me the lives of my children."

"I understand and if you can't help, there are no hard feelings, but keep in mind, I'm only asking you to speak with Professor Williams and then report directly back to me. Shouldn't take more than a couple of hours and you'd be doing your country a great service."

Flores knew his weakness. Serving his country was important to Randall, and the offer seemed rather harmless. "Okay, I'll do it."

"Wonderful! I arranged a meeting with her this afternoon at 3:00 p.m. Her last class will be over and she will be at her home. I'll have my secretary get you the address."

Flores stood, and the men shook hands. He then turned to leave, but stopped and looked back at Randall. "Of course, this meeting and anything you glean from your discussion with Dr. Williams are classified. Please don't discuss this with anyone. Not even your daughter or son."

At least he didn't bring up the offer to join his team again. "Understood."

Chapter Three

Georgetown, Washington D.C.

May 9, 2:59 p.m.

Randall sat in the driver's seat of his Ford F150 pickup, glancing at the house where Dr. Williams lived. Having gotten the address from Flores' assistant, he had double checked to make sure it was the right place. On the drive over, he had considered how to introduce himself and the question at hand. Most academics were less than enthusiastic about responding to questionable inquiries and this situation certainly fell into that bucket. There was no way of knowing how Dr. Williams would reply, he just had to hope that she had an open mind.

He exited his truck, walking toward the colorful group of row houses. The three-story structures were built in the traditional colonial style, frequently used in this part of the city. Nestled between two brick colored buildings was the canary yellow colored home currently occupied by Dr. Williams. Randall hustled up the steps and was about to knock when he noticed the door was slightly ajar.

He rapped his knuckles lightly on the door and called out to the professor. There was no reply. He pushed the door inward, stepped into the home and called out to her again. Still nothing. Randall walked into the foyer of the home and discovered unpacked boxes stacked against the wall, which were freshly painted a light crème color. Stepping down the short hallway, he exited into the living room. This fully furnished area, painted light blue, had a matching flower-patterned sofa and loveseat and brown coffee table. The only thing missing was Dr. Williams.

Randall walked further into the home, softly calling out the professor's name, not wanting to scare her. Reaching another hallway that fed into the back side of the house, he paused, not sure if he should proceed. Listening closely, he heard muffled voices coming from the room at the end of the left side of the hallway. It was Dr. Williams, and she appeared to be conversing with someone. As she finished speaking, he heard a man's voice.

Feeling sheepish, he began a slow retreat into the living room, but stopped when the man raised his voice in anger. Randall walked toward the back room again, this time hugging the wall to avoid being seen. A loose wooden floorboard creaked beneath his foot. He stopped immediately, holding his breath, hoping they hadn't heard him.

"I'm telling you, there is no such book. President Washington did not produce a document in which he predicted future events. That's simply rubbish!" Dr. Williams said.

"I'm going to give you one final chance. Either you tell me where the book is hidden or I'll let you discuss it with my associate and I promise you, he won't be nearly as kind as I've been," the male voice threatened.

"How in the world can I tell you the location of something that doesn't exist? Your request is ridiculous!" Williams replied, clearly not backing down.

Randall moved closer to the door, careful not to step on the loose board again. He craned his neck to peer around the doorframe and into the room. Dr. Williams sat in a high-back chair with two men standing on both sides, their backs to the door. One man, the one addressing the professor, was wearing a charcoal tailored suit, the other was sporting jeans and a sweater.

"I warned you, professor, now you've left me no choice," the suit man said, turning to his associate, who grabbed Dr. Williams by the arm.

"Let go of me!"

Randall slinked back into the living room and grabbed a glass pitcher and plate from an end table. He crept back down the hallway and stopped just short of the doorway. He then tossed the plate onto the far end of the wooden floor, causing it to shatter.

"What the hell was that?" One intruder yelled out. "Go out there and check!"

Randall raised the pitcher over his head and waited for the gunman to exit the room. He heard footsteps from the room and tensed. The sweater man exited into the hallway, caught Randall out of the corner of his eye and spun in his direction, gun in hand.

Randall dropped the pitcher onto the man's outstretched gun hand, knocking the gun from his grip and shattering the pitcher and the man's hand. The sweater man yelped in pain. Randall rushed him, tackling him into the wall. The sweater man's head snapped back and into the wall, making a loud cracking sound. His body flopped back onto Randall who fell, rear first, to the ground, the sweater man landing on top of him.

The suited man strode into the hallway, clearly having heard the commotion. Upon seeing his comrade unconscious, his eyes went wide with anger. "I'll kill you for this, you son of a bitch!" He drew his weapon from beneath his coat.

Randall shielded his face from the impending gunshot, helpless to stop the attacker. Dr. Williams sprinted from the room, jumped onto the gunman's back, and yanked at his hair. "Take that Yank!"

The gunman slapped at her, trying his best to knock her off. Randall wasted no time, pushing the slumped intruder's body off and jumping to his feet. He rushed the gunman, who was too busy fighting Dr. Williams to get off a clean shot. The gunman fired wildly into the air, his view obscured by Dr. William's fingers which dug into his eyes.

Randall yelled, "Lookout!" as a warning to Dr. Williams, before tackling the second gunman to the ground. The three tumbled to the floor, a tangle of legs, arms and bodies.

The gun skittered to the ground, out of reach of the gunman, who flopped off to the side of the scrum, leaving Randall straddling Dr. Williams. She looked up at him; her face mere inches from his own. She wore a concerned look on her face. "I'm not sure who you are, and appreciate your help, but I'd appreciate if you got off of me."

The gunman moaned, calling Randall's attention back to him. Randall stood, walked over to the pistol, and picked it up before the gunman could regain his feet.

"Hold it right there," Randall said, pointing the gun at the intruder's chest. The man slowly stood and took a single step toward Randall, who cocked the hammer. The man immediately stopped. "Call the police," Randall said to Dr. Williams.

"Right!" Dr. Williams exited the room.

"Who are you, and what do you want?"

The man said nothing. Randall could see the resolve in his eyes. Whoever these guys were, they wouldn't talk.

Dr. Williams returned from the other room. "The police are on their way."

Randall nodded, keeping a close eye on the gunman.

"I'm glad you came along when you did. Those fellas looked like trouble." Williams said, stepping next to Randall. She stood close to him, a look of relief on her face.

"I'm glad too Dr. Williams."

"Please, call me Liz," she cocked her head to the side. "I'm assuming you're Nick?"

"That's right. I guess General Flores explained why I was coming to speak with you."

Before Liz could answer, a knock came at the door.

"I'll get that. I'm sure it's the police," Liz said before disappearing down the hallway. She returned a minute later, four metropolitan officers following closely behind. Moments later, they were joined by the paramedics who tended to the sweater man while the police took the suit man into custody. "Mr. and Mrs. Randall, I'll need the two of you to come down to the station to answer some questions and file a report."

"We're not married," Randall replied, shaking his head.

"That's right, officer. Dr. Randall had just stopped by for a visit," Liz said.

"I see. We'll still need both of you to come down to the station," the officer said.

"Of course, I just need to make a call first," Randall replied.

"Make it fast."

Randall slipped into Liz's back office, calling Flores to explain what had happened. Hanging up, he rejoined her. The police then escorted them down to a waiting police car and loaded into the back.

"What did General Flores say about the reason for my visit?"

Liz smiled. "He said it had something to do with your President Washington. I'm guessing this might be related to the book those two men were searching for?"

"General Flores was curious to find out what you know about the book and thought we might speak as peers."

"I see. So, what would like to know?" Liz pursed her lips.

"To start, what do you know about this book by President Washington?"

Liz brushed a hair from her face. "It's a fairy tale. A lark! There's absolutely no truth to the story about the book! It was concocted by someone wanting their fifteen minutes of fame by invoking the name of your president."

"Then why are these guys looking for it? And who are they?"

Elizabeth shrugged. "Crackpots I guess." She crossed her legs, cupping her chin in her hand. "What exactly does General Flores do and how does it involve you?"

"That's a long story."

"We seem to have plenty of time," Liz replied.

She had a point. Randall began his explanation as the police cruiser pulled from the curb.

Chapter Four

The police escorted Liz and Randall to the D.C. Central Detention Facility on D Street. Sitting near the Anacostia River, the facility's sorted and colorful history was best summed up by a long-time inmate of the DC Jail who claimed that 9 years in the DC Jail was equivalent to 20 years in another prison. The inmate told of moldy jail cells, questionable strip searches, broken locks on cell doors, and a litany of other offenses against inmates. Blocky in design, the brick colored facility stood in stark contrast to the cobalt blue sky. As the squad car carrying them pulled up to facility, Randall immediately recognized a familiar face wearing the unmistakable dress blue uniform issued to Air Force officers.

The tall, handsome man stood at attention, his brown eyes following the police officer, who opened the back door of the squad car for Randall and Liz to exit. The hint of a grin on the officer's face belied his feelings at seeing the professor for the first time in nearly a year.

"Professor Randall, good to see you," Michael Flores said to Randall, extending his hand.

Randall ignored the outstretched arm, choosing instead to grip Michael in a hug. "Great to see you, Michael! I guess you're working for you father now."

His professional veneer all but worn away, Michael wore a full-blown smile now. "It's good to see you too, Nick. Yeah, I guess dad figured it was better to keep me close by so he could keep an eye on me."

Randall noted Liz had joined them, standing to his right and slightly behind him. Michael's eyes shifted to her. He extended a hand. "Michael Flores, pleasure to meet you."

"The pleasure's mine," Liz said, smiling warmly.

"Sorry, where are my manners?" Randall said.

"I don't know. Where?" Liz jabbed.

Michael laughed. "Why don't we go inside?"

The three followed the police officers into the jailhouse and into a meeting area near the main squad room, past the officers' desks. Michael requested time alone with Randall and Liz, earning a hard glare from the arresting officer, who was clearly irritated with his interference. The officer grudgingly agreed.

"So, what happened?" Michael asked.

"When I got to Dr. Williams' home…"

"… it's Liz."

"When I got to Liz's home, I found her front door open and those two guys questioning her. From the sound of their tone, it looked like things were getting testy."

Liz sighed and nodded. "All joking aside, I owe Nick my life. If he hadn't arrived when he did, there's no telling what those men would have done to me."

"What did they want from you?" Michael asked.

"They were looking for a book allegedly written by President Washington," Liz answered.

"What did you tell them?" Michael asked.

"That they're bloody crazy! There is no book of predictions, which is the same thing I was going to tell Nick to relay to your father."

Michael blinked at Liz's directness, then furrowed his brow, causing Randall to smile. *Nice to see someone else in her crosshairs.*

"With all due respect Dr. Williams…"

"…Liz."

"There was another attack yesterday by men trying to find the book, and they killed several people. Highly trained men carried out that attack using military tactics similar to those used by our own armed services. It's highly unlikely that they would be engaged in such an exercise if they didn't have concrete proof of the book's existence."

Liz's demeanor softened. "I'm sorry Michael. I don't doubt you, but unfortunately, I'm not sure what I can do to help. In all of my years of researching Washington, I've never come across anything that leads me to believe in the book's existence."

"But you've heard of the book?" Randall asked, joining the conversation.

Liz nodded. "Yes, I've heard of the book, but mostly from fringe sources—the kind you find in the tabloids. There's never been a single historical researcher of any significance who has lent any credence to the idea."

Michael turned toward the squad room. "Hopefully, we'll be able to get some answers from those two."

Chapter Five

Ivangorod, Leningrad Oblast, Russia

May 10, 6:29 a.m.

Warm air poured from Vasily Aminov's mouth, forming small clouds whipped into whirlpools of white by the frigid air as he walked along the outer wall of the citadel overlooking the Narva River. Ivangorod Fortress had seen much turmoil in its long history. Built by Ivan III in 1492, the Russian medieval castle was intended to reaffirm Russia's right to access the sea and form a bulwark against the Teutonic Order, which dominated the Baltics.

Aminov tugged up the collar of his fur lined wool coat against a blast of artic air rising from the river as he turned the corner of the outer wall before ducking inside the main entrance to the fortress. He strode by a line of tourists waiting impatiently to buy tickets, brushing past a man attempting to flag him down with a question. He had no time for such foolishness today. Awaiting him in his office was his team leader, whose men were unsuccessful in capturing the British academic in America.

Fools. How could they have failed at such a simple task?

He hurried as he punched his way through the door marked *Стой, только частный персонал* in Cyrillic letters. Roughly translated to *Halt, private personnel only* the warning dissuaded anyone from trying to follow him in.

Aminov moved past the gray cubicles manned by museum staff forming the outer ring of the office complex. He grunted as he glared at the men and women manning the phones and computers, no longer hiding his disdain at the intrusion into his operations.

Soon we'll no longer need to maintain this facade.

During the inception phase of the project, the museum had served as a convenient cover for the operation. Aminov, a former Spetsnaz agent, had leveraged his experience running covert operations behind the guise of a legitimate business to ensure the project's success, carefully disguising the hidden operation taking place beneath the surface of the fortress. Playing upon the emotions of his former contacts, his plan to deal a crippling blow to the United States had garnered him a high level of financial and political support from fellow operatives and those in a position of power within the new Russian government.

Now, after decades of planning, he was on the verge of pulling off something that the previous communist regime had only dreamt of doing — ending American hegemony throughout the world. The prospect was intoxicating, and Aminov had to frequently remind the others that several key events still had to fall into place before their plan could come to fruition. Failing to execute all remaining steps could still result in utter failure. This prospect served as a sobering reminder that decades of planning could result in nothing more than public humiliation, and failure would be met with swift and thorough punishment. The remains of operatives who had failed to deliver for their masters littered the history of the Soviet Union and Aminov needed no help to understand what would become of him if he failed.

The guard stationed outside the door to his office snapped to attention, saluting his commander as he held the door open. Aminov brusquely returned the salute, moving through the doorway without breaking stride. As he entered, the enormous man seated on the opposite side of his desk popped to attention. "Commander Aminov."

Aminov glared at the man whose eyes went wide with fear despite his size advantage.

"You failed me Sasha."

"Commander, they ambushed my men while interrogating the subject. There was little they could do."

"A fifty-year-old academic and a female professor overpowered your men?

"Sir, the American has ties to a secret branch of the military. Apparently, he's been involved in at least two other operations, according to our sources."

Aminov's brow raised at the news. "Are you saying he's an American operative?"

"We're uncertain, but we're seeking additional information."

Aminov eased into his seat, Sasha still standing at attention.

Good, he knows his place. "Sit down."

Sasha did as instructed, dropping quickly into his chair.

"What do we know of this American?"

"Here is the information we've been able to gather," Sasha handed his commander a dossier titled Nick Randall.

Aminov snatched it from his hand, then read it carefully. Professor Nick Randall was an archeology processor at Georgetown University, an appointment which almost didn't happen. Apparently, he had a knack for angering those in a position of authority by questioning their decisions. Aminov smiled inwardly at the assessment, one which was certainly on a folder bearing his name somewhere in the Byzantine archives of the former Soviet republic. The feeling quickly evaporated. Such men were dangerous adversaries, their behavior difficult to predict, especially under duress.

He continued reading. The professor had taken part in a top-secret military operation in the Antarctic known as 'Operation Ice Hammer.' While details were sparse, he had apparently assisted the military in acquiring top secret technology in a surgical military strike against a well-equipped faction of the Chinese military. While this was impressive, it wasn't his only field experience. He had played an instrumental role in foiling a plot to assassinate the President and other assembled leaders at the recently completed G20 summit in Germany. Clearly, this man wasn't a simple professor. But if not, then what was he? It wouldn't be the first case of an American spy posing as an academic. Aminov closed the folder, resting his hands on the desk.

"As you can see, commander, this man is clearly a trained operative. With the benefit of surprise, my men didn't stand a chance against him. "

Aminov lifted his eyes to Sasha, who was clearly seeking to quell his commander's anger. What did the Americans call it? He was covering his ass. Still, there was something about the situation that warranted further examination.

"Your assessment of the American is highly presumptuous. The details about his background are incomplete."

Sasha inhaled deeply.

"Your captured men. Can we count on them to resist interrogation?"

Sasha snatched at the ray of hope offered by his commander. "They are two of my most loyal men. I will attest to their allegiance. They will disclose nothing."

"For your sake Sasha, I hope you are right."

Chapter Six

Randall leaned back into a round leather chair, staring out the window onto the Potomac River. Though partially obscured by the tall, white posts framing the long window panes, the riverfront view was majestic. Small boats plied their way down the waterway, the tree lined shores of the Potomac serving as their serene backdrop. After leaving the police station, Michael had suggested they grab dinner and discuss the day's events. Having not eaten anything except a piece of toast and fruit for breakfast, Randall willingly agreed. When the question of where to eat was raised, Liz had suggested Fiola Mare, a beautiful Italian restaurant where she had eaten with a colleague upon her arrival.

Given the situation and the secrecy Flores had spoken to, but also knowing that John would love to speak with Liz, given his interest in all things George Washington, Randall had asked Liz and Michael if John could join them. Neither had taken issue with this, so Randall had invited his son to join them. John had jumped at the chance, telling his father he would join them after work.

Drink in hand and enjoying the view, Randall had to admit her recommendation had been a good one. As the fog lazily rolled in and the setting sun slowly dipped below the horizon, Randall felt perfectly content enjoying his Vodka Tonic, waiting for dinner to arrive. He and Liz had driven over together, Michael having to report in to his commanding officer before joining them. The ride had given the two a chance to get to know each other and he and Liz had hit it off, sharing stories about teaching, family, and a love of history.

"Did you miss me?" Liz said, returning from the lady's room.

Randall turned to face her. Somehow, despite the calamitous series of events that had befallen them, Liz looked absolutely stunning. So much so that Randall momentarily found himself at a loss for words. He quickly recovered. "Great pick for the restaurant. There's an incredible view from here."

Liz grinned. "Dr. Randall, you say the sweetest things! It's amazing what a little makeup and a hair brush can accomplish."

Blushing, Randall stood from his chair, holding Liz's seat as she sat down. "I hope you don't mind, but I ordered some middle neck clams as an appetizer."

"Sounds wonderful," Liz said, smiling.

Liz opened the beverage menu and inquired about his choice of drink.

"I've never had a Vodka Tonic. I think I'll try one!"

The server brought Liz her drink, which she sipped while thumbing through the menu. She placed it down, apparently having decided what she would order. "I'm excited to meet your son, John. We professors can rarely say we have fans."

"Rest assured you do. He'll be just as excited to meet you. He really enjoys American history, especially about the Revolutionary War and George Washington. I'm sure he'll enjoy hearing about how he's perceived by British scholars."

Almost as if on cue, John walked into the restaurant. Spotting his father, he waved, saying something to the maitre de, who escorted him to their table.

"John, I'd like to introduce you to Dr. Liz Williams."

"It's a pleasure to meet you. I've heard a great deal about your work and was excited to hear that you were coming to teach here. I don't know if my dad told you, but I'm a big George Washington buff and I'm looking forward to speaking with you about him."

Liz stood, extending her hand. "The pleasure's mine, John. Yes, your father was just telling me about your interest in President Washington. He was asking me what the English thought about him. A bit of colonial spying, you might say." Liz winked.

A broad smile spread across John's face, "I guess you could call it that. Unfortunately, my dad really didn't tell me much about his visit. Guess he's not cut out for the spy business."

Randall shook his head, serving as the subject of everyone's humor. He chuckled as John took his seat.

"So, how was the visit?" John asked, folding his hands on the table in front of him.

"Your father makes quite a first impression," Liz said, smiling.

John's gaze shifted to his father, the look on his face conveying his confusion.

"Do you remember General Flores?"

John nodded.

"He asked me to pay Liz a visit today. He called me this

morning when I was editing a student's graduate paper." Randall said.

"Nohel?" John asked, knowing his father had promised to help him.

"Right. He needed it back today, so I got up early and headed to the office to finish reviewing it. Anyway, when I got to Liz's house, the front door was open, so I went inside and found two thugs were questioning her about a book that President Washington allegedly wrote. Things were getting heated, so I stepped in to help," Randall explained. He then shared the rest of the story with Michael, taking through the meeting with Michael at the jail.

"I'm so glad you're okay, Dr. Williams. Sounds like a scary situation," John said, his voice conveying his concern.

"Thank you, John, and please call me Liz."

"Liz, what do you think about this secret book? Have you come across anything that leads you to believe you might know its whereabouts?"

For the first time in the evening, Liz's expression turned serious. "At first, I told your father it was just the figment of the imagination. Something concocted for one of those conspiracy shows, but now I'm not so sure."

"Do you think it could have something to do with the Freemasons? I understand General Washington was a high-ranking member of the organization," John stated.

"I guess it's possible. On the way over, I started thinking about some of the more outlandish tales concerning your late president and something struck me. It was something a fellow Washington researcher had uncovered, and he asked if I could verify it."

"What is it?" Randall asked.

"I don't know how familiar you are with the specifics of

the relationship between Washington and Ben Franklin, but the two were very fond of each other."

"Franklin was one of the few people Washington felt safe confiding in. When he was at Valley Forge, several state representatives were trying to remove him from his post as General of the revolutionary forces," John commented.

"Very good John. You know your Washington history. As you say, the war with England deeply divided the colonies and there were some who also became jealous of General Washington."

"But not Benjamin Franklin?" Randall asked.

"Correct. Mr. Franklin was 26 years older than Washington and was already an elder statesman by the time General Washington faced this crisis. In 1775, at 69, Franklin traveled from Philadelphia to Massachusetts to meet with Washington after he was named commander-in-chief of the Continental Army. Despite the opposition from certain politicians, Franklin was one of Washington's strongest supporters in the congress. He also spoke highly of Washington to the French Court while serving as a diplomat there. Franklin and Washington engaged in a long exchange of letters, starting from the early days of the imperial crisis to the last days of Franklin's life."

"What does that have to do with the book of predictions?" Randall asked.

"In May 1787, Washington arrived in Philadelphia, a day prior to the constitutional convention. The first thing he did was to seek Franklin, to speak about the upcoming proceedings which would either lead to a stronger central government for the young nation or for the splitting of the country along state lines," Liz Explained.

"There was concern that states wouldn't compromise

enough to create the framework for a unified country," John added.

"Correct. However, there were rumors that the nature of the meeting between the men veered away from planning to keep the union together."

"What do you mean?" Randall asked, his eyes narrowing.

"This researcher, who approached me, claimed that Washington disclosed an odd encounter he had at Valley Forge to Franklin. It seems the general was seeking Franklin's counsel." Liz replied.

"What sort of encounter?" Randall asked.

Liz bit her lip, hesitating to disclose any additional information.

"It's okay, Liz, please continue," Randall offered, placing his hand on her arm to encourage her.

Liz exhaled and shook her head as if doubting she should even utter the words. "This researcher claimed that a spirit who disclosed events about the future of the country visited the general. Apparently, Washington was so moved by the experience, he allegedly recorded the events in as much detail as possible so he wouldn't forget them."

"Washington's book of predictions," Randall said. "What else did this researcher say?"

"Not a great deal more. He asked me my opinion, and I told him the story was nonsense and that I had never heard of such a thing. I also advised him that if he wanted to be taken seriously as a researcher, he should stop pursuing such silly notions and focus on real research," Liz explained.

"What happened next?" Randall asked.

"He was quite upset. I tried to explain that as a serious researcher and professor, I couldn't be associated with such madness, but he stormed out before I could finish. Now, I'm less certain about the encounter and I feel bad for turning him away."

"What was his name?" John asked.

Liz's cheeks turned a deep shade of red. "I don't know. He was in such a hurry to see me he never introduced himself. He just started talking quickly about the book and once I replied to his question, he left without telling me. I hope you both don't think less of me for the way I treated that young fellow."

Randall could see the sadness in Liz's eyes. He grasped her hand to comfort her. "Don't worry Liz. I understand the pressure to conform in the academic world and how difficult it can be for those who don't follow the narrative."

Liz smiled, clearly relieved by Randall's response. She squeezed his hand to convey her thanks. Randall spotted Michael entering the restaurant and speaking to the same maitre de John had spoken to earlier. The man pointed at their table, and Michael made his way over, joining the others. Randall noted the serious expression on his face.

"Any news?" Randall asked as Michael took an open seat.

"Yes, and I'm afraid it's not good," Michael said, pulling a folder from his bag. He paused, looking at John. "I'm sorry, but I don't believe we've met."

"John Randall, nice to meet you," John said, extending a hand to Michael.

"Nice to meet you. I apologize, but this is classified information, and I'm only permitted to show it to your father and Dr. Williams."

Randall grinned. "Just so you know, John helped with the first mission I had with your father in the Antarctic."

Michael looked at Randall, then shifted his gaze to John. "If it makes you feel any better, your dad really didn't like me tagging along on the tour of the Dulce facility he supervised," John said.

"You saw the facility?" Michael asked, his voice dropping in tone. He shrugged, then shook his head. "I guess for the Randall family, the normal rules don't apply." He removed a picture of a man's arm, bearing multiple tattoos. He pointed to one, a black-winged bat, superimposed over a gun sight drawing with Cyrillic writing in concentric arcs above and below the picture.

"What's that?" Randall asked.

"Spetsnaz."

"Russian special forces?" John asked.

Michael nodded.

"You think the Russians are behind Liz's attempted kidnapping and the break-in at Mt. Vernon?" Randall asked.

"It's possible. We're checking our database to see if we get a hit on someone matching the prints or facial features of our two friends downtown. It's a bit of a long shot, but Colonel Rawlings thinks it's worth a shot," Michael replied.

"Colonel Rawlings?" This time, it was Liz.

"He's my commanding officer. One stipulation of joining my father's unit was that I wouldn't report directly to him. The service frowns on nepotism. Even the appearance of it."

"Did they say anything that might help?" John asked.

Michael shook his head no. "We'll keep interrogating them, but if these guys are Russian Special forces, the chance of actually getting information is slim."

"What would the Russians want with a book of predictions from General Washington? It makes no sense," John said.

"Liz, why don't you get Michael up to speed on what you told us?" Randall asked.

Liz explained her encounter with the researcher and his theory about Washington.

"Then there's history to this claim about the book existing. I get the feeling that whoever is after it has been planning this for a long time," Michael said.

Randall cocked his head to the side. "You have a theory you'd like to share?"

Michael shook his head. "Not really. It's just that the Russians aren't known for chasing things down rabbit holes. If they're looking for something, they usually have a good reason for it."

"So that puts us back to square one about where to look for it," John said.

"Maybe not. If that young man I spoke to years ago was right, then maybe we can find some clues in the correspondence between Washington and Franklin. From what I remember, the two wrote each other a series of letters. Perhaps that's a good place to start," Liz said.

"Where would we find the letters?" Michael asked.

"The largest collection of Washington's documents is in the Manuscript Division of the Library of Congress, but there's also documents held at Mount Vernon and with the University of Virginia," Liz replied.

"If the original attackers targeted Mt. Vernon, then there must have been something that led them to that location," Michael said.

Liz nodded. "Right, but most of the Mt. Vernon documents are at the Library of Congress. They had requested the documents as part of compiling the President's documents into one digital library."

"Sounds like the Library of Congress should be our first

stop, but it's closed right now. Plus, I don't know if they're going to agree to let us thumb through their documents. I'm sure they're extremely protective of any materials in their care. How's the best way to go about getting access?" John asked.

"If we've figured this out, then we have to assume the enemy, whoever they are, has figured it out as well. We need to move quickly and cut through the red tape. I'll contact Commander Rawlings. He should be able to get us in there quickly, maybe early tomorrow morning," Michael replied.

Randall smiled, removing his phone from his pocket. "I think I can get us in tonight."

"How?" John asked.

"Remember Phil, the graduate student who used to work for me?" Randall replied. "After the incident in Peru, he switched gears and focused on American history. He works at the Library of Congress now." Randall dialed Phil's number and, after a brief conversation, made arrangements, then hung up.

"When do we go?" Liz asked.

"He'll meet us there in an hour," Randall replied.

Michael pulled out his cell phone. "Great, I'll notify Commander Rawlings."

Chapter Seven

Library of Congress, Washington D.C.

May 9, 9:47 p.m.

After leaving Fiola Mare, the team piled into John's Jeep Grand Cherokee for the trip to the Library of Congress. The ride was quick, taking them on a scenic tour south along the Potomac River, past a lighted Lincoln Memorial and onto Independence Avenue, driving parallel to the National Mall. Randall knew the area well, realizing that beyond the tree-lined avenue lay the memorials to the men and women who sacrificed their lives for their country's freedom. He paused a moment and said a silent prayer in their remembrance.

They continued east, passing the Washington Monument, the sprawling Smithsonian complex of museums and eventually past the United States Capitol itself, the Jefferson building coming into view. Having spent time there, he understood the incredible history contained within the walls of the de facto national library of the United States.

Boasting the largest collection of books in the world, the Library is housed in three buildings, the Jefferson Building, the Madison Building and the Adams Building, clustered near the southeast corner of the Capitol grounds. The Jefferson Building, serving as the main public access building, was flanked on the North by East Capitol Street, the South by Independence Avenue and the West and East by 1st and 2nd Streets, respectively. Serving as the primary hub, tunnels connected the Jefferson Building to the Adams Building, the Madison Building and the Capital visitor's center.

Lesser known to the public is a tunnel, running under 1st Street, connecting the Madison Building to the Cannon House Office Building. This was the tunnel Phil would take to meet them so he could show them the Washington documents housed in the Madison Building. Since the Library was now closed, Phil had agreed to meet the team by the back entrance to the Madison building, on the ground floor, near the corner of 1st and C streets.

John pulled his Jeep into the underground parking structure used by a select group of employees, accessing the secure area with a key code Phil had provided. Parking, they climbed the driveway back up to street level and walked to the Madison building. Randall stepped to the door and knocked. A loud clicking noise arose from inside the building, causing Randall to step back. The door slowly swung inward and Phil stepped out, propping the door open.

"Thanks for agreeing to meet us, Phil," Randall said, stepping forward and hugging his former graduate student.

"Anything for you, Dr. R. Come on in."

The group filed into the building as Phil held the door

open. Once inside, Randall introduced everyone, then Phil led them deeper into the building.

"The letters written by George Washington should be with the material on loan from the Mt. Vernon documents. I called a buddy of mine who's involved with the project and he brought what he could find to the Manuscript Reading Room on the first floor," Phil said, heading for the stairs ahead and to the left.

"I understand you used to work with Dr. Randall when you were a graduate student," Liz asked, following closely behind Phil. "What was that like?"

Phil paused a moment, then continued his upward climb. "Dr. Randall's the reason I chose this field for my career. He was the best teacher I've ever had. He brought archeology to life and treated each one of us like family."

"Sounds like you followed in his footsteps." Liz said.

"Not exactly. After a field assignment with the professor, I switched my focus to early American culture. That's how I ended up working here," Phil replied, waving his hand in the air as he reached the landing on the first floor.

"What made you want to switch?" Liz asked.

A grin formed on Phil's face. "Let's just say that working with Dr. Randall was a little too exciting for my tastes." He turned to look back at the stairs just as his former mentor stepped into the hallway.

"I think I know what you mean," Liz said, winking at Phil. The two turned to Randall, both smirking.

"What did I do?" Randall asked, furrowing his brow.

"Come on," Phil said, nodding his head to the right. "The letters are this way."

Liz laced her arm into Phil's, the two leaning in to each other, whispering and giggling as they walked. Occasionally

Liz glanced over her shoulder at Randall, who walked, hands in pocket, shaking his head.

"Looks like she has your number, Nick," Michael commented, smiling as well.

Randall sighed.

The hallways were dimly lit, Phil turning on the minimum number of lights needed to traverse the building. The group walked to the corner of the building and turned right, passing the human resources service center and arriving at a four-way intersection with the main entrance to their left and the atrium to their right. They went right. Just prior to entering the atrium, the team turned left and entered their destination, the Manuscript Reading Room. Neatly arranged on the tables were several boxes containing the documents on loan from Mt. Vernon. Next to the boxes were two pairs of white gloves and a simple note, notifying Phil that he, along with one chosen member of the team, could search the files, but were required to wear the gloves.

"I'll help to look for the letter," Liz announced, donning a set of gloves. Phil did the same, while the rest of the group took seats around the long wooden tables.

"I apologize, Dr. Williams, but I need to make sure you're trained in handling documents of this nature. I'm sure you've done so during past research, but as part of the staff here, I need to ask," Phil asked.

"I understand entirely Phil and take no offence. Yes, I'm trained in multiple methodologies, including your Society of American Archivist procedures," Liz replied. "And please, call me Liz."

Phil smiled, clearly relieved that he hadn't offended Liz. "Did you know that this building was the last of the three Library of Congress structures to be built?" Phil asked, gingerly removing a single file from the first box. "In 1957,

Librarian of Congress L. Quincy Mumford started studies for a third building, Congress approved the construction, and then appropriated $75 million to build it."

"I didn't know that Phil," Liz said, carefully removing a single folder from a separate box.

"Yep, it's also our nation's official memorial to James Madison, who's considered the "father" of the U.S. Constitution and the Bill of Rights."

Liz smiled warmly. "Marvelous!"

"As a member of the Continental Congress, Madison became the first sponsor of the idea of a library for Congress by proposing a list of books that would be useful to legislators," Phil explained.

"Any luck yet?" Randall asked, peering over Liz's shoulder.

"We've only been at it for a few minutes, Nick. These things take time," Liz replied.

"I think I'll go for a walk," Nick turned to leave.

"Hang on, I'll join you," John said, jogging to his father's side.

The two men exited the room.

"I think he's perturbed that I'm helping you search Phil," Liz commented, returning the first folder and retrieving a second.

Phil refiled his folder as well. "He likes to keep busy. Not a big fan of just standing around. I learned that working for him for a couple of years at the university. I can appreciate that. He taught me the importance of hard work."

"I can see why Nick spoke so glowingly of you. It seems you two are close."

"We speak every couple of weeks and get together for lunch or dinner every month. He's like a second father to me."

"He clearly feels the same way about you too," Liz said.

Phil grinned. "Thank you, Dr. Williams."

"You're welcome and please, Liz."

Randall and John slowly wound their way back through the path they had taken from the first-floor stairs, enjoying an area normally off limits to the public. Serving as the reading area for members of Congress, Randall realized that, if not for Phil, he would never have seen the inside of the building.

"Phil's doing well," John said.

Randall nodded. "I'm not surprised. He was always an outstanding student and worked his butt off to earn this post."

"You sound like a proud father."

Randall looked at his son. "Sorry. I guess I've had a habit of taking home work with me in the past."

"Don't worry about it. After all these years, Sam and I are used to sharing you with your favorite students," John said, referring to his sister Samantha.

The two turned left at the corner, walking back to the stairs they had come up earlier.

"Do you think Phil and Liz will find something that will lead us to the book, or at least help explain what these people are after?" John asked.

"Your guess is as good as mine." Randall replied as they drew close to the stairs. The men closed within 10 feet of the top of the staircase when a soft clicking sound arose from the bottom of the stairwell. As quickly as it started, the noise ended.

"Did you hear that?" Randall asked.

"What are you talking about?" John replied.

Randall walked slowly towards the stairwell, turning to face the opening. He looked down at the first deck. A single beam of light splayed the poorly lit deck, slowly panning back and forth.

"I thought Phil said no one else was supposed to be here," Randall said as John joined him.

The light immediately cut out.

"Shit. We better get back to the Manuscript Room," Randall whispered. He grabbed John's arm.

"What's going on?" John asked as his dad tugged him down the hall.

"Did you see how light went off? Someone didn't want us to know they were there."

"The Russians," John said.

"I think so."

The two sprinted back to the Manuscript Room, arriving at the door out of breath.

Phil's face lit up upon seeing them. "We think we found something! A letter from Franklin to Washington, and get this. It's dated October 15, 1787, right after the Constitutional Convention ended!"

"What does it say?" Randall asked.

"In the letter, Franklin responds to Washington about his help on the matter they spoke of the night before the convention and refers to a package Washington sent him. Franklin said that he reviewed it carefully and, understanding its unique value, had it transferred to a fellow man of science, and a close friend, who could keep a closely guarded secret."

"He didn't say who he was sending it to?" Randall asked.

Phil shook his head no. "But he said his friend could be

trusted because the man owed Franklin for assisting him with a matter of grave concern."

"We've got to get out of here. Bring the letter and let's go," Randall said, motioning for the group to follow.

Liz furrowed her brow. "What's going on?"

"Phil, you said no one else was here, right?" Randall asked.

"Yeah. We're it."

"Someone was at the bottom of the flight of stairs with a flashlight and the minute I spoke, the beam went out," Randall said.

"I better check this out," Michael sprinted past Randall, pulling out his Beretta as he exited the room. A moment later, two gunshots confirmed Randall's worst fears.

"Phil, we need another way out of here," Randall said.

"There's another set of stairs down the hall and to the left."

The group exited the room, spotting Michael peering around the corner of the wall into the hallway. He fired two additional shots, then pulled back as gunfire raked the hallway. Bits of drywall splintered under the automatic gunfire.

Randall hustled to Michael's side. "Can you tell who they are?"

"Russian. I heard one of them giving orders."

"Do you have another gun?" Randall asked.

Michael reached down to his ankle and removed a second smaller Beretta px4 and handed it to Randall, who checked the chamber to make sure it was loaded.

"Phil said there's another stairway to the left."

"We can't go that way. They'll rip us to shreds," Michael replied. "Is there another way out through the atrium?"

Phil pulled up next to Randall and heard Michael's question. "No. that's a dead end."

"Bad choice of words, dear," Liz said, smiling grimly as she joined them.

"I have an idea," Randall said, hustling back into the Manuscript Room.

Michael popped back around the corner, firing an additional two rounds, then diving back to safety moments before a hail of bullets obliterated the corner of the wall.

"I can't hold them off much longer," Michael said.

Randall hustled back to join the group, a fire extinguisher in hand.

"What do you plan to do with that?" John asked.

"Michael, if I toss this down the hall, can you hit it?" Randall asked.

A broad grin spread across Michael's face. "You bet!"

"When this thing blows, everyone follow Phil to the stairs." Randall said. He nodded to Michael. "Ready?" Michael nodded back.

In unison, the two men popped around the corner. Randall tossed the extinguisher towards their pursuers, while Michael took aim, firing a single round when the extinguisher had traveled several feet. The explosion was deafening, white powder spreading out in every direction, creating a great cloud in the middle of the hallway.

"Go!" Randall yelled.

Phil sprinted down the hallway to the left, the others close in tow. Michael brought up the rear, firing a round toward the Russians, who blindly returned fire. A moment later, they arrived at the top of the steps. Upon seeing everyone had arrived, Phil turned to go down. Randall grabbed his arm.

"They're going to be down there, Phil. We need to go up."

Phil nodded, then pivoted up the staircase. "I think I know another way out."

The group hustled up the steps, following Phil up to the second floor. He didn't stop. He turned and started up the next flight of stairs.

Randall sprinted next to him. "Where are we going?"

"This is the Congressional library, so they designed it with a tunnel that runs to the Cannon House Office Building in the basement. That's how I got here. It's sometimes used as a secret evacuation route for congressmen."

"But we're going up."

"The access is on the sixth floor in the cafeteria. There's a service elevator that can take us straight down."

Randall nodded.

Phil continued his mad dash up the stairs, occasionally looking back to make sure the rest of the group was keeping up. Randall stayed close by in case they discovered trouble at the top of the staircase.

The team reached the fourth floor.

"Hang on, I need to take a break," Liz said, clutching the side rail on the stairs.

Phil took a quick head count.

"How do we access this emergency exit?" John asked.

"The entrance is behind a bank of wall files," Phil replied.

"How did you find out about it?" Liz asked.

"I made friends with a Congressional Aide. We were coming back from lunch one day and he told me about it. It's a closely guarded secret, and he made me promise not to tell anyone, but I guess I have to break my promise."

Liz grinned. "And we couldn't be more thrilled."

Phil laughed, Liz's sense of humor contagious.

"We have to get moving again," Michael said, looking

down the flight of stairs toward the 3rd floor. As if to support his statement, the echo of heavy footfalls bounced up the stairwell, announcing their pursuers were closing in. He fired a single shot to slow their progress and the slide of his Beretta jammed open, announcing he had spent his last round. He thumbed the magazine release, causing it to tumble onto the stairs. It clicked loudly on the stone steps. Michael jammed a new magazine into this gun and chambered a round. "This is all the ammunition I brought."

The group resumed their dash up the steps, reaching the 5th floor in short order. As they hit the landing to the entrance to the floor, the dim lighting was pierced by flashes of fire coming from down the hall as they were greeted with gunfire from the Russians.

"Get down the stairs!" Randall yelled, returning fire in the direction of the muzzle blasts.

The sound of gunfire from the 5th floor intensified, as did the sound of boot steps climbing the stairs.

"We can't stay here. They'll catch us in the crossfire," Randall said.

"You're right. The fire team on the 5th floor is making their way towards the entrance now. Their job is to cut us off to allow the team coming up to catch us," Michael said.

"What do we do?" Liz asked.

"I'm going back up. When you hear me yell, get your asses up the stairs to the 6th floor! Don't stop when you hear the shooting," Michael said, turning and walking up the stairs, hugging the wall as he went.

The others followed close behind, but stayed below floor level. As promised, Michael yelled, charging out of the darkness towards the Russians, drawing their attention as he fired his Beretta.

"Move!" Randall yelled.

Phil ran first, followed by Liz and then John, Randall bringing up the rear. Bullets tore at the staircase, knocking bits of rock and drywall loose from the walls, causing the debris to rain down on them as they scrambled up past the 5th floor entrance. Heeding Michael's advice, they didn't stop, sprinting straight for the 6th floor.

"Where's the entrance?" Randall asked, following closely on Phil's heels.

"This way."

Phil sprinted down the dimly lit hall, making a right turn at the center of the building. To his right was the Library of Congress Federal Credit Union, to his left, the cafeteria. He tugged on the glass double doors. They didn't budge. A moment later, Randall arrived at his side.

"Why are you stopping?" Randall asked.

"It's locked and I don't have a key," Phil replied, stabbing his fingers into his hair. "Damn it! I didn't think about this!"

"Watch out!" a voice called out from behind Phil and Randall. The two turned to see John sprinting towards the door, a long, black cylindrical trash can in hand. He closed his eyes as he rammed the trash can into the glass door. Glass spilled inward, raining in small pieces on the floor inside as the tempered class crumbled under impact. Randall ducked through the huge opening into the cafeteria, John and Phil on his heels. Liz arrived a moment later.

"The elevator is back this way!" Phil yelled, heading to the cafeteria counter. He approached a small ledge inset into the counter, with an open space beneath. Reaching under the counter, he flipped the ledge up, creating an open space to access the kitchen. He turned left, arriving at the elevator a moment later.

"Hopefully this will work," Phil said, removing his staff

I.D., and running it through the card reader. The light blinked green. Phil hit the call button for the elevator car. A small binging sound announced its arrival.

"Everyone get in," Randall said, watching as Liz, John and Phil entered the car.

"Come on Nick," Liz said.

"You head back to General Flores and give him the letter and let him know what happened. I'm going back for Michael."

John stepped out of the car. "You can't help Michael by yourself. I'm going with you."

"No, you need to make sure that letter gets to Flores. I'll be okay, please John, just do as I say."

John looked at his father, then at Liz and Phil.

"John, go and you need to do it now. The Russians could be here any minute, and if they get to the tunnel before you, it's all over for us."

John set his jaw and nodded, then entered the elevator car. "Good luck Dad."

Chapter Eight

Randall watched as the elevator door closed, sensing a finality when they clicked together. He ejected the magazine from his gun. He had eight rounds left and one in the chamber. That would never be enough to hold off multiple Russian mercenaries. He would have to improvise. Relying on his previous military experience, he made a mental list of items he could use as weapons: knives, pots, pans, anything sharp and/or heavy. He walked behind the counter and a lighted, refrigerated display case. He flicked the light on his phone, shining it on the shelves, which were empty except for a couple of heavy skillets and pots. The kitchen staff must have put everything else away.

He moved deeper into the cafeteria, heading towards the kitchen area to see what he could find. Finding storage cabinets, he tugged on the handles. Locked.

This isn't good.

He tried another cabinet. It was locked, too. Randall knew the clock was ticking. He needed a plan, fast! He scoured the entire kitchen area, finding little more than a broom and a carton of small jawbreakers. *How the hell am I going to fight off trained mercenaries with treats?*

Randall stared at the jawbreakers while holding the broomstick. A thought suddenly occurred to him. He set the broom aside and took the carton of jawbreakers down from the shelf. He tore the box open, finding dozens of smaller boxes inside.

He carried the carton onto the main floor of the cafeteria, balancing the broomstick on top and stopping to turn off the light in the display case. When he reached the shattered glass door, he opened the first box of jawbreakers and spilled them on the floor. The candies mixed with the glass, the small spheres nearly the same size as the tiny pieces of broken tempered glass. Next, he reached up with the broom and broke the light directly above the spilled candy. Randall repeated the exercise , breaking every light until a four-foot wide swath of broken glass and hard, round candies covered the floor in front of the doorway into the cafeteria. Bathed in darkness, it would be difficult for anyone to tell the difference between the jawbreakers and the glass pieces.

He kept the strip of floor near the counter, completely bare of the jawbreakers. A soft clicking arose down the hallway. Someone was coming. Randall crept behind the counter, resting the broom against the back wall. He needed one last thing for his plan. Something heavy. He spotted the cast-iron skillet resting on a shelf below the counter. It would have to do. Picking it up, he crouched behind the counter. When the action started, he'd have to hurry.

Randall closed his eyes, wanting them to adjust as much as possible to the darkness to afford some vision in the blackened room. Fortunately, the room had never been brightly lit and after breaking all the lights; he had already been in darkness for some time. His eyes closed, he willed his body to relax, breathing deeply. It worked. His other senses were keener now, and he was rewarded with the faint sound of rubber soles gently padding across the floor. He opened his eyes and craned his neck to peer around the corner of the opening in the counter, towards the smashed glass doors. A tiny ribbon of filtered light which leaked from a room next to the hallway near the smashed door was the only thing keeping the room from being pitch black. It wasn't much, but it was enough.

Faint movement near the cafeteria entrance caught his attention as a dark figure crossed in front of the faint light at the end of the cafeteria, about fifteen feet away. A single mercenary had arrived.

Randall crouched back behind the counter. A light crunching sound announced the mercenary had crossed into broken glass. He was getting closer.

The sound stopped. Had the Russian spotted him or the trap he had set?

Randall quieted his nerves and readied himself, his gun tucked in his belt and the skillet in his hand. He would have to incapacitate the soldier without firing his gun to keep from alerting the mercenary's comrades.

The crunching sound appeared again, followed shortly by the rushing sound of gumballs and glass rolling across the floor. A loud crashing sound, followed by clicking metal and a grunt, announced it was time to move. Randall hit the light switch in the display case and charged from behind the counter, skillet in hand. A lone mercenary lay sprawled on the floor, looking like the proverbial deer in the headlights, bathed in the light from the display case, his weapon lying several feet to his side.

Randall charged at him. The mercenary struggled to regain his footing, slipping and falling again, but pulled a knife from a leg sheath. Laying on his back, he raised his knife hand at Randall, who swatted the weapon from his hand with the skillet, likely cracking the mercenary's fingers.

The Russian cursed in pain, but used a leg sweep to knock Randall to the floor. Randall fell hard on his ass, yelping as he hit the hard floor. He landed only inches away from the mercenary's assault rifle and scrambled to pick it up.

The Russian realized what Randall intended to do and grabbed his leg, pulling Randall towards him. Randall lunged, grabbed the assault weapon, and turned it on the Russian. He fired wildly, missing his target, but causing the mercenary to scramble backwards to avoid being shot by the automatic gunfire.

So much for not alerting others.

The mercenary used the round candies to slide several feet away from Randall and back onto clear ground. He jumped to his feet, his hand going for the handgun kept in his chest webbing. Randall, still on his back, had only seconds. He raised the weapon and fired a stream of bullets, tracing from the floor and up the mercenary's leg and torso. The man's body shuddered as Randall peppered him with automatic gunfire. The Russian fell to the floor, his handgun making a loud clicking sound as it skittered to the side.

Randall dropped the weapon and lay on the floor, breathing in large gasps. His entire body shook because of the rush of adrenaline flowing through his veins. He needed moment to gather himself, but knew he had little time. Having heard the battle, more mercenaries were certainly on their way.

Michael heard the sounds of a scuffle coming from the sixth floor above his head, followed by several bursts of automatic gunfire. That didn't bode well for the rest of the group's escape. The only positive aspect of the battle had been to draw away several of the mercenaries who were chasing him.

His initial plan had worked, charging at the Russians and drawing their attention long enough for Randall and the group to make it up to the sixth floor. Unfortunately for him, it had worked a little too well. His stunt had drawn the main concentration of fire from the Russians and he had barely escaped being cut to shreds by a torrent of gunfire.

As luck would have it, there had been a door into a workroom on his left that had granted him a slight reprieve from the Russian counterattack. The reprieve had been short-lived as three mercenaries had followed him into the room. He had dispatched the first coming through the doorway, but had run out of ammunition. This had left him with one option. Run.

He had exited the workroom through a door near the opposite side and had been maneuvering through the fifth floor ever since. After successfully eluding the Russians, he had stumbled upon a gear bag containing night vision goggles, a Glock, and submachine gun. Somewhere, an angry Russian cursed him for finding his gear.

Now equipped as well as his Russian counterparts, he had an additional concern. It sounded like his friends had either been killed or apprehended. He needed to find out which, hoping it was the latter.

The wailing of sirens in the distance, growing louder, announced that the authorities knew things were amiss. A situation noticed by his Russian pursuers who withdrew in anticipation of the police's arrival. Michael had spotted two of them hurriedly exiting the fifth floor through his newly acquired night goggles. They were going down the stairs, in the direction they had come.

Michael shifted his attention to the commotion on the sixth floor. He carefully worked his way toward the staircase his friends had taken earlier. He walked a few feet closer, each time scurrying into the safety of side doorways and alcoves to check for signs of the enemy. There were none. He finally made it to the stairs, walking in a crouch as he ascended, craning his head and weapon around each bend, anticipating a firefight. He cleared the last steps, exiting into the sixth-floor hallway.

It was much darker here than on the other floors. Michael was thankful for the night vision goggles, which afforded him sight in the poorly lit area. He snaked his way towards the cafeteria, where Phil had said they would find the elevator to the basement. He turned the corner into the walkway into the cafeteria and immediately noticed a body lying on the ground. The thermal profile showed that, while it was still warmer than the surrounding area, it was considerably cooler than a normal person. Whoever it was, he or she was dead.

Michael gingerly stepped over the shattered, broken glass, scanning the cafeteria for signs of life. A radio on the dead man cackled to life. His compatriots were trying to reach him. Michael grasped the device, putting it to his ear and listening in on the conversation. Just as expected, most of the Russians were exiting the building while two were trying to reach their fallen comrade on the sixth floor.

"Sorry boys, but your friend is dead," Michael said into the radio in response to the conversation on the chatter.

"Michael?" A voice called out from behind the counter.

Michael dropped the radio, taking aim in the counter's direction. "Who's there?"

"It's Nick!" Randall said, popping out from behind the cooler.

"Thank God, I thought you and the others might be dead. Where's everyone else?"

"They made it down the elevator. I stuck around to see if I could find you."

Michael grinned. "Your handiwork?" He said, motioning to the lifeless body on the ground. Randall simply nodded.

"We better get out of here. Sounds like the police are nearly here," Randall said.

Chapter Nine

Colonel Leonid Kapralov surveyed the staged battlefield from his vantage on a hillside overlooking his troops. They had been drilling for five days straight as Operation Glorious Summer slowly wound to a close.

The training, a mock defense against invading NATO forces, had been a rousing success on all fronts as his 1st Guards Tank Brigade had lured the enemy battalion into a low-lying depression within the earth, outflanked them, then caught them by surprise in a crossfire, destroying most of the 58 'NATO' tanks while only suffering minor losses. Kaprolov smiled as he read the report on the exercise. 42 enemy tanks entirely destroyed and an additional 11 partially incapacitated. Only 5 enemy tanks had survived unscathed. Meanwhile, the forces under his command had suffered 11 total losses and 6 damaged tanks.

Our tactics worked nearly flawlessly. Imagine what we'll be able to do when we deploy our T-14 Armatas later this year.

His chest swelled with pride as he once again stared

across the battlefield through his binoculars. As reality set in, the good feelings waned. The exercise, while a success, never would have been necessary had it not been for the provocation of NATO by the Russian annexation of the Crimean Peninsula. The resulting saber rattling by the Americans had, at first, been dismissed as nothing more than an attempt to save face in the aftermath of the successful Russian invasion. But the Latvians had changed that. The former Soviet satellite had seized the opportunity to push for a NATO naval base at the port city of Liepaja, a former site of the Soviet Union's Baltic fleet. While Kapralov understood the rationale behind the invasion of the Crimea to maintain a naval presence in the Black Sea, their actions had inadvertently led to a fresh crisis. If NATO were to construct a base in Latvia, then they could restrict the movement of Russian naval forces through the Baltic. This would be a disaster for the Russian Navy. Their leaders had traded one waterway for another.

Someone's head should have rolled for not seeing this possibility.

Even though he couldn't see it from his current vantage, Kapralov knew NATO had already begun surveying the Liepaja port area, the early phase of a feasibility study to determine if the Latvian plan held merit. If they moved forward with the base, they would complete construction in phases, providing them with a naval presence in Russia's backyard. Making matters worse, the Americans were also insisting on having a tank battalion deployed to Latvia, to help secure the border between the small NATO member state and Russia.

Kapralov frowned. Despite decades of spying during the cold war, the Americans still did not know how the Russian mind worked. The scars from hundreds of years of war and occupation at the hands of foreign powers had caused a sort of paranoia to set in. When they had annexed the Crimea, it had been nothing more than self-preservation. The deployment of a brigade of American tanks to the Russian border was just short of an overt declaration of hostilities by the United States. How would they feel if Russia were to do the same along the northern border of neighboring Canada?

"Colonel, General Berezin is on the phone for you," a voice called from behind, snapping Kapralov back to reality.

"Notify the men to gather for a full debriefing of the exercise at 14:00 hours," Kapralov said to his second in command.

The Captain snapped to attention, saluting his commanding officer before jogging off to the officers' quarters to address his tank commanders.

Kapralov hopped in the rear seat of his vehicle, his driver handing him a satellite phone. "General, you asked to speak with me?"

"Colonel Kapralov, we need you to report to St. Petersburg immediately. You will find a plane waiting for you at the airfield. Go there now. You're expected here by 16:00 hours," the General replied.

"Sir, Operation Glorious Summer has just concluded. We need to do a full assessment of tactics and strategy. It's imperative that this take place shortly after the exercise to ensure maximum benefit."

Kapralov heard a grunt on the other end of the phone. He knew the General wasn't accustomed to having his subordinates question his commands. Normally, such indiscretions could lead to a demotion or worse, a long stretch in the gulags, but Kapralov had served bravely under the command of the General in the Afghan war. Though a mere lieutenant, he had led a rescue attempt of a downed helicopter crew in a remote village. By the end of the day, virtually all of Kapralov's platoon had been killed. Only the young Lieutenant, and two subordinates remained. They charged the village camp where the helicopter crew was being held with little more than their side arms and had rescued the crew and a special passenger. A newly appointed Major and rising star of the party. Kapralov had suffered two gunshot wounds, but fought valiantly, killing five Afghan rebels single handedly.

For his bravery, they had awarded him the Hero of the Russian Federation, the highest title of honor in the nation. While at the hospital recovering from his injuries, a special guest paid him a visit. Major Konstantin Berezin had conveyed his deepest gratitude for Kapralov's heroic act. The meeting marked the beginning of a long friendship and professional relationship which had lasted to this day.

"Leonid, we have a serious situation here and I need your expertise. With each passing hour, the situation grows more severe. If we don't confront it now, it could lead to a grave conflict with the West."

Kapralov raised an eyebrow at the disclosure. "What is the nature of this situation?"

"I am not a liberty to discuss this matter by phone. As you know, enemies of the state are everywhere, and this situation warrants the utmost care and secrecy."

That Berezin refused to discuss the situation by phone spoke to its serious nature and a realization and admittance that all was not as well as portrayed within the ranks of the military. Spies abounded and as long as the West held the lure of riches, sunny weather, and beautiful, scantily clad women, the brutal tactics employed to maintain loyalty would only work so well.

"Very well, General, I will gather my things and leave immediately."

"Very good Colonel. I remind you not to speak of this to anyone of this. Secrecy is of the utmost necessity, as is moving quickly."

Chapter Ten

Arlington, Virginia

May 10, 6:27 a.m.

The morning sun crested the horizon, showering the earth with light, and announcing the beginning of a new day. Randall sat at the counter of the 2nd story home, sipping a hot cup of coffee which Liz had brought him. After escaping the Russian assault at the Madison Building, Randall and Mike had eluded the police and contacted the rest of the group. They arranged to meet at the home of Liz's colleague in Arlington, Virginia, a quaint city next to Washington, D.C. If D.C. was the center of power of the country, then Arlington was where many of the power brokers laid their heads to rest at night.

Liz and John had arrived at the home first, and Phil had waited to see Randall before going back to his own place.

Much to Randall's chagrin, Phil had told his former mentor that the prior evening's events had confirmed that he had made the right choice, foregoing a swashbuckling life of adventure for the staid atmosphere of his job at the library. After failing to reach Colonel Rawlings, Michael had pulled the family card and had contacted his father directly. The senior Flores had guaranteed that he would contact the Director of the Library of Congress to explain that Phil had operated under the direction of his unit on a matter of high national priority, smoothing any ruffled feathers. Phil appreciated the gesture. John had also taken photos of the letter and gave the original back to Phil to return it to the library. He had then hugged Randall and set off for home.

By the time Michael and Randall had joined Liz and John, their host, Beverly Johnson, already had coffee and breakfast ready for them. Liz explained Beverly had volunteered to show her the ropes and aid in her adjustment to her new surroundings when she had arrived from England. The two had become close over the several months since Liz arrived. Randall rubbed his tired eyes as Liz filled in her friend about the events which had transpired.

"Thanks again for letting us meet here, Bev. I wasn't sure where else we could turn," Liz said, cradling her coffee mug for warmth.

"I'm just glad that you're okay. I can't believe gunmen attacked you! You certainly lead a more interesting life than me." Beverly replied.

As if reading Randall's mind, Liz addressed her friend in an even but serious tone. "You understand that everything we've told you is classified Bev. You need to guarantee that you won't tell a soul."

Beverly nodded. "Understood. So, what's next?"

John sat across the table from his father and Liz, scribbling notes on a legal pad in front of him. He lifted the pen, staring down at what he had written.

"What do you think, John?" Randall asked, taking another sip of coffee.

John angled his eyes up from the paper and toward his father. "I've looked through the letter again to see if we've missed anything and couldn't find any more clues." He sat up straighter. "If we assume the letter from Franklin to Washington referred to the book Washington wrote about his visions, then he would have sent it by horseback to Franklin. As far as the timeline, Washington went back to Mt. Vernon after the convention and would have sent the book from there. The trip from Mt. Vernon to Philadelphia is about 160 miles, so it would have taken about 3-4 days for the book to reach Franklin."

"But we still don't know who Franklin sent it to, after he read it," Michael replied.

"Looks like we're back to square one," Liz commented.

John sat back in his chair and folded his arms, a smile forming on his lips. "Maybe not."

Randall raised a brow. "If you know something, don't keep it to yourself."

"Okay, but to follow my thinking, first, you need to think like a colonial American," John said.

"Do I need to wear a blue overcoat?" Michael joked.

"No, but it might help," John said, eliciting a smile from Michael. "First, we need to consider who wrote the letter. Benjamin Franklin had a sense of humor, but also loved codes and riddles," John said.

"You think he used code in his letter to Washington?" Randall asked.

"I think it's possible. Let's look at his word choice. In the letter, he referred to a 'grave matter'. That's not an uncommon turn of phrase, but for Franklin, there could be a hidden meaning."

"Like what?" Randall asked.

"If you were a well-known colonial American and had something you wanted to hide, something of great value you didn't want anyone to discover, where would you hide it?"

"Bury it somewhere on your property?" Randall offered.

"Give it to a friend and tell him or her to hide it?" Beverly asked.

"Send it to bloody England," Liz said, hands folded on her lap, her eyes transfixed on John.

"Exactly Liz," John said. "Actually, you all have a piece of the puzzle."

Randall scratched his head. "Am I the only one who's not following this?"

Liz placed her hand on Randall's. "When Mr. Franklin was serving the colonies in England, he lived in a tall narrow Georgian house in the heart of London, at 36 Craven Street. He became close friends with William Hewson, a student of anatomy who wished to study it more closely."

Randall frowned. "What does that have to do with Washington's book?"

"At the time, they frowned on the study of anatomy and anyone wishing to study it had to do so secretly. Hewson used Franklin's Craven house to conduct research and to dispose of used material," Liz said.

"Skeletal remains to be exact," John added. "As you know, Franklin was a scientist and enjoyed making discoveries more than just about anything. In 1998 conservationists were doing work on the Craven house to restore it. When they excavated the basement, they found over 1,200 bones and fragments buried there. The best guess is that Franklin let Hewson run an anatomy school in his basement."

"But that still doesn't explain what happened to the book," Randall said.

"If Franklin let Hewson bury bones in the basement, who's to say there aren't other things buried there?" John asked.

"That's a bit of stretch," Randall said, folding his arms across his chest, considering the proposition. "But it's certainly possible."

"There's a fairly easy way to find out if we're on to something. We can go to England and check," John said.

Michael exhaled. "I realize that you all know far more about history than I do, but I have to agree with your father. That's a pretty thin lead. I'm not sure I can muster much support on my end to follow up."

Randall exhaled slowly, then looked into the eyes of his son. "How sure do you feel about this, John?"

John grinned. "Pretty sure. It all fits the pattern. Washington was busy with helping to keep the nation together and he trusted Franklin implicitly. When Washington's enemies were trying to bring him down, Franklin was a rock of support. If he was going to trust anyone with something of value, Franklin would be his man."

"You're right Michael. It is thin. But it's the only thing we really have to go on. Besides, John knows his stuff about Revolutionary war history," Randall said, clearly warming to the idea.

"How do we check?" Michael asked.

"I think I know someone who can help," Liz said.

Randall pivoted to look at Liz. "Who?"

Liz didn't reply. She stared out the window, as if trying to spot a distant ship on the horizon.

"Liz?" Randall asked.

Liz sighed, then turned to look at him. "Someone I'd rather not ask."

Chapter Eleven

Training Camp, Pakistan

May 10, 4:07 p.m.

A blazing sun hovered in the sky, scorching the Earth below as the thermometer continued its upward march. The radiating heat from the rocky landscape caused the superheated air to expand, wreaking havoc with the light waves trying to cut through it. The result was a shimmering effect as the air appeared wavy when looking at it from a distance. Aminov checked the thermostat, the temperature was 99°. His dry lips bent into a smile as he watched the battalion marching in lock-step, carrying full gear packs, easily weighing over 60 pounds. Colonel Bai showed no remorse as he pushed his troops through their rigorous training regimen.

The soldiers marched over the barren terrain, the brown and red streaked mountains forming a desolate backdrop. The hot, empty country belied the fact that Pakistan held the world's sixth largest population, but aside from these soldiers, there was no sign of life in this rock-strewn desert.

This is truly a younger man's job.

Aminov sat beneath a shaded canopy, sipping his chilled water as he watched the soldiers march in the searing heat of the Northern Pakistani afternoon. The day had only grown hotter and worse for them.

So, what? They're well paid, and many was the time I longed for relief from the frigid Siberian winters spent on patrol. I would have welcomed this heat.

"Are they ready?" Aminov asked his direct report.

"Affirmative, sir," Colonel Bai answered in perfect English. A graduate of the prestigious Republic of China Military Academy, Bai had followed in the footsteps of many previous Chinese commanders, graduating near the top of his class with honors. His mastery of the English language was a prized commodity for the People's Liberation Army. A skill he now used for his new employer.

"And the other assets. Are they in place?"

"Yes, awaiting your orders. When the time comes, they will be ready to carry out your wishes."

"How can you be sure?"

Bai lowered his binoculars and turned to face the Russian. "My men do not fear the enemy. They fear me."

Aminov nodded, taking another sip of water.

"Sir, do we have an updated timeline for the operation?"

"We are awaiting one last chip to fall into place and we are close to acquiring what we need. When we do, I will give you the order to launch the attack. Remember Bai, it's critical to make sure it looks like the PLA orchestrated this.

We need our Indian friends to blame China and their Pakistani allies for the destruction."

"Understood sir. We received the last shipment of weapons from our contacts in the PLA, and we have integrated our Pakistani team members into our troops. We will leave nothing to chance."

"You had better not."

Chapter Twelve

London, England

May 10, 5:18 p.m.

"I think I need a drink," Liz said, fending off the questions she was being peppered with by the team. Since the 747 had lifted off from National Airport, everyone had inquired about what she had meant about seeking help from someone she'd rather not ask. Everyone except Randall, who had watched in amusement from across the aisle of the jumbo jet, which was quickly approaching Heathrow.

"It was just an interesting response to the question, and it sounds like there's more to the story," John said, pressing the issue.

"Besides, we need to know if there's someone you'd like us to rough up for you," Michael said, adding his own two cents.

All Liz could do was sigh and shake her head.

"You haven't told us where we're going to meet this friend of yours. Is he a teacher, or is he in some other line of work?" Randall asked, coming to Liz's aid and changing the subject.

"He's the Director of the Benjamin Franklin House," Liz replied, thankful for the lifeline. "Someone invited him to be a guest speaker at my university and a colleague introduced us, because I'm an expert on President Washington. Since we were both Brits with an affection for American revolutionary war era figures, my friends thought we would hit it off."

"Did you?" Randall asked.

"Let's just say he was an extremely colorful chap and leave it at that."

Sensing Liz's unease, Randall redirected the conversation once again. "Michael, were you able to have a security expert meet us?" The group had enlisted the help of an expert to defeat the security system at Franklin House to allow them to search for the book.

"Affirmative. I spoke with Colonel Rawlings and she'll be waiting for us when we touch down."

"What's her name?"

"Lieutenant Catherine Walker."

Satisfied, Randall nodded his head.

Silence fell over the group as the plane descended to Heathrow. A short time later, they were on the ground and walking up the enclosed walkway toward the terminal. The area was packed with people sitting, standing, and hunched over tablets and laptops. Everyone ignored them as they entered the terminal. Everyone except for a single woman, with a hawk's like focus on the stream of passengers exiting the plane.

Randall judged her to be several of inches shorter than

he, which pegged her at about five foot seven inches. She had her dark hair pulled back into a ponytail and wore a charcoal gray suit with a light blue shirt. To any passerby, she would have looked like another business traveler heading to her next appointment.

She approached Michael. "Captain Flores?"

"Lieutenant Walker, nice to meet you," he said, shaking her hand, not wanting to tip anyone off that this was anything but two business associates meeting.

"I didn't get much information about this assignment; do you mind if I ask what we're planning to do?"

"Let's talk about it in the cab."

They exited the terminal and hailed a taxi.

A short time later, the cab rolled to a stop at the curb, in front of a four-story brick building on Craven Street. A black, wrought-iron fence framed a small area in front of two tall windows, inset into a white block wall, which formed the first story of the structure. Between the two windows was a dark, copper sign which read, "Benjamin Franklin (1706-1790) lived here."

Directly to the left of the windows was the doorway and standing on the doorstep, hands folded behind his back, stood a portly man, sporting a black derby, ascot and handlebar mustache. He looked like a character from an episode of Sherlock Holmes. The only thing missing was a monocle. He contorted his lips into something resembling a smile.

"I'm guessing that's Dr. Edwards?" Randall asked.

Liz simply sighed and reached for the car handle. Popping it open, she exited the cab and forced a smile onto her face. Randall followed closely behind, with the others trailing.

Randall watched Edwards' eyes follow Liz's every move,

slowly panning up and down her frame. He was no longer watching her. He was leering at her like a horny teenage boy staring at the foldout picture in a men's magazine.

Edwards licked his lips. "Couldn't keep away from me, eh Liz?"

"Oh Winston, always good to see you," Liz said, giving him a quick hug, then pulling away. She was too slow. Edwards enveloped her in his thick arms, pulling her close and squeezing for far too long.

Randall stopped next to Liz, extending his hand. "Dr. Nick Randall, nice to meet you."

Edwards didn't budge, maintaining his iron grip on Liz, who pried herself from his lecherous grip. "Winston, my friend Nick Randall."

Edwards titled his head, giving Randall a quick sideways glance before turning back to Liz. "What brings you to my doorstep, my dear?"

Randall's smile evaporated, and he lowered his hand. He set his jaw, his brown eyes boring into the back of Edwards' skull as the chubby Englishman led Liz through the front door.

"What was that about?" John said. He had walked to his father's side.

Randall cleared his throat and entered through the reddish-brown door into Franklin's English home. It immediately transported him back in history, overwhelmed by the prospect of standing in the same room as one of America's great statesmen. Voices carried down the hallway and Randall followed them, arriving in the white paneled study. Edwards propped his elbow onto the mantle above the fireplace as he leaned into Liz, speaking in a whispered tone. To his left, near one of the two street facing windows, stood another man of much smaller stature. He tapped his foot, and shook his head in small, nearly imperceptible arcs, staring at the ground.

Liz shot Randall a glance. "Winston was just telling me about the work they've completed recently. They just removed a section of flooring in the basement for more excavation."

Edward's eyes rolled in his head, coming to rest in Randall's direction. He didn't bother turning his head. "One of our benefactors recently requested we search for more bones from Dr. Hewson's anatomy school. Apparently, you Yanks seem to have an unquenchable thirst for such morbid curiosities."

John and Michael joined the group, falling behind and to the right of Randall. Catherine wasn't with them.

"If you don't want to look for more artifacts, then why are you excavating?" Randall asked.

"Money, my dear man. The benefactor provided us with a rather large endowment and has agreed to underwrite the cost of the excavation," Edwards replied, barely hiding his contempt at the question.

"Can we see the area?" John asked.

Edwards ignored him. "Liz, you still haven't told me why you're here." He grabbed her arm and pulled her closer. "Aside from obviously wanting to see me."

"Oh Winston, always such a charmer." She leaned away from him. "My friend here is writing a book about Mr. Franklin and wanted to see his English home in person, for the sake of research," Liz said, motioning to John.

"Liz has said tremendous things about you," John said, realizing Winston enjoyed having his ego stroked. He extended his hand to Winston, who shook John's hand vigorously, lapping up the compliment.

"I'd be thrilled to regale you with stories about this

charming home, but, I must ask, why the hurry? You seemed somewhat desperate to meet, when we spoke on the phone?" Winston asked, directing his question to Liz.

"I'm on a tight publishing deadline and needed to confirm a few facts before we go to print. My editor is already unhappy that I won't sign off on moving forward and I'm pushing my luck just asking for a couple of days," John replied for Liz.

Winston drew his mouth into a tight bow and nodded. "Well, we're here now. What would you like to learn?"

"Can we start with a tour of the basement, where they discovered the skeletal remains?" John asked.

Winston chuckled. "You Yanks and your infatuation with the macabre. After you!" He extended his hand in magnanimous fashion, bowing deeply to John and Liz.

The group walked in single file, down the narrow staircase to the basement level with Randall bringing up the rear behind Michael. As they reached the lower level, the group crowded around a narrow strip of wooden floor, lying at the edge of an open dirt pit. Someone had clearly been excavating the area, which was marked with small flags.

"Have they found any additional skeletal remains?" John asked.

"As of this time, no," Winston replied.

"How can you be sure?" Randall asked.

Winston sighed, closed his eyes, and rocked his head from side to side. "Mr. Randall, nothing happens in this house without my knowledge. If the researchers working on this project found anything, I would be the first to know."

Randall restrained himself from reaching out and grabbing Edwards' thick neck. Anything he said seemed to rub the man the wrong way, and he simply couldn't stand his arrogance, but they needed him at this moment.

John, clearly sensing the tension between his father and Edwards, stepped between them. "I'm sure there have been incredible finds here, Dr. Edwards. If another researcher wanted to search for additional artifacts here, would you allow them?"

Edwards frowned. "No. This is a onetime special arrangement for our benefactor. If anyone else tried to excavate here, I would march them back out of this house." He pointed up the steps to the ground floor for emphasis.

"John, why don't you ask Dr. Edwards the questions you have for your research, while your father, Michael, and I look around the house? You wouldn't mind that, would you Winston dear?" Liz said, touching Edwards' arm.

"I'll be a most gracious host to your young friend, and I'm happy to answer all of his questions. However, please touch nothing on the fourth floor behind the roped off area." Winston pointed a chubby finger at the group. "We're having restoration work done there and," Winston closed his eyes and sighed. "We already had one… gentleman, nearly damage it!"

"Wonderful. We'll leave you boys to it then," Liz said, not missing a beat, as if she had heard such rants from Winston before.

Liz turned to go up the steps, grabbing Randall's arm and pulling him along. Michael followed behind, patting Randall on the back as they ascended the stairs.

The three had barely reached street level before Randall erupted. "That guy's a serious piece of work. If you weren't here, I'd have hit him. And what exactly was your relationship with him?"

"Nick, he's a pompous windbag, and our relationship was entirely professional," Liz said.

Before Randall could respond, Catherine materialized from the adjacent room.

"What do you think?" Michael asked.

"Basically, it's a home security system. Nothing we should be concerned with. I'll be able to disable it easily."

Voices coming up the stairs announced that John and Dr. Edwards were returning. John was in front, rolling his eyes as Edwards followed close on his heels, lecturing him about how British researchers were superior to their American counterparts.

"Did you get what you needed?" Liz asked John as he approached the group.

"Yes, I'm ready to go."

Liz turned to Edwards, cutting him off in mid-sentence. "Winston, thank you for kindly showing us the place and answering John's questions."

Winston blinked several times. "Are you going?"

"I'm afraid so. We have to make another stop. We haven't even unpacked yet," Liz said, slipping her arm into Randall's, and pulling him to the door.

"But we've barely even spoken. I thought we might have tea," Winston moaned like a small child.

"Perhaps next time. Until then," Liz waved, not turning to face him.

The group walked to the front door, past Edward's assistant, who had been watching with amusement. Clearly, he didn't frequently see someone best his boss. "Sir," he said as John walked by.

John turned, and the man handed him a card. "In case you have any further questions, I'd be happy to speak with you."

"Thanks. I appreciate it."

With that, they left.

Chapter Thirteen

The group sat in Randall's hotel room, discussing their plan of action. While the others had spoken with Edwards, Catherine had surveyed the alarm system and found the power feed running outside of the building. She and Michael would approach the front door in tandem, then Catherine would veer to the side and cut the power, disabling the security system while Michael popped the lock, and they entered before someone spotted them and notified the authorities. Michael would then serve as a lookout and let the rest of the team know when it was safe to enter. Once everyone was inside, he would take a position by the fourth-story window and keep an eye out for signs of trouble, and Catherine would guard the door while the others searched for the book.

Michael checked his watch. 1:15 a.m. The streets would be quiet, but if a police officer should stop them, they could simply say they were out for a night on the town. Despite most pubs closing at 11:00 p.m., one local establishment near the Craven Street home was open until 2:00 a.m. With their alibi in place, they headed out.

A short while later, they entered the Soho area. Despite the late hour, a small, but loud group still roamed the streets, undoubtedly louder because of an extended visit to one local pub still open. As they passed it, a small herd of twenty-something's spilled out the door, and down the steps, nearly crashing into Michael.

"Sorry fella," one man said to Michael, who simply smiled back.

"O'Neill's?" John said. He looked quizzically at the name of the establishment, clearly bemused that the only pub nearby that was still open spoke to an Irish surname.

Randall grinned. "Only in London."

As they approached 36 Craven Street, the team broke into two groups, Michael and Catherine in one and Liz, Randall and John in the other. Michael and Catherine slipped around the corner onto Craven Street, while the others lagged, walking at a leisurely pace.

"We're in," Michael quietly announced over the radio Randall held concealed in his hand.

"On our way," Randall replied, slipping the radio into his pocket.

A short time later, they were in Franklin's home. Randall, Liz and John climbed down the wooden flight of stairs to the basement, tools in hand. John erected the battery powered work lights, illuminating the white paneled wood walls, and exposed pit area. He then joined his father, who was already in the excavation area. While the two men searched for the book, Liz held the radio that Michael had given her and watched the stairs.

"How do you want to do this?" John asked.

Randall scratched the black and gray stubble on his chin. "I know this breaks every scientific convention, but I think we just need to dig as fast as we can and hope that, if the book's buried here, Hewson put it in some sort of container for protection."

"That makes sense. He would have realized that the book would have decayed if they buried it in dirt for years."

The two decided they would work in shifts, each man taking his turn digging in the exposed six by eight-foot pit, while the other rested and helped remove any accumulated dirt piles in the other's way. John, being the younger of the two, took the first shift. The damp soil made for easy digging as John drove the rounded shovel point into the dark dirt.

Randall watched, flinching as John dug past the markers set by the previous researchers who had been digging in the pit. Under normal circumstances, such disregard for proper excavation protocol—slow and careful removal of each layer of earth using small hand trowels and brushes—would be unthinkable. But these weren't normal circumstances. They had a few hours to find the book. Any damage they caused would have to be chalked up to the grave nature of the situation they found themselves in.

Despite the short time frame, they still needed to conduct the search methodically, cutting six inches into the dirt, excavating the entire opening and lifting the dirt onto the section of flooring on the pit's edge. Randall tugged at his coat, zipping it up to the collar to stave off the chilly night air. John, in contrast, had removed his jacket and worked in short sleeves, his back collar and armpits soaked with sweat.

After 30 minutes of digging, John stopped.

"Why don't you hop up and get a drink of water and let me have a turn?"

John nodded, driving the tip of his shovel into the soil. "Works for me." He climbed out of the pit and picked up the jug of water they had brought as Randall hopped down, taking his place. The two worked in this fashion for over two hours, stopping occasionally to chat with Liz, who reported that Michael and Catherine had provided regular reports of the occasional passerby.

Randall, having just finished his shift, took a seat in a chair Liz had fetched from the upstairs sitting room. He wiped his brow with the back of his dirt covered hand and took a long drink of water when the sound of the shovel hitting something solid pulled his attention back to the pit.

"I think I found something," John said, probing the dark soil with the end of the shovel, trying to find the edge of the hidden object.

Randall got up and hopped into the pit to help. "How big is it?"

"I'd say maybe a couple of feet long. Oh, it's just a bone," John's voice conveyed his disappointment, like a small child opening a birthday gift, only to discover it was socks and underwear.

Randall patted him on the back. "At least you found something."

John laughed, redoubling his efforts.

An hour and a half later, they had still failed to find anything, aside from several additional skeletal remains. Normally, such finds would be much cause for excitement, but tonight, their prize eluded them.

"Nick, grab John and get up here!" Liz called from the top of the stairs.

John abandoned his shovel, joining his father on the stairs. When they reached the top, Liz's ashen expression let them know something was wrong. Catherine stood by her side, communicating with Michael on the radio. The two men jogged over to them.

"What's going on?" Randall asked.

Liz lowered the radio and peered out the corner of the glass above the front door. "We have visitors."

"Who?" John asked.

"Don't know, but they're armed. Michael spotted them walking down the street thirty minutes ago. Now they're back and staying low and hugging the sides of the building."

"Reconnaissance," Randall said.

Catherine nodded in agreement.

"How many?" Liz asked.

"Three."

"We have two more approaching from the opposite side," Michael's voice called from the radio.

"Everyone up the stairs to the top level," Catherine said, removing her side arm from her jacket and checking the magazine to ensure it was loaded.

The other three hurried up the stairs as Liz took a crouching position to the side of the door, with a clear view of the entry.

They hustled to the fourth floor, finding Michael crouched down, his gun trained on the stairwell. His glance shifted from the stairs to the window. He lifted the radio to his mouth. "Catherine, the three to the left are waiting for the other two to join them. I expect breach in under two minutes."

"Can we fight them off?" John asked.

Michael shook his head. "There's five that I can see in the front, and we can assume more on the backside of the building. They'll breach the lower level and sweep each floor until they have us pinned down. We need to find another way out." He moved to the stairs.

"Where are you going?" Randall asked.

"To help Catherine. There's no way she can hold them back on her own."

"We're going to look for a way to the roof. Be ready to get back up here. We'll call you both as soon as we figure something out," Randall said.

Michael nodded, then disappeared down the staircase.

"Spread out and look for a flight of stairs, or some other access to the roof," Randall said.

Liz and John headed in opposite directions, while Randall searched the room he was in. The inset panel walls were painted a crème color and stretched to the ceiling. There were no vents or other openings. He moved to the adjacent room. No luck there as well. John jogged to his side.

"Anything?" Randall asked.

John shook his head. "You?"

"No. Hopefully Liz is having better luck."

"Unfortunately, I've fared no better," Liz said. She entered the room and came to a stop by Randall's side.

A loud crashing sound emanated from below, followed by a small explosion and the clattering sound of gunfire.

Liz's eyes went wide. She grabbed Randall's sleeve. "The window."

Randall understood. He sprinted to the window and looked down on Craven Street from the side of the glass. To his surprise, he saw no gunmen. They had all entered the building. Gunfire erupted as Michael and Catherine struggled to keep the intruders at bay.

Randall searched for a way to open the window. He

found the locking device, turned it, and pushed up. The window wouldn't budge.

"Why won't it open?" Liz asked.

"I think it's painted shut," Randall replied.

"We'll have to break it," John said. A look of determination filled his eyes.

Randall punched at the side panels on both sides, then pushed up again. The window slid open, and Randall climbed onto the sill. He shivered as the chilly night air washed over his face and collar. The involuntary movement caused his arm to jerk, and Randall tumbled out.

John, realizing what was happening, grabbed his father's belt and held him in place. Randall dangled for a moment, half in and half out the window, staring at the cobblestone street below. His hand struck a pebble on the ledge, and the small stone tumbled to the ground, making a cracking sound when it struck the road below.

Randall's heart beat like the wings of a hummingbird. *That could have been me.* He recovered his composure and climbed onto the sill and stood facing the building. "Thanks son." He looked up at the gently sloping roofline and realized there was no way to climb up.

"Can we get to the roof?" John asked.

Randall scanned the area and noticed a small, black pipe, several inches beyond the seam where the roof flattened out. He judged it to be about three feet away. Too far to reach.

"I think I have an idea," Randall said. "Find a rope or something about six feet long."

Liz and John disappeared from the window and into the old building. Randall clung to a piece of decorative trim, balancing on the ledge. An icy wind gnawed at him, and he felt his body temperature dropping.

The sounds of the gun battle below raged on as Randall heard orders being shouted to their attackers. From his vantage, he could also hear footsteps running up the staircase. He could only hope it was Michael or Catherine retreating up a level. A few moments later, John and Liz jogged into the room.

"We found a rope," John said, panting.

"Great. Tie a loop in the rope, hand it to me, and then hold my legs," Randall said to John, who passed him the rope and then held his father's legs through the open window.

"What in God's name are you doing, Nick?" Liz said, concern in her voice.

"I'm pretending to be a cowboy."

Randall released his grip on the wood trim and balanced on the windowsill, rope in hand. He tossed the rope towards the black pipe, overshooting it by a couple of feet.

"You've gotta warn me when you're going to move like that! I almost lost my grip!" John yelled.

"Sorry John. I've got to lean out a bit more to get this rope around a pipe."

"It won't do us much good if you fall out the damn window and splatter your brains on the street! Liz, can you hold the back of my belt to steady me before my dad kills himself out there?"

John braced his knee against the wall and clutched his father's legs while Liz grabbed his belt to help steady him. "Okay, go ahead."

Randall tried to lasso the pipe again and missed once more. This time, overshooting to the left.

More footsteps from the lower levels, this time much

closer. The sound of grunting and something heavy crashing followed them.

We're running out of time!

"Dad, if you're going to do this, you better make it quick!" John said.

Randall tried again, this time hitting the mark. He tugged on the rope to make sure it was secure. He pulled with all of his weight, dropping to his knees, once again drawing a curse from John. Certain the rope would hold his weight, he climbed down from the sill, the rope dangling out the open window.

"John, do you think you can pull yourself up to the roof, then haul Liz up on the rope?"

"Bloody hell Nick! I'm not climbing out there!" Liz cried.

The sound of footsteps coming up the steps called their attention to the stairs. Randall stepped in front of Liz, shielding her from the approaching intruders. Two figures sprinted from the stairs, guns in hand.

"Thank God it's you!" Randall said, relaxing his body as he recognized Michael and Catherine.

"We've got to move. They'll be here any minute!" Michael said, pulling to a stop next to the group, placing his hands on his knees to catch his breath.

"We think we have a way out," Randall said, turning to search for John.

"Liz, grab the rope," John's voice called through the open window.

Randall and Liz popped their heads out the window, finding John standing on the top of the building by the black pipe. Randall grabbed the rope and tied it around Liz's waist.

"I'm not sure I can do this," Liz said, her voice wavering.

"Out you go," Randall replied, lifting her onto the sill.

Liz begrudgingly stepped onto the ledge as Randall held her hand.

"Pull her up!" Randall yelled to John, who did as ordered.

Liz shrieked. "I'll get you back Nick!"

Despite the circumstances, Randall couldn't help but smile. Minutes later, John tossed the end of the rope back down.

"You're up," Michael said, appearing by Randall's side.

"No way, Catherine's next."

"You're a civilian. You go before me," Catherine protested.

A loud thudding sound reverberated up the staircase. The attackers were closing in.

"We blocked the door with an armoire and another piece of furniture. I'm not sure how long it will hold," Michael said.

"Then you better get going," Randall said to Catherine, who stared at him, holding her ground

"Lieutenant, you're up. We don't have time to argue, and that's a direct order," Michael said.

Catherine sighed heavily, climbed onto the ledge, and shimmied up the rope in athletic fashion.

"Okay, now you," Michael said to Randall.

"I don't think so."

Michael shifted on his feet. "Nick, that might have worked with the Lieutenant, but it's not working with me. You need to get your ass out there."

A blast came from down the stairs, followed by shouts.

"They're shooting out the armoire. A few more shots

and they'll be through. They'll be here in minutes," Michael said, nodding for Randall to go.

"Right, and you're younger, stronger, and faster than me. If you go first, you'll be able to pull me up much faster."

"Damit! We don't have time for this!"

More blasts from the lower level.

Randall grabbed the rope through the window. "You're right, so you better get moving." He handed the rope to Michael, who shook his head and snatched it from Randall. He slipped onto the sill.

"Get out here and tie the end around your waist!" Michael shouted as he hauled himself up the rope like a top athlete.

Randall grinned, then tied the rope around his waist as Michael completed his climb. He had just finished the knot when he heard another blast, followed by a crashing sound, and boots thudding on the wooden stairs. He stared back into the room, wide eyed, as two dark figures appeared at the top of the stairs.

Randall stepped onto the sill and climbed.

"The window!" a voice called from the room below. Randall was several feet up when a head popped out the smashed window. Randall tried to climb faster but was suddenly jerked up the building, causing his arm to be dragged across the exterior of the building, his jacket sleeve torn to shreds.

Chapter Fourteen

Randall soon found himself hauled onto the rooftop like the catch of the day being dragged aboard by a fishing trawler. He rubbed at his raw right arm.

"Are you alright?" Liz asked.

"Never better," Randall replied.

A bullet ricocheted up the side of the building, causing everyone to pull back from the edge. Suddenly, the rope they had used to access the roof went taut. "Someone's climbing up!" John said, reaching for the rope.

Michael produced a serrated knife from his pack and hacked at the rope, which frayed under the attack. In a moment's time, the rope split, the end skittering off the rooftop, followed by the sound of cursing and screaming as one attacker tumbled to the street below.

"That'll slow them down, but it won't stop them. Come on!" Michael yelled.

The group scurried across the rooftops, the frosty night wind howling like a mournful ghost. They headed Northwest, toward Hungerford Lane, careful not to get too close to the edge.

"How did they know we'd be there?" John asked.

"That's a good question," Randall said, looking back in the direction they had come.

Catherine led the way, gun drawn, and ready to defend the group. Michael brought up the rear to cover their flank. They reached the end of the relatively flat brick roofs. An alleyway filled a small gap between the buildings and stairs leading down to the street.

The sound of sirens wailing in the distance grew louder, announcing the police were on their way.

"This way," Catherine said, stopping at the top of the staircase, which resembled the fire-escapes back home. She assisted John, who went first, to help Liz transition from rooftop to stairs. Randall followed her, and Catherine jumped down next. Michael arrived a moment later.

"I haven't seen anyone, so I think we're safe," Michael said.

The group traversed down the stairs as police cars screeched to a stop on the street below. The officers exited their vehicles, taking aim at them.

"You, on the staircase, don't move!" One officer shouted. "Drop your weapons! Now!"

The group waited in the squad room, having just been released after a visit from a grumpy diplomat from the American Embassy. The man was clearly unhappy at being woken at such a late hour, but had been given no choice. Michael had wisely used his one call to contact his father back home, resulting in the diplomat's late-night call upon the authorities.

"I don't know who the hell you people are, but you're damn lucky that you won't be sitting in those cells rotting for a long time," he said.

"We appreciate your help, especially at such a late hour," Randall replied.

"I trust that you'll stay out of trouble for the rest of your visit. It's not like the Brits need any more reason for thinking Americans don't give a shit about how the rest of the world lives," the diplomat said, scowling at Randall before walking to the elevator.

"That went well," John said, stepping next to his father.

"Something's not right," Randall said.

"What do you mean?" John asked.

Randall's mind turned, thinking about the day's events. "How did the Russians know we would be here? It seems like they know what we're going to do before we do it."

"If they knew about the letters we were looking for, maybe they saw the same connection that we did," John offered.

Randall had considered and dismissed this possibility. The Russians had known about their visit to the Library of Congress and this trip to London. The odds of them being able to predict both sets of events were low, but there was no reason to alarm John. He would have to carefully consider who they had spoken to find a connection. "Maybe you're right."

A loud ping from down the hallway announced an elevator car. As the door slid open, a familiar face exited the elevator. Edwards had arrived.

Great, just what I needed.

The portly Englishman locked eyes with Randall and

trudged down the corridor directly at him. "Exactly who do you think you are, breaking into my museum and disturbing our excavation? Have you no shame man! The damage you've caused by your ham-fisted methods is immeasurable! I promise you, I'll do everything in my power to see that you're barred from any research in this country ever again!"

Before Randall could speak, Liz stepped directly into Edward's path. "You'll do no such thing, Winston! I still remember your indiscretion at the Rotterdam conference, and unless you'd care for me to share it with your colleagues, you'll keep your mouth closed."

Edwards shrunk like a flower wilting in the desert sun. His upper lip trembled, and his eyes glassed over. "I can't believe you're saying this. I just—."

"You'll do well to turn around and march back home, and never mention this again!"

Edwards nodded, turned and slunk back to the elevator. He called the car, entered it and was gone.

"I'm not sure what that was about, but thank you," Randall said, turning to Liz, his back to the elevator.

"It looks like we settled here things, but we're still no closer to solving this riddle," John said.

"You're right, but we can eliminate the possibility that they buried the book at Franklin's house. If it was there, we would have found it," Randall said. The sound of someone clearing his throat startled him. Randall spun and looked into a vaguely familiar face. The gentleman was dangerously thin and slightly taller than Edwards. He wore round, dark-rimmed glasses that hung off a triangular nose. It took Randall a minute, but the cloud of uncertainty parted and he recognized the man. It was Edward's assistant from The Franklin House.

"Sorry, I didn't mean to disturb you," the man said, grimacing.

"You work with Dr. Edwards," Randall said.

"He called to complain about having to come down to the station to deal with you. He wasn't happy when he found out what happened."

"Sorry for getting you rousted from bed at such a late hour."

"It's fine. My name is Ethan Davies. A pleasure to meet you," Davies said, shaking Randall's hand.

"Did your boss ask you to come and speak with us?" Randall asked.

Davies laughed, pushing his glasses back up his nose as they drooped. "Oh no. If Winston knew I was here, he'd be exceptionally angry with me."

"I thought you said he called to complain about us?"

"He did, and that's the only reason he called. He wanted to make sure I knew he was angry. It's just the way he is."

Randall smirked at Davies' honesty.

"Anyway, I came because I have some information that might interest you. I understand that you're looking for something that Mr. Franklin may have sent to Mr. Hewson. Is that correct?"

Randall's expression became serious. He studied Davies carefully. "That's right."

"Then I have something you'll want to see," Davies said, slipping a flash drive into Randall's hand.

"What's this?"

"Scanned copies of correspondence between Franklin and Hewson. We found them concealed in a wall panel during construction. Of course, I can't give you the originals. They're priceless artifacts that we'll soon be including on our tour. However, I believe the images will suffice for your needs."

"Why are you giving me these?"

Davies grinned broadly now, revealing tea stained teeth in need of whitening. "Because it would drive Winston crazy!"

Randall closed his eyes, shook his head, laughing at the reply. "Thank you. We'll review them on our flight back to the States."

The men shook hands and Davies turned to leave, walking at a crisp pace to the elevator. He pushed the call button and waited for the car to come back up.

"What do you think we'll find?" John asked, calling his father's attention.

"I have no idea."

Chapter Fifteen

Alexandria, Virginia

May 11, 4:58 p.m.

After leaving the police station, Michael had arranged a military flight home, deeming travel on a conventional carrier to be too dangerous, given what had transpired at Franklin's House. Upon returning to D.C., he had also used his contacts to arrange safe lodgings for everyone. Catherine now stood guard, while the rest of the group tried to solve the riddle of Davies' flash drive.

He pushed back in his seat, casting his eyes about the rest of the group seated around the rectangular wooden dining room table. No one looked any more rested than he did, each member of the team getting little more than a few hours of fitful sleep on the flight home. The only thing causing a semblance of wakefulness being the contents of the flash drive that Davies had given them.

"I'll go make some more coffee," John announced, pushing up from the table and walking to the kitchen at the far right of the dining room. The home, while not large, a tick over 1,800 square feet, featured an open floor plan, the dining room flowing directly into the kitchen on one end and the living room on the other.

"What do you make of it, Nick?" Michael asked, rubbing his tired eyes and yawning.

The 'it' in question had been a letter from Hewson to Franklin, sent approximately a year and a half after Franklin's correspondence. The letter referred to other correspondence between the men, but, unfortunately, it was short on details.

"It looks like we were right about Franklin sending the package to Hewson for safekeeping," Randall said, referring to the first letter in which Franklin asked his friend to watch over the package. "But the book, or whatever was in the package, came back to Franklin about 18 months later, so it looks like we were on a bit of a snipe hunt here. The question now is where did it go once it came back to the states?"

"Looks like we're back to square one," John said, fetching fresh cups of coffee from the kitchen.

"Maybe not," Randall said, eliciting a confused look from his son. "First, you can tell from the symbol on the letter from Hewson to Franklin that they were both freemasons."

"What do you mean?" John asked, as he set a cup of black coffee in front of his father.

"See those three squares?" Randall asked, jabbing a finger at a picture in the letter's corner. The symbol featured a large square base with two smaller squares stacked on top, but sitting at odd angles, their corners raised and touching in the middle, forming a triangle with the top of the square.

John nodded.

"47th Problem of Euclid."

"What's that?" John asked.

Randall smiled. "It's a masonic symbol known as The 47th Problem of Euclid, also called the 47th Proposition of Euclid, or the Pythagorean Theorem."

"What does that mean?" Liz asked, joining them.

"The Masons are an ancient, fraternal organization, which traces its origins back to stone masons in the Fourteenth century, so learning to apply mathematics to create elaborate structures was a critical skill set to learn. Back in the day, they didn't have modern equipment for construction, so they needed to create a structurally sound base, and this was that method."

"How?" John asked. He was clearly enjoying hearing the explanation from his father.

"If you remember your math, The Pythagorean Theorem says that in any right triangle, the sum of the squares of the two sides is equal to the square of the hypotenuse, or the longest side."

John raised an eyebrow.

"In ancient Egypt, there were architectural specialists known as Harpedonaptae who were called in to lay the foundation lines of buildings. They were highly skilled and relied on astronomy and mathematical calculations to form perfect square angles for each building. They would lay a building's cornerstone at the northeast corner of the building."

"Why in the northeast?" Liz asked.

"The Harpedonaptae first laid out the north and south lines by observing the location of Polaris, the North Star, which they believed was in a fixed location in the sky. After laying out a perfect North and South line, they used

Pythagorean's Theorem to create a square to establish perfect East and West lines for their foundations," Randall said.

John's face morphed into a smile and he closed his eyes and nodded his head.

"That's great, Nick, but it still doesn't help us find the book," Liz said.

"I'm getting to that. Read the stanza just below the figure."

In unison, John and Liz bent over each of Randall's shoulders, Liz his left and John his right.

> *If his knowledge you seek to gain,*
> *Euclid's Problem will lead the way.*
> *A giant's rest shall be its bed,*
> *Upon his home, the brave will tread.*

"You think this is a clue to point us to Washington's book?" John asked.

"Yes. I think we need to find a building, or structure with the symbol on it."

Liz dropped her glasses from her eyes. "Like a Rune stone, leading the way to the book?"

"Right. We find the building with that symbol and we've found the book."

Chapter Sixteen

Randall absentmindedly dragged the back of his fingers across the stubble that had formed on chin. He dug his palms into his tired eyes and rubbed. He then glanced up from the computer screen and saw Liz dozing on a brown sofa, an open book lying across her midsection. To her right, curled up with a blanket, asleep on a brown leather recliner, was Catherine, clearly wiped out from pulling the early guard duty shift.

Randall's eyes swept the room and came to rest on John, who was standing next to a picture on the far end of the room. He traced a finger across it, then looked down at his phone. The right corner of his mouth was curled up into an expression Randall knew well. It was the look his son got when he made an important discovery.

Randall quietly pushed himself up from the table and walked to John, careful to keep the noise of his footsteps to a minimum, lest he wake Liz or Catherine. A moment later, he was by John's side and realized it wasn't a picture, but a diagram of Mt. Vernon with directional bearings. "What did you find?" He whispered.

John turned his head toward his father, then looked back at the diagram of Mt. Vernon. "What do you notice about the buildings in this diagram?"

Randall turned to face the poster, leaning in to look closely. The Mansion was at the center, top of the map. Directly below it, lying to the West, was the Bowling Green, flanked to the left, or South, by the Upper Garden and the right by the Lower Garden. To the left and above the Upper Garden, forming two sides of a square, were a series of red-roofed buildings. Beyond the buildings, farther South, was the largest structure on the map, The Ford Orientation Center.

"They're all colonial style, white-washed buildings with red roofs, or brick structures."

"How are they oriented?"

Randall squinted now, trying to understand where John was taking him. "They're all oriented the same way, parallel to each other."

"Very good, Dad, but look closer. Are they all aligned the same way?"

Randall scanned the map and immediately caught his error. He turned to look at John, his eyes wide. "All except the Texas Gate and Washington's tomb. They seem to line up with the true North-South line."

John was grinning like a school kid who just found out school was closed because of a heavy snow.

"You think it's there?" Randall asked.

"After you explained the Mason connection, I had a hunch, then did an internet search for pictures of the tomb. I couldn't find the symbol on any of them, but I saw these," John showed his father his phone.

The Washington Prophecy

Randall adjusted his glasses and peered down at the screen. There was a picture of a courtyard split down the center by a red stone walkway. Flanking each side of the walkway were white stone obelisks surrounded by black wrought iron fences. The walkway ended at a brick building with a black arched gate at its center. Resting behind the gate were two white sarcophagi.

"Do those look familiar?" John asked, pointing at the obelisks.

"Like mini-Washington monuments," Randall replied, studying the picture carefully. He looked up from the phone. "But you didn't see the symbol on any of the pictures?"

John frowned and shook his head. "There's a good chance it's not in an obvious spot. After all, we're talking about a secretive society, and, if we're right about this, a passage to something that wasn't meant to be discovered.

Randall took a deep breath and once again ran his fingers over his chin. After a moment, he looked at his son. "You think we should check it out?" It was more a statement than a question.

"I do. It all makes sense. Remember the second stanza of the verse?"

A giant's rest shall be its bed,
Upon his home, the brave will tread.

"Washington was a formidable figure during the Revolutionary period of our country. Many of his supporters, and historians, feel the country never would have survived without him as the leader."

"And this is his final resting place, his bed," Randall said.

"Right, and if we're brave enough to tread there, I believe we'll find the book."

Randall gripped his son's shoulder and smiled. "Then we better get everyone up. We have a trip to plan."

Chapter Seventeen

Fairfax County, Virginia

May 11, 10:22 p.m.

The landscape changed dramatically over the short drive from the Alexandria safe-house to the Virginia countryside, suburban sprawl replaced by gently rolling hillsides. Colonel Rawlings gave the team a black Chevy SUV for their drive to the estate. The trip along the George Washington Memorial Parkway had offered stunning views of the Potomac River at night, but as the suburbs fell away into the distance, an inky blackness had enveloped them as they passed the final community of Riverside Park and traversed the final winding roads to Mt. Vernon.

The wind buffeted the SUV as they made the turn onto their final approach to the estate. The headlights burrowed through the darkness like inverted yellow cones, puncturing the black, as the first signs of manmade structures came into view. A final, bending arc to the right and they had arrived at the Texas Gate. The structure shone in the Suburban's headlights, its arching black gate and enclosure framed by two separate white, colonial style structures with red-tiled roofs, attached to a long brick wall that formed the outer perimeter of the property.

Michael hopped down from the driver's seat and walked to the black iron gate, flicking on his flashlight. John followed closely behind, bolt-cutters tucked beneath his jacket. The two arrived at the locked gate in less than a minute.

John studied the entrance and quickly determined that there were two ways in. Over the wall, or through the gate. Given the distance to Washington's tomb, the first option was out. They needed to drive if they were to have any chance of successfully exploring the tomb, finding the book, and leaving before staff arrived to open the facility in the morning. That meant going through the gate.

"Are you ready to do this?" Michael asked.

John took a deep breath and nodded. He slipped the bolt-cutters from his jacket and went to work on cutting the lock while Michael watched the road for signs of vehicles approaching. Cutting through the reinforced metal latch was difficult, but after a moment, a loud snap, followed by the sound of the heavy metal lock hitting pavement, announced they were through.

"You're sure we don't need to worry about the security cameras?" John asked, pulling the chain through the gate and propping one side open.

Michael shook his head and picked up the main part of the lock. "Our contact says they don't monitor it overnight. When the morning shift arrives, if there was a problem overnight, they review the tape and our guy will make sure that there's no trace of us."

"So, we have about five and a half hours to find the book?" John asked, slipping the bolt-cutters back under his coat.

"More or less. I think the quicker we can do this, the better," Michael replied. Both men walked back to the SUV.

They got back inside the Tahoe and Michael slipped through the open gate, stopping on the other side. John hopped down, closed the gate, and fed the chain back through, and reattached the lock as best he could to make it appear the gate was properly secured.

Michael threaded through dark looping roads, the ghostly silhouette of trees swaying in the wind on either side, illuminated by the Tahoe's driving lights. Given the circumstances, Michael opted not to have on the headlamps of the SUV. They traveled away from the primary home, navigating to the far end of the estate, arriving a short time later outside a simple brick structure. Michael pulled off the road onto a dirt path, tucking the Tahoe into a small stand of trees next to the building. They had arrived at Washington's tomb.

The group filed out of the SUV, flashlights in hand, swinging around the building until they arrived at front of the structure. As with the front gate, a fence secured the area. John made quick work of the lock, and the group entered the courtyard to the main tomb area. They approached another black wrought-iron fence with yet another lock.

"Do we just need to cut this one and we're in?" Liz asked.

Michael shook his head. "There are motion sensors inside."

As with Franklin's house, Catherine went to work, disabling the alarm. It didn't take her long.

"Nice work," John said.

"Thanks, it's one of my specialties," Catherine said. She walked back over to the Tahoe and removed a long slender bag, then slung it to her back before rejoining the group at the gate.

"What's that?" John asked. He nodded at the bag on Catherine's back.

"Drag bag. I use it to store my rifle," Catherine responded. She pushed the gate open and Michael went in first, gun drawn. A moment later, he signaled for the others to join him. Given the recent encounters with the Russians both at the Library of Congress and in England, Randall had also asked for and received a side arm.

The inside of the Washington Family Tomb was tiny, forcing the group of five to crowd into the small space between two stone sarcophagi.

"Where should we begin?" Liz asked.

"We need to look for a symbol. If I'm right, it will point us in the direction we need to go," John replied.

"Do you really think they hid the book somewhere in here? It's not a very big place to hide something so valuable," Michael said.

"I guess that means we won't have to look for very long then," Randall said, patting Michael on the shoulder. The younger man just shook his head and grinned.

"I think we should split up into teams. Two people inside, two searching outside, and I'll stand guard," Michael said. He distributed a hand-held radio to each team.

"Makes sense. Dad, you and Liz search inside.

Catherine and I will look for the symbol outside. If you find something, let us know and we'll do the same," John said.

John, Catherine, and Michael departed, leaving Randall and Liz to search inside the tomb.

"It's strange," Liz commented from the far side of the vault.

"What's that?" Randall asked.

"When you consider how important Mr. Washington was to your country, how accessible his remains are."

Randall paused, then shone his light in Liz's direction.

"What?" Liz asked.

"I've never thought of that. You're right. It was pretty simple for us to just break in," Randall said. The gravity of their actions immediately settled on him. They had broken into the tomb of the first President of the United States and were now rummaging around his remains. A student of history, Randall held places such as these as venerated grounds, and once again, he found himself disturbing them. Sadly, this wasn't the first time a situation had forced him to do so, having broken into the Vatican grotto previously, along with other sacred areas. Although each time he had done so with good reason, the thought of desecrating an honored area still bothered him.

"Are you okay?" Liz asked. She had clearly picked up on his mood change.

Randall nodded. "Why do you ask?"

"Your face. You look like you saw a ghost," Liz replied.

A smile broke out across Randall's face, causing Liz giggled loudly.

"Having fun in there, you two?" A voice called out from the courtyard. It was Michael.

An enormous grin spread across Randall's face. He then turned back to the search for the symbol. After thirty minutes, they had searched the entire vault and found nothing.

"Any luck?" John called through the radio.

"Nope," Randall replied. "How about you?"

"We've circled the building twice now, but no sign of the symbol."

Silence fell between them. Had John been wrong about the book being here? If so, they were back to square one. Worse than that, everything their theories were based on might be wrong.

"Dad, are you there?"

Randall rubbed his stubble covered chin. It was becoming a full-blown beard. Mostly grey. John had been right about Hewson, and something told Randall that John was right about this, too. Washington had been a Mason, and it made sense that the book was here.

"Catherine and I are coming back," John said through the radio.

A few minutes later, John re-appeared back inside the tomb. He walked up to his father, his head cocked to one side. "Is everything okay? You didn't answer me on the radio."

"Sorry about that. I was just thinking about the riddle from the letter. Where's Catherine?"

"Michael called her on the radio. I guess I was wrong about that."

"I don't think so. We must have missed something. Let's walk through this again. We know that Hewson and Franklin were both Masons and used Masonic symbols in their correspondence. We also know that Washington was a Mason, and that the 47th Problem of Euclid played some kind of role here, otherwise why did Hewson refer to it in his letter?"

"He might have just put the symbol on the letter as a nod from one Mason to another."

"No way. These guys operated in code, to where a simple play on words held the key to finding the clue that's leading us to the book," Randall said, referring to the grave reference that led them to Franklin's London home. "The symbol on the letter isn't an accident. The book is here and we need to keep looking for it."

"Let's assume you're right. We've searched the tomb, inside and out, and can't find the symbol anywhere. Where could it be?"

"When was this tomb constructed?" Liz said, interjecting herself into the conversation.

"They built the tomb in 1831, and they lay Washington to rest here in 1837, along with the remains of Martha and several other relatives," John replied.

"Do we know if there have been any renovations since then?" Randall asked.

"They've probably painted and patched holes inside since then. Maybe they covered the symbol was in the process?" Liz said, her voice rising in excitement.

John frowned. "If we assume everything my dad said is correct, and these men were using Masonic code to create a trail to the book, then they would have built the clue so that it would have survived improvements." He turned to look at his father, who was grinning broadly. "What?"

"They would have built the clue so that it would have survived improvements. You've solved the mystery."

"What do you mean? I'm not following you?"

Randall could see by his expression that John didn't see how his play on words had provided a critical clue. "They built the clue. These men were Masons. Master builders!

The tomb lying along true North and South, the 47th Problem of Euclid. It all fits a pattern."

"My God, you're right!" Liz blurted, then covered her mouth in embarrassment.

John's glance bounced back and forth between his father and Liz. "Will someone please tell me what's going on?"

"The clue is on the cornerstone of the tomb, where they would have started construction!" Randall said.

John's eyes went wide. "Ivy. There's ivy growing on the walls outside! It may have covered the symbol!"

The group raced outside, flashlights bouncing wildly as they followed John to the true North-South wall. John stopped, shining his light at the bottom corner. A thick patch of ivy draped the wall, several inches thick at the bottom, and tapering to a single layer halfway up the building.

"Help me get this off the wall, but be careful not to pull the brick off," John said to his father, before dropping to his knees and pulling a single strand of the vine away at a time. By the beams of the flashlights, the two men worked slowly, careful not to damage the brick wall. After nearly thirty minutes of meticulous work, they peeled back the last layer of ivy.

Father and son turned to face each other in unison, smiles on their faces. They had found the symbol.

Chapter Eighteen

"Well done, boys!" Liz said, patting the Randall boys on their shoulders.

A tired Randall mopped the sweat from his forehead before wiping his gritty hands on the front of his shirt. He pushed himself to his feet, joining John, who was already standing and looking at his phone. "What are you doing?"

"I took a picture of Hewson's letter. I'm comparing it to that," John said, nodding his head to the message inscribed on the cornerstone.

Randall shifted his eyes to the wall and read the inscription. The brick was discolored, red interspersed among the streaks of white calcium carbonate and black soil, but the engraving was clear. At the top sat a large square base with two smaller squares stacked on top, sitting at odd angles, their corners raised and touching in the middle, forming a triangle with the top of the base square. Beneath the figure, the inscription read:

WASHINGTON
III, IV, V

At the very bottom of the writing was an elaborately drawn striped shield, with a doubled headed arrow at its top edge. Draped on either side was bunting, which hung loosely, forming small loops, which met at a final loop beneath the shield. Perched atop the shield was a majestic eagle, claws gripping the top of the shield, its head turned to the left.

"What are you thinking?" Randall asked.

John's eyes flashed from his phone to the wall, and then his father. "I think this is the clue we're looking for, but I'm not sure how to decipher it."

"Do you think there's a secret lever built into the inscription?" Liz asked, a hint of hope in her voice.

"Good idea Liz, let's see," John said, once again kneeling by the cornerstone. He examined each feature, searching for a raised edge or some hint of a hidden seam. John pressed, pulled, and traced along each figure, but nothing happened.

"Maybe this is supposed to point to the entrance somewhere else," Randall said, scratching the back of his neck.

John considered this and nodded. "You could be right. We've seen the Euclid symbol and writing before. Except the eagle crest."

"Do you think that's what's supposed to lead us to the entrance?" Randall asked.

"Maybe. But how?" John asked.

Liz pushed her glasses closer to her eyes, then folded her arms, gaze locked on the inscription. "I've seen this somewhere." She closed her eyes, clearly trying to recall where. Her expression morphed from determination to glee. "I've got it!" She grabbed Randall by the arm, hauling him back towards the crypt, flashlight in hand.

"Where are we going?" Randall asked, following along quickly so as not to trip.

They arrived back inside the vault. Liz released his arm. "Here, take this." She handed him the flashlight. Randall pointed the beam at Liz, who removed her glasses, then gestured with both hands, like a game show host, to the top of Washington's sarcophagus. Randall swept his light from Liz to the stone slab.

"Great job Liz!" Randall said. He grasped her hand in his and squeezed.

John joined them. "What's all the commotion?"

"Liz found the eagle."

John frowned. "Where?"

Randall once again illuminated the top of Washington's coffin.

"Well, I'll be," John said. "What do we do next?"

"Each clue has led us to the next step. The stanza and Euclid problem pointed us to this estate, the true North-South building technique to the cornerstone, the Eagle to the sarcophagus. The only clues we haven't used yet are Washington and III, IV, V," Randall said.

"And we have the word 'Washington' on the top of the coffin," Liz added.

"So, we need to figure out the meaning of III, IV, V?" John asked.

"Right," Randall said with a nod. "We know from Pythagorean Theorem that the numbers 3, 4, 5 are significant because of the relationship between the sides of a right triangle, but they're also important numbers to the Masons. My guess is this is a code we need to use on the letters of the word 'Washington.'"

"Like the order of the letters?" John asked.

"That would be my guess," Randall confirmed.

Liz was already examining the top of the coffin with her flashlight. "The third, fourth and fifth letters of the word are the letters SHI."

"Okay, so let's try that," John said, touching the letters in sequence. Nothing happened.

"Press a little harder," Randall suggested.

John shrugged, leaned on his finger as he pressed the letter 'S'. The rock crumbled under his weight, his index finger sinking into the stone lid. He pulled it back out. "What just happened?"

"The Masons were master builders. Although we can't see it, they hollowed out the space in the rock behind the letters to create false facades. Only someone who knew their code would know to check." Randall said. He tried again with the letter 'H'. This time, the stone held. He made additional attempts on both 'H' and 'I' but the stone held firm.

"What gives?" John asked.

Randall shrugged. "I'm not sure."

"Perhaps we're not applying the code correctly," Liz said. "Maybe we need to begin counting again from the next letter?"

Randall started on 'H' and counted to four, his finger coming to rest above 'G'. "Here goes." He pressed on the letter with the force of his body. It crumbled like the 'S'. "Liz, you're a genius!"

Randall repeated the pattern, beginning with 'T' and counting around to the beginning of 'Washington' until he reached the 'A', the fifth letter. It crumbled like the others. As Randall removed his finger, the sound of stone grinding against stone arose from their left.

John shone his light toward Martha Washington's coffin. It had rotated ninety degrees.

Randall grabbed the radio from his pocket. "Michael and Catherine, we found something. Get in here!"

"On our way."

By the time Randall had put his radio back in his pocket, both Liz and John were by Martha's coffin, staring into a hole in the vault's floor. Randall walked over to them.

Through the beam of John's light, Randall could make out steps descending beneath the floor of the building. The opening was just wide enough for an average size man to fit through, without having to turn sideways. Randall heard footsteps coming to a stop behind him. John, hearing the same sound, turned and pointed his flashlight in that direction. Michael and Catherine had arrived.

"What did you find?" Michael asked.

"Take a look," Randall said, motioning to the opening in the crypt's floor.

Michael pinched his brow, then walked over to the steps, shooting the beam of his flashlight into the now open passage. He let out a small laugh. "How do you Randall boys keep finding these things?"

"Who should go in?" Liz asked, hovering behind Randall.

"After what happened in London, we need to maintain surveillance. Catherine, find a spot out there with a view of the crypt and keep an eye out for anyone who might have followed us, but make sure you're concealed. If you see anyone approaching, call it in on the radio. Don't engage unless I give the order. Everyone else goes in. I'll lead, to make sure it's clear."

The group nodded in agreement. Catherine opened her drag bag and removed her sniper rifle. She checked to make sure it was ready before slinging the drag bag onto her back and slipping out through the courtyard.

"Does everyone have a light?" Michael asked. Once again nods from everyone. "Let's go."

Michael descended into the blackness beyond, his gun-mounted flashlight providing illumination. Randall followed closely behind, stepping onto the first stone step, then the next, quickly disappearing beneath the floor of the crypt. Michael's light cast a cone-shaped beam of yellow-white illumination into the subterranean chamber. He'd move down a few steps, then sweep his light in a small arc to see what lay beyond.

The staircase was little more than a rectangular chute, enclosed on both sides. As they descended, Randall sensed the temperature drop, the air becoming thicker, a tinge of mustiness filling the space. The stairs ended about thirty feet down, feeding into a narrow corridor of hewn rock.

Randall turned the narrow hallway just wide enough to do so. Behind him was Liz, followed by John in the rear. As he turned back to face forward, Randall nearly bumped Michael from behind, the latter having halted. Randall craned around Michael's hulking figure, able to see only what Michael's gun mounted light afforded. He immediately understood why Michael had stopped.

The corridor fed into an underground chamber, appointed with items found in America's colonial era. Randall pushed past Michael and stepped into the chamber. He shone his light around for a better look.

The stonework was exquisite, matching that found in the halls of the nation's capital. Sandstone sculpted blocks, stacked in geometric perfection, formed the walls, which rested on marble floors. Each stone was fitted with perfection, making the seams virtually undetectable.

A sudden explosion of light sparked from behind Randall, who turned in surprise. Michael squatted next to a halogen work lamp he had removed from his gear bag. The brightness of the light created the appearance of day in the chamber, allowing Randall to take in the full beauty of the room.

"I'll be right back," Michael said. He jogged back up the stone steps, disappearing from view.

Randall hardly noticed his departure. He was too awestruck by the sight that befell his eyes. Hung on one wall was a portrait of Benjamin Franklin seated at a red velvet-covered table, studiously studying a manuscript with a small stack of books resting on the corner. Directly to its right, a second portrait of Franklin featured the statesman, gavel in hand, standing at a podium. He was standing on an elevated platform between two ornate columns, appearing to hold court. But it was his outfit that drew Randall's attention. He was wearing a Mason's apron.

Beneath the portraits, in rosewood and glass display cases, were several sets of bifocals, and shelves of leather-bound books. Set against the wall to the right of the display case was a wooden hutch desk, with matching cloth bound chair, resting atop a beautiful mosaic patterned, black and white checked floor. Sitting atop the desk was a quill pen resting in an inkwell.

"It's incredible," Liz muttered, awestruck. She was standing next to the display case full of books, running her fingers across the glass covering them. Randall joined her.

"Can you imagine the value of these? They belong in the Library of Congress," Randall said. He squatted to get a better look at the case. Two overlaid pieces of glass, each a little longer than half the length of the case, sat in parallel grooves cut into the case. Randall slid one piece of glass to the side, exposing a set of books. He looked at Liz, whose eyes were wide, a smile running from ear to ear.

Randall motioned to the books. "After you."

"Gladly," Liz said. She pulled a kerchief from her pocket and delicately lifted one book from the shelf and set it on Franklin's desk. She then used the kerchief to carefully clean and dry her hands before opening the book.

Randall appreciated the gesture. There was some disagreement in the antiquarian community about whether it was best to use white gloves or clean, dry hands when handling antique books. While Phil's friend had required the use of the white gloves, the British Library had eschewed the use of gloves in favor of clean, dry hands. The thought behind this favored method was that gloves reduced manual dexterity and increased the likelihood of causing damage.

Liz clearly prescribed to the latter school of thought. Following her gesture, Randall borrowed Liz's kerchief and carefully cleaned his hands. He then picked a book whose cover was well worn and cradled it gingerly in one hand. He adjusted his reading glasses and then carefully turned the delicate pages with his bare hands and read several entries. It was a scientific journal kept by Franklin, filled with observations about electricity and its interaction with different materials. He flipped through several more pages and found detailed drawings and notes from Franklin's early experiments.

Randall returned the book to the shelf and carefully lifted a second. This one contained Franklin's notes on the printing business and writing. He described, in vivid detail, his interactions with other business people and the growth of his industry. More pictures filled the pages, along with notes in the margins written in a different color from the other writing.

"Anything interesting?" Randall asked Liz.

"It's all interesting," Liz replied, still grinning like a schoolgirl on her first day.

Randall laughed, then nodded in agreement. This was a truly incredible find beyond the dreams of most researchers. He was reading previously unseen manuscripts penned by one of the giants of American history for the first time in over two-hundred years. His third choice was a thick, black covered book. He lifted it from the case, immediately feeling its heft, then carried it over to the desk and set it down next to Liz's book. He flipped it open, immediately realizing it differed from the first two.

"… upon receiving the correspondence from my friend Washington, I realized this was a matter of grave importance to our fledgling democracy. Of such impact were the potential ramifications that I immediately spirited away the device and his letters. Had any other man shared the genesis of this technological wonder, I would have truly considered him mad. But General Washington is anything but mad. He is a man of solid timber, the sort upon which made him the natural choice to lead our nation."

"What in the world?" Randall muttered, goose pimples forming on forearms.

"Did you say something, Nick?" Liz asked.

Randall thumbed through more pages, stopping on a full-page diagram, which was drawn sideways, so he rotated the book in his hand. Franklin listed 32 symbols in table form, with English letters beneath only a few, but with question marks beneath most. The symbols were unlike any Randall had ever seen. Sharp lines and soft round shapes intermingled to form the symbols Franklin had sought to translate.

"Nick, what's the matter?" Liz called out, her voice seeming to come from nowhere and everywhere all at once.

Randall felt a tug at his arm. "Nick!" He turned to see Liz pulling on his elbow and tapping his arm, trying to get his attention. His eyes followed her arm until they came to rest on her lips.

"You're scaring me!" Liz said, worry in her voice.

He finally snapped out of the trance. "I'm sorry Liz, I just can't believe what I've found."

"Dad! You need to get over here! Now!" John yelled from another room.

Randall's head shot up and looked around the room, realizing for the first time it was just him and Liz. He looked to the opening from Franklin's room to the next space, deeper in the chamber. He tucked Franklin's book in his pack and hurried to find John, pulling Liz with him.

Michael had set up another work light, illuminating this room like the first. Randall's eyes swept the space, which was considerably larger than the Franklin room. As with the latter, the walls and flooring were crafted to perfection, but using wood instead of sandstone. Long slender columns running floor to ceiling graced the walls, spaced evenly along each side. Beautiful, life-sized portraits of Washington adorned tall, white wooden panels in the walls.

"Incredible," Randall said, reverence in his voice.

A dark wooden desk and upholstered chair sat in one corner, but it was the far corner that caught Randall's eye. John and Michael stood by a long, narrow soffit, cut into the wall, their bodies shielding whatever was inside.

"What took you so long?" John asked, turning to grab his father. He yanked Randall to the corner, Michael stepping to the side so father and son could properly examine the artifacts.

Randall stopped two feet short of the soffit, eyes locked on the contents within.

Set into a half-sphere-shaped depression in the soffit was a round object, the size of a large medicine ball. It glimmered in the beams of the work-light, at times appearing metallic, while from a different angle, seeming like glass. On it were the markings from Franklin's journal. Next to the sphere was a shoe-box size wood and glass case containing a section of bone and strands of hair. Inscribed on the box were the initials G.W.

"What is that?" Liz asked, pointing at the sphere.

John put his hand on his father's shoulder. "Michael and I studied it while you were in the other chamber. This is going to sound nuts, but I think it's an electronic device."

"What makes you say that?" Randall asked. He kneeled next to the object, carefully studying its smooth surface.

"When I touched it, the symbols lit up."

Liz's mouth went slack for a moment, and she cocked her head toward John. "Did you say it's an electronic device?"

"Yes."

"Who would have hidden an electronic device here?" Liz asked, her voice rising.

"I don't think it's a book that Franklin and Washington referred to in their letters. I think it was this," John said, nodding at the device. "While Hewson was hiding this in England, Washington must have had this space built to house it."

"It would explain the book I found in Franklin's collection," Randall said.

John twisted his head toward his father. "What book?"

"Excuse me, gentleman," Liz said, pushing her way between Randall and John. "What exactly is going on here? You can't possibly believe that Washington and Franklin possessed an electronic device in the 1700s. It's simply impossible!"

"Actually, that is what I'm saying Liz. Somehow Washington came into possession of this machine and wasn't sure what to do with it, so he hid it."

Liz turned to face Randall, her face filled with confusion.

Randall grimaced. Liz didn't understand, but that wasn't her fault. She hadn't been involved with any of his past escapades. He placed his hand on her arm. "I know this will come as a shock, but it's not the first time we've seen something like this."

Liz knitted her eyebrows.

Randall took a deep breath. "My specialty is, what some would call, abnormal archeology. Years ago, I developed alternate theories of human evolution, involving interaction with more advanced species."

Liz blinked. "More advanced than humans?"

"Yes."

Liz shook her head. "What in the bloody hell are you talking about?"

"In the jungles of Peru, I discovered a tribe unlike anything known to science. They showed me an underground city, powered by a volcano. The city possessed advanced technology beyond anything we're capable of. We also found a secret base in the Antarctic Circle with beings that built devices that destroyed advanced Chinese military hardware without a struggle," Randall replied.

"Is this some sort of joke?" Liz asked, shooting a glance at John, then Michael. Both men looked down at their shoe tops to avoid her glare. She refocused on Randall.

"I know this is hard for you to accept, but we might be dealing with powers far greater than anything currently known to man," Randall said, taking her hand.

Liz recoiled, pulling her hand away. She blinked, wet her lips about to speak, then stopped, staring into Randall's eyes.

"I know this all sounds crazy, but it's true. It's part of the reason Michael became involved. His father helped us in the past."

Liz glanced at Michael, who nodded.

"I know this is asking a lot, but please trust us... trust me."

Liz closed her eyes, taking several deep breaths. She nodded, looking at Randall. "Okay Nick. I'll play along... for now."

"Thank you."

The crisis averted, John refocused on the sphere. "Okay, let's take a closer look at this," John said. He joined his father, kneeling by the device. The two men looked over the exposed surfaces, searching for clues about how it operated.

"I need to pick it up to examine the rest of it," John said, garnering a worried look from his father.

"How do we know it's not dangerous?" Randall asked.

"Nothing bad happened when I touched it. Besides, Ben Franklin and George Washington both handled it. If they risked it, then I think I should, too."

Randall frowned. It was one thing for him to risk his life on such things, but he didn't like the idea of John endangering himself. He looked at his son, whose eyes were wide with wonder, his face filled with eagerness to explore. Randall reluctantly nodded in agreement.

John grasped the device, gingerly lifting it from the soffit. "It's not too heavy. I'd say about five to six pounds." He rotated it in his hand. As he did, the symbols on its side blinked to life, a soft blue glow emanating from them.

"The book I told you about mentioned these markings," Randall said, pointing a finger at the inscription on the device. "Maybe it will help us figure out how it works."

"Worth a try," John said, running his palm over the Sphere.

Randall reached for his bag, which he had set on the ground near the device. A cool breeze washed over his hand as he retrieved the book. "That's funny. I feel a draft."

"I felt it too," Liz said.

Randall looked at Liz and realized Michael was no longer in the room. "Where's Michael?"

"I'm not sure. He left a few minutes ago," Liz replied, arms still folded across her chest. But her face had softened, her curious scientific mind clearly wondering about the device.

Randall retrieved the book from his bag and thumbed through the pages until he arrived at Franklin's diagram. He studied the diagram, but unfortunately, Franklin had only deciphered several of the characters, and none matched the symbols on the device. Randall sighed.

"No luck?" John asked, still examining the device.

"The symbols on the sphere are in this journal, but Franklin wasn't able to decipher any of them. He figured out what some meant, but unfortunately, not any on the sphere."

"That means there're more symbols on something," Liz said, drifting closer to Randall and John.

Randall laughed. "You're right Liz. I hadn't thought of that."

"What do you think the bone and hair are for?" Liz asked.

John glanced up at the glass case. "I'm not sure."

Randall laid a hand on the case. It was frosty to the touch. He pulled his hand back in surprise.

"Everything okay?" Liz asked.

"I wasn't expecting it to be so cold."

Liz knelt between the two men. "They might be trying to preserve the DNA in the bone and hair. Light and heat break down DNA samples more quickly."

Michael ran into the room. "We need to set up a defensive perimeter. Now!"

"Why?" Randall asked.

"I haven't been able to reach Catherine, and something tripped the motion sensor I left at the top of the stairs. We only have a couple of minutes before they get here," Michael dropped his gear bag on the ground, opened it, and started handing out guns.

"They?" Liz asked.

"I don't know who's coming, but someone tripped the sensor. Based on what happened in London, we have to assume the worst," Michael answered, handing a Glock to Liz.

"I will not use that thing!" Liz pushed the handgun away.

"I know you don't want to, but it might be our only chance of getting out of here alive," Michael said. His expression was all business, and he offered her the gun again. "I'll show you how to use it." Liz grudgingly accepted the firearm.

"Maybe there's something else we can do," Randall said, moving his hand along the floor.

"What did you have in mind?" John asked.

"The breeze I felt. Maybe whoever built this place used natural air currents to cool the bone and hair sample," Randall answered.

"There could be another opening that leads to the surface," John said, his voice rising in anticipation.

"Right. We just have to find it. Liz, help me search. John, you help Michael get ready!"

Liz and Randall followed the cool breeze along the floor to the adjacent wall. It was strongest beneath a portrait of Washington kneeling in prayer beside his horse at Valley Forge.

"Help me get this off the wall," Randall said to Liz, grasping the painting on one side as she handled the other. "Lift."

The two hefted the picture from the wall, gently laying it on the ground. Inlaid into the wood panel in the now vacant spot was an inscription:

Procurva ingens scala, quae ducit ad medium cenaculum.

Laying in a neat row, beneath the inscription, were small tiles containing the Roman Numerals 1-10.

"It's Latin." Liz said. "The winding staircase that leads to the middle chamber."

Randall frowned. They didn't have time for riddles.

"There's an inscription on the wall. It says the winding staircase that leads to the middle chamber, and there are Roman Numerals beneath it!" Randall said.

"Any ideas?" Liz asked, worry in her voice.

"Winding staircase. It could be several things. They were builders…" John's voice trailed away.

Seconds ticked by.

"Whatever you're doing, you better hurry!" Michael

called out, crouching behind the wooden desk, taking aim at the opening from Franklin's room.

"Wait," John's face lit up. He ran over to his father. "I think I know."

"Great, you help Liz," Randall removed his gun and ran over to the bookcase, switching places with John.

"The winding staircase, it's got to be a reference to the steps of masonry, which are 3, 5, and 7," John hurriedly pressed the number sequence. Upon pressing 5, the sound of metal clinking on stone arose from the Franklin room, followed by a bright flash of light and a loud explosion. Smoke and stone fragments streamed from the adjacent room, followed by the staccato sound of automatic gunfire.

"How the hell did they find us?" John yelled.

Randall and Michael opened fire into the approaching maelstrom, alternating suppressive fire.

John pressed 7. A six by four-foot section of wall opened on the adjacent panel. He sprinted to the display case. The sphere was gone. "Dad, Michael, we have a way out! Where's the sphere!"

Neither could hear him. He grabbed the display case with the bone and hair, and shoved it into his bag. He started for his father, who was crouching behind the upended book case, but a stream of lead pushed him back near Liz, who crouched by the open wall panel.

"Dad, come on!" John screamed. He waved his arms wildly, trying to get his father's attention. He failed.

More lead rained down on Randall and Michael. The intruders were pinning them down so they couldn't move.

For a fraction of a moment, the shooting stopped.

"Dad, Michael, over here!" John yelled.

Both men spun to look in John's direction. They saw the opening.

"Go!" Michael yelled to Randall, who rose to a crouch. A stream of hot lead poured in from the Franklin room, forcing him back into a prone position.

"Get the hell out, John!" Randall yelled, slamming a fresh magazine into his Sig Sauer.

John stared helplessly at his father. There was nothing he could do.

"John, we have to get out of here!" Liz said, tugging at his arm.

John stood motionless. A tree rooted in place.

"You have to go! I'm going to lay down cover fire. Get ready!" Randall ordered. He popped above the bookcase and opened fire again as Michael reloaded.

A metallic cylinder arced through the air, bouncing onto the marble floor of the Washington room. A stream of smoke poured out of one end, obscuring Randall and Michael from John's view.

"Come on!" Liz screamed, yanking John backward through the opening. The two tumbled into the passageway, dropping to the ground as the wall closed behind them.

Chapter Nineteen

Smoke filled the Washington room, obscuring everything from Randall's view, but not before he had seen John and Liz escape. John's answer to the clue on the wall had clearly been correct, and he was thankful that John and Liz had gotten away. Unfortunately, he and Michael hadn't been so lucky. Although the gunfire had ceased, he knew it was only a temporary reprieve. Whoever had followed them into the tomb wanted the device and wouldn't give it up without a fight.

Randall looked to his side. The sphere was still there. He had carried it with him behind the bookcase.

"Nick, you still with me?" Michael called out in a low voice.

"Still here," Randall ejected his magazine. He only had three rounds left. He slapped the magazine back in.

It was a waiting game now. Their attackers had clearly driven them into a corner, so they couldn't move. The question was, did they want to kill them, or capture them?

Randall heard a single set of boot steps drawing closer, then stop.

"In the room. Put your guns down and bring out the device," a voice called from the Franklin room.

"And if we don't?" Michael replied.

"Then I'll have no choice but to kill you."

The smoke settled closer to the ground, causing Randall to cough, his eyes burning and watering.

"Who am I speaking with?" Michael asked.

"Does it matter? We have you outnumbered and the crypt above ground is surrounded."

"I have a feeling if we come out, you'll just shoot us," Michael said, drawing a laugh from the other man.

"If I had wanted you dead, you'd all be dead by now. Dr. Nick Randall, are you in there?"

Randall frowned. How did this guy know his name? "Why do you want to know?"

"You're probably wondering what that device is. If you come out, I can show you."

The guy was probably playing him, but the funny thing was that he was right. Randall wanted to know what the device was.

Randall could hear two voices conversing from the other room, but he couldn't make out what they were saying. They were speaking an unfamiliar language, but Randall couldn't place it. Then he heard a single word he understood. 'Nyet.'

"Do you know these guys?" Michael asked.

Randall shook his head no.

"I've been more than patient, but you're leaving me no choice. If you fail to come out in the next thirty seconds, my men will finish you."

Seconds ticked by. Randall searched for something,

anything, to help. He looked at Michael, who stared back. Words weren't necessary. They were trapped with no way out.

Footsteps drew closer.

The smoke still obscured most things from view, but Randall could now make out at least three silhouettes which had entered the Washington room.

"Ten seconds."

Randall said a silent farewell to Sam and John.

"Five, four, three."

"We'll come out," Michael yelled. "But I need assurances that you won't harm my friend."

"Ah, Captain Flores. Yes, a soldier always puts the safety of others ahead of his own. As one soldier to another, I assure you, no harm will befall Dr. Randall. As I said before, if it was my intent to kill you, you would already be dead."

"Who are you, and why do you want the device?" Michael asked.

"Captain Flores, you're in no position to ask questions. Send out Dr. Randall now."

Michael had bought enough time for more smoke to clear. Randall could see his face pressed against the stock of his assault rifle, one eye tracking targets through his scope. "Nick, get up and move slowly to them. I have you covered if they try anything."

Randall rose to his feet, hands in the air. "I've set my gun down. I'm not armed." He moved toward the opening, back into the Franklin room.

"Hands behind your head Dr. Randall."

Randall complied, reaching the threshold which took him into the Franklin room. No sooner had he cleared the entry when a pair of meaty hands dropped onto his shoulders, spinning him around, pinning him against a wall.

Before he could react, his hands were behind his back, zip tied together. His captors marched him to the far end of the room, turning him to face the Washington room.

"On your knees!" one mercenary told him, shoving him to the floor.

There was little smoke in this room, only the remnants of what had wafted in from the Washington room. Randall noted six burly men in black fatigues stationed around the room, which was now severely damaged by the blast. Charred pock marks marred the once pristine sandstone walls and marble floors. Franklin's bookcase was overturned, glass smashed to bits, and the charred remains of the books he had just held minutes earlier splayed on the marble floor.

Despite the situation, Randall was angry. These men had destroyed priceless artifacts that the world deserved to see. Now, instead of ending up in a museum for the public to enjoy and scholars to study, they were burned beyond recognition. The only consolation prize were two dead mercenaries lying on the ground. He and Michael had at least gotten two of them.

"Now you, Captain Flores," one mercenary said. He was the only one not wearing a black mask. His steel gray hair was cropped into a short buzz, the color matching a thick mustache beneath a flat nose. Cobalt blue eyes followed Randall's every move, a light smile playing on the man's lips. Randall immediately recognized his voice as the one who had called out to him earlier.

"Nick, are you okay?"

"They have my hands zip tied behind my back, but I'm fine."

"I'm coming out," Michael said. Slowly rising to his feet, hands in the air. He left his rifle on the ground and walked slowly toward the Franklin room... and into the teeth of their enemies. Three mercenaries tracked his every move with their weapons.

Michael crossed the floor, entering the Franklin room.

"Turn around!" One mercenary yelled. Michael complied. The mercenary unleased a brutal blow to the back of Michael's head, sending him to the marble floor.

"What the hell did you do that for!" Randall yelled, trying to rise to his feet. He was met with the same set of beefy hands, pushing him back down roughly.

"On your knees!" the mercenary barked at Michael, who complied. The soldier zip tied Michael's hands together, then jerked him to his feet, and dragged him over to the older mercenary.

The older soldier surveyed Michael, sizing up his opponent. He pulled his service pistol from his belt and fired a single round into Michael's upper thigh. Michael crumpled in pain, dropping to knees, blood spurting from the wound on his leg.

"What the hell!" Randall said, struggling to pull away from the mercenary holding him. "You said you wouldn't hurt us!"

The older man sneered. "I said I wouldn't harm you. I may need your expertise, but this one," the old soldier said, waving his pistol at Michael, who gritted through clenched teeth. "This one is simply a soldier, and soldiers are expendable."

"If you kill Michael, there's no way in hell I'll help you."

"Perhaps, then, your friend serves a purpose. Bring him to me," the old soldier told his men, who lifted Michael to his knees, dragging him over to their leader. The old soldier pointed his gun at Michael's temple. "Dr. Randall, if you value your friend's life, you won't fail me. Do you understand?"

Randall nodded.

"Where did your son and Dr. Williams go?" He pushed the barrel into Michael's head.

Michael set his jaw. "Don't tell him anything."

Randall looked at Michael, then at the old soldier. "I'm not sure," he lied, trying to buy John and Liz more time to escape.

The soldier cocked the hammer of his gun.

Randall relented. "They were looking for another way out through one wall in the other room," Randall nodded toward the Washington room. "They may have gotten out that way, but I'm not sure. The smoke was so thick, I couldn't see them."

The old soldier narrowed his eyes, locking his gaze on Randall. He nodded to his men. Two mercenaries sprinted into the Washington room, returning a moment later. One of them had the sphere.

"There was no opening, Colonel Aminov, but they removed a picture from one wall and there was a symbol and the word 'Washington' written on it," the mercenary said.

Aminov holstered his gun. He took the sphere from his soldier and gazed longingly at the device. He now had what he had come for. Randall's son and the female academic were unimportant. A thin smile snaked across his face. "The legends were true." He glanced at Randall and Michael. "Load the prisoners into the truck. We have some research to do."

Chapter Twenty

John and Liz followed the corkscrew shaped pathway back up toward the surface, the beam of John's flashlight serving as the only illumination. They spoke no words along the way, John's thoughts turning again and again to abandoning his father and Michael. Were they dead? Captured? He couldn't bring himself to accept the former, but the thought nagged at the periphery of his mind.

There had been no gunshots or explosions after the secret panel had closed. Only quiet and darkness, the sound of their footsteps on the rocky floor the only noise to accompany them as they wound their way back to the surface.

The dark, musty tunnel was devoid of anything but hewn rock, one turn leading to another. After what seemed an eternity, they reached the endpoint of the pathway. Engraved into the wall were the same symbols and numbers from the Washington room. John punched the sequence, stabbing at each letter as if they were responsible for their predicament. The wall opened.

John stepped out into the moonlight and immediately heard footsteps.

"Don't move," a thickly accented voice growled. John froze in place, but not before Liz exited the structure, bumping into him. The unmistakable sound of the action of a gun racking rose from behind.

"Wait!"

Before John could say another word, a whizzing sound, followed by a soft thud, like the sound of celery striking a burlap sack, arose from behind him. The next sound of was the sound of something heavy dropping onto the ivy-covered ground.

John stood motionless for several seconds, then finally turned slowly, aiming the beam of his light in the voice's direction. Laying on the ground was a dead mercenary, a single crimson colored hole in the side of his head.

"John, are you okay?" A female voice called from his pack.

John tore open his pack, retrieving the radio. "Catherine, is that you?" He whispered.

"Affirmative. Where are the others?"

"Liz is with me, but my dad and Michael are still inside. Mercenaries attacked us."

"Roger that. They came in from the West. I tried to contact Michael, but lost signal. Can you move?"

"Yes, Liz and I can walk."

"I need you to go South, behind you. There's a trail that runs Southeast. Take it to The Wharf, but stay off of the main trail. Hug the sides and follow a line of vegetation so no one can see you. I'll meet you there."

"What about my dad and Michael?"

"We're no good to them if we get caught. I radioed in

for help and there'll be a boat waiting for us. We'll have to plan our next move."

John sat staring at the radio. Once again, he faced a choice of whether to abandon his father and Michael.

"John, did you copy my last message?"

"There has to be something we can do for them."

"The only thing we can do is get back to base and get some help. I planted a tracking device on one of their vehicles. We'll know where they're taking them. We need to move now. Those mercenaries could come up the same path you just took out of the crypt."

John exhaled. "Okay, we're leaving now."

"Roger, see you in twenty minutes."

John tossed the radio back into his bag in disgust.

"I'm sorry John," Liz said.

"We better get going."

The two departed, finding the trail that Catherine had described. John paused a moment, looking back at the crypt, not knowing if he had just seen his father for the last time. Twenty minutes later, they rendezvoused with Catherine at The Wharf. As she had promised, there was a boat waiting. They boarded and crossed the Potomac to a waiting SUV. John opened the rear door. Waiting inside was a familiar face he hadn't expected to see.

"We need to talk, John." General Flores was waiting.

Chapter Twenty-One

The black SUV wound its way by the Potomac River, heading back to the Pentagon. Having already explained the discovery of the device, Liz and John sat quietly as Flores explained what he and his team had uncovered.

"We have a mole in our operation. He's been feeding information to someone operating outside of the United States," Flores explained.

"How did you discover it?" John asked.

Flores bit his lip. "One of our analysts discovered several unauthorized transmissions sent to an unknown IP Address from somewhere in my section. She tracked the origin of the messages to a secure system in the wing housing one of my direct reports. We pulled surveillance footage and narrowed the possibilities down to two individuals."

"Two?" Liz asked.

Flores nodded. "We put the two subjects under surveillance, then fed them information about the investigation, hinting about a fake lead generated from a second team. We watched them until someone used the compromised system."

"Who is it?" John asked.

"Colonel Rawlings."

"Michael's commanding officer?" John asked, clearly disturbed.

Flores nodded.

"Did you arrest him?" Liz asked.

"No. We determined it's best to let him continue to operate. We need him to lead us to his handler. It's our best chance to finally get a leg up on whoever is behind this."

John frowned. "But how do we make it happen?"

"The group has taken your father and Captain Flores hostage. They also have possession of the device, so we need something to entice them. Something they missed."

"John, you haven't told the General about the bone fragment and the hair," Liz announced.

"You're right Liz. General, this could be our bait." John removed the case with the bone fragment and the hair follicles from his pack.

Flores took the container from John. "What's this?"

"We think it's hair and bone from Washington," John replied.

"What's its purpose?" Flores asked.

"This is just a guess, but I believe the device must somehow need the D.N.A from George Washington to function."

A look of confusion crossed Flores' face.

"The story goes that an apparition, which helped him see visions of the future, visited Washington, but what if the machine generated the visions instead?"

Liz nodded. "Like virtual reality!"

"Exactly!" John replied.

"Do we have any way to test your theory?" Flores asked. John shook his head.

Flores frowned. "I'd prefer to know for certain that your theory is true before we feed the information to Rawlings, but I don't think we have another choice."

John nodded. "I agree. How do we do this?"

"We've set up a lab for you back at the Pentagon to create the appearance of a major discovery in the case to draw Rawling's attention. We've informed him that Michael and your father were apprehended, so he's waiting to hear from you about what you've found. Once he does, he'll excuse himself as soon as possible and send the message."

"You said your analyst tracked the message to an unknown IP address. Do you have a location?" John asked.

Flores shook his head. "The transmission was scrambled, and they ended the message before we had time to track it to the source."

"Then we're out of luck."

"Maybe not. I might have a way for us to find them."

"What did you have in mind?"

Chapter Twenty-Two

Atlantic Ocean

May 12, 8:07 a.m.

Air Force One soared high above the Atlantic Ocean, unescorted, but tracked closely by NORAD. President Mercer removed his glasses and rubbed his temples as he sat in the presidential suite in the aircraft's front. He stared out from his leather recliner at the two beds flanking the short walkway through the room, each bed sporting matching navy blue comforters with the presidential logo embroidered on them. He contemplated the circumstances facing the United States and its NATO allies in Europe.

Following the Russian invasion of Crimea in 2014, all of Europe, especially the former members of the Soviet Bloc in Eastern Europe, had been on edge about the possibility of further Russian expansion. Memories of the cold war, while not as prominent as once before, were still fresh enough in the minds of Europeans to cast a long shadow over the event. It didn't help that Russian President Anatoliy Volkov was a big fan of sabre rattling, favoring a display of force over the subtlety of political negotiations. Regardless of how the West viewed the Russian leader, a healthy segment of his people approved of and actually enjoyed his displays, harkening back to a time when their country was a military superpower on par with the United States.

Mercer closed the folder on his lap and sighed. Making matters worse, his major NATO partners weren't on the same page about to how to handle the growing potential threat. While Britain supported greater sanctions, along with an increased military posture against the Russians, France and Germany were less enthused. The latter citing its excessive dependence on the Russian Federation for petroleum as a serious consideration when dealing with its neighbor to the East.

While the ally schism was maddening, it wasn't fully surprising. Even at home, there was disagreement on how to handle the Russians. Vice-President Ron Sanders had made his opinions plainly clear, willing to push a limited military confrontation if necessary. While not one to shy away from a fight, Mercer had countered that any military intervention, no matter how limited in scope, could easily escalate, enveloping the entire continent in war. Worst still, the specter of the limited use of tactical nuclear warheads couldn't be discounted. And once they crossed that threshold, the situation could easily escalate out of control, plunging the world into a full nuclear war.

Besides, the United States was already involved in the protracted conflict in the Middle East and the last thing the country needed was to wade into yet another armed conflict on another continent. Between the fighting in Syria,

Afghanistan, and other regional disputes, along with the protracted operations against ISIS, Al Qaeda, and an assortment of other terrorist groups, the American military was stretched thin. A military option, while kept on the table, had to be the last resort. That was the message he would carry to his allies.

He flipped the folder onto the end table next to his chair. The very act seeming to lift the seriousness of being the head of state for the most powerful nation on Earth, at least for a moment. He turned his attention to the encrypted tablet sitting on his lap. He hit the power button; the screen glowing to life. This would be his reward for dealing with the potential of world-wide nuclear annihilation.

On the tablet was the update he had requested from General Flores about the progress being made on finding Washington's secret book. A bit of a Revolutionary War wonk, Mercer reveled in the idea that he, and his greatest hero George Washington, shared the same role as leader of their great nation. Now, if Flores' team could find the book, he would be the first person to directly experience Washington's thoughts on possibly the single greatest defining moment of the young country. More than that, he would get first-hand knowledge of Washington's predictions about the future.

As he skimmed the document, a smile crossed his lips as he read about the exploits of Nick Randall. How an ordinary academic could be at the center of such a momentous occasion was mind-boggling. Yet Mercer knew there was no one better to lead the expedition. He had first-hand experience of Randall's capabilities under fire; the man having saved the free world in the not too distant past. Or at least a good chunk of it.

Mercer's smile evaporated as he read about the latest update. Lieutenant Walker had reported that half the team, Randall and Flores' son Michael, had been taken captive. Making matters worse, the enemy had acquired a device the team had found in the secret rooms discovered under Washington's tomb. Mercer had to reread the line twice. Exactly what was the device they had found and how in the hell was this group constantly getting the drop on Flores and his team?

Mercer slammed the tablet onto the end table, walked to his door, and threw it open. "Ken, get me Brennan on the phone," he said, referring to the NSA Director. "Once you get a hold of him, patch him through to me on the secure line in my office."

Chapter Twenty-Three

Arlington, Virginia

May 12, 6:17 a.m.

John stared out the window of the safe house and onto the tree-lined street. The homes in this subdivision were spaced at greater distances than the closely placed homes of the former safe house. The streets were still quiet, the morning rush yet to come, only the occasional jogger or stray animal breaking the stillness. The eastern horizon was alight with the rays of the rising sun as the morning shrugged off the darkness of the long night they had spent escaping from their attackers at Mt. Vernon.

John sighed, hoping his father and Michael had survived. Although he now had a mission to complete, he couldn't entirely push the thought from his mind.

The news of Rawlings being a mole had hit everyone hard, but it explained how this group, whoever they were, had stayed one step ahead of them. It also spoke of their incredible influence and power to place an agent within one of the most secure and secretive organizations in the United States. Regardless, now was their chance to turn the tables on their enemies and take the initiative, placing them on the defensive and hopefully exposing their plans.

Flores' idea had been simple. Rawlings was unaware that he and John had spoken and may not have even been aware that John and Liz had escaped. John would call Flores' office, claiming to have gotten the number from his father's phone. Flores would be present to ensure that they put the call through to Rawlings and have his technicians monitor all messages coming from the compromised server, and all communications related to Rawlings and his area. John would explain that mercenaries had taken Michael and his father hostage and that he was trying to contact Rawlings to give him an update and ask for help, not knowing who else to contact. He would mention that they had found the Washington DNA at the site and that he and Liz were keeping it at a safe location until Rawlings could collect them. Knowing Rawling's superiors would want all loose ends tied up, it was a safe bet that he would contact them. When he did, Flores and his team would track the outbound call or electronic correspondence from Rawlings and pin down the location of anyone he contacted.

In anticipation of the attempt to apprehend John, Liz and the DNA samples, Flores had dispatched a team to guard John at the new safe house and to move Liz to a separate safe location. He had also strategically placed a sniper to offer cover fire and provide oversight of all activity near the house, and four agents were waiting in their cars, two in each vehicle, down the street and around the corner.

Waiting in the home with John was a frightening-looking member of Flores' task force, Agent Joshua Padua. His craggy face and bald head bore a large, crescent-shaped scar, the result of an improvised explosive device, or I.E.D., encountered during a tour of duty in Afghanistan. Despite his outward appearance, Agent Padua had a wonderful sense of humor, his demeanor as diametrically opposed to his persona as possible.

John glanced at the clock. It was time to make the call. He dialed the number Flores had given him and after a moment, was transferred to Rawlings and waited for him to pick up. He didn't have to wait long.

"Rawlings. Who is this?" a deep baritone voice asked.

"My name is John Randall. I was working with Captain Michael Flores, who was captured a short time ago. Are you Commander Rawlings?"

"Hold for a moment."

The line went quiet, but Rawlings returned moments later. "You said someone captured Captain Flores. How were you able to escape?"

"I found a secret panel with access to the surface. I'm not sure what to do next and need your help. We found DNA samples we believe belong to President Washington. We think they might be related to the device we found," John said.

"Who has the device now?"

The fact Rawlings wasn't surprised about the mention of a device when the team had initially thought they were searching for a book confirmed John's suspicions. Flores was right, the Commander was dirty. "The group who attacked us. They got the device when they captured Captain Flores and my dad."

"Where are you now?"

"Dr. Williams and I are at a friend's home in Virginia.

He's out of town on business, but I have a key. What should we do?"

"You did the right thing calling me. Give me the address and I'll send a team out to pick you up."

John gave Rawlings the address.

"My men will be there in 10 minutes. Stay put and don't contact anyone else!" Rawlings hung up.

"Great job John," Padua said. He hung up the phone he had been using to monitor the call. "You sounded completely natural."

"Thanks. What do we do now?"

"We wait."

Chapter Twenty-Four

Arlington, Virginia

May 12, 6:39 a.m.

John sat on the gray sofa, watching Joshua as he spoke with General Flores on the phone. It was difficult to follow the discussion since he could only hear one side of conversation, but Josh and Flores were speaking about their plan of action. John caught the words fortress and Russia, but that was about all he could gather. Joshua clicked his cell phone off.

"What's happening?" John asked.

"Rawlings took the bait. We traced his call to Russia. Whoever he was speaking with was calling from somewhere near Leningrad."

"Looks like it is the Russians. What happens next? Do you send in a team to see if my dad and Michael are there?"

"First things first. We need to make sure you're safe."

John frowned. Flores men surrounded the safe house, and he had Joshua as his personal bodyguard. His own safety wasn't an issue. "With all due respect, I'm not worried about me. I'm worried about my dad and Michael."

Padua's radio buzzed. "We have movement on the perimeter," the team sniper, Don Price, reported.

"I need location and numbers," Padua replied. "Here, put this on." He handed John a set of body armor.

"Two armed men coming in from the Southeast, three houses down from the alley," Price reported.

"Affirmative. Gomes, Donnelly, intercept," Padua said calmly.

"Roger that."

Padua glanced over at John, who had strapped on the body armor. "Get on the floor, behind the sofa."

John complied. Lying on his stomach on the blue and white area rug near the center of the room. All he could do now was wait.

Small bursts of semi-automatic gunfire erupted down the street, followed by the sound of several gun blasts.

"Price, what's going on?" Padua asked.

"Three more men blindsided Gomes and Donnelly. Donnelly is down. Gomes is taking cover down the alley."

"Price, engage the gunmen! Haddock and Wilkerson, get over and assist Gomes and Donnelly."

More semiautomatic fire, this time from West.

"Haddock, Wilkerson, report!" Padua yelled into his radio.

"We're taking fire. We're pinned down," Wilkerson replied.

"Shit." Padua moved from the window, over to John. "Come on, we've got to get you out of here."

John popped to his feet, following Padua as he made his way to the rear door.

"Base, this is Padua. We're under attack and need backup. We have an agent down," Padua crouched by the back door and motioned for John to take cover down the short hallway by the kitchen. He looked through the side window panel into the backyard. The area was clear.

He opened the door, leading with this gun. Not seeing anyone, he motioned for John to join him.

The two men sprinted down the stairs and into the backyard. They followed the exterior wall of the house toward the gate in the Northwest corner. Reaching the center of the yard, John heard a loud pop, followed by the feeling of a sledgehammer hitting him in the back. He dropped to the ground, unable to breathe.

"Man down! Price, we have sniper fire coming from the South!" Padua yelled into his radio, dropping to cover John, his handgun stretched out over him. He grabbed John and dragged him a foot before a second loud pop sounded. A round struck the earth inches from John's head.

A single cracking sound emanated from a short distance away.

"Picked up his muzzle flash. Got him," Price reported.

Padua searched John's back, finding a lead slug buried in the body armor.

John gasped for breath. "Son of a bitch, it hurts like hell."

Padua helped John to his feet and led him to the back gate to their waiting getaway car. The sound of sirens echoed in the distance, the wailing noise growing closer.

The gate kicked inward and two black-clad men scurried into the yard.

Padua dropped one immediately, then turned to face the

second gunman, who had gotten a bead on them. Before either could get a shot off, the gunman's head jerked to the side, his body slumping to the ground.

Price was 2 for 2.

"You have two more inbound, about 20 feet out," Price announced over the radio.

"Come on, we need to go back," Padua said, pulling John back toward the house.

They crashed through the back door, John sprinting down the short hallway to the kitchen, while Padua slammed the door shut and locked it.

"I need an update," Padua called into his radio.

"We got two, but Haddock is down," Wilkerson reported.

"Gomes, you there?" Padua asked.

No reply.

Small bursts of gunfire continued to sound off in the distance.

"You have three about to breach the front door," Price reported.

"Get down!" Padua yelled.

John dove behind the kitchen counter as gunfire ripped through the front door.

Padua held his fire, aiming down the hallway to the front.

The knob turned, the front door bursting inward.

Padua unloaded his clip, dropping the first gunman into the room. The door swung partially shut.

Padua slapped a new magazine into his gun and racked the action.

The sound of sirens grew louder, screeching tires skidded to a stop outside the home.

"Bogies are leaving," Price said.

Padua exhaled deeply, but didn't let his guard down.

"Padua, are you there?" this time it was General Flores on the radio.

Impressive that the top dog had come himself. "Roger. Randall and I are here, and we're okay."

"Good work protecting the asset," Flores said. "We have multiple agents arriving on scene. I'm coming in the front door."

Padua stood, then signaled to John that it was safe. They turned in unison as the front door swung inward. Two agents, service pistols in hand, entered first, sweeping the area. "All clear."

Flores strode through the front door, caught sight of John, and headed straight for him without breaking stride. He reached John just as the younger man removed the body armor and put his hand on John's shoulder. "I'm glad you're okay. I wouldn't want to face your father if something had happened to you."

The greeting caught John off guard and he chuckled in response, forgetting for a moment that the Russians had captured his father. Then he remembered he wasn't the only one in the room with a personal interest in this matter. "I heard you traced the call."

"That's correct."

"Good to know that our plan worked. What's next? Are you sending in a team to find my dad and Michael?"

"I wanted to speak to you directly about that."

Chapter Twenty-Five

John followed Flores out the front door of the home and into a waiting black SUV, its rear door held open by a uniformed soldier. Safely ensconced in the rear seat, the vehicle sped away from the safehouse. The acceleration pushed John back into the gray leather seat, causing John to yelp in pain from the spot where the sniper's bullet had struck his body armor. Flores smiled knowingly. "The body armor keeps you alive, but the injury still hurts like hell."

"Tell me about it," John said, arching his back away from the seat.

"We traced Rawlings' call to Ivangorod Fortress, a medieval castle near Leningrad. The fact that he made the call from his cell phone instead of using a secure system tells me the information about the D.N.A was big."

"Did you pick him up?"

Flores frowned, providing an answer before he spoke. "He slipped away."

"How?"

"Apparently our organization is more compromised

than we thought, which also explains what happened at the safe house. The Russians shouldn't have been able to get so close to you. We're going to have to work outside the agency until we can address the situation."

John sighed, rubbing his back. The pain was a testament to the veracity of Flores' words. "What happens next?"

"There's someone I'd like you to meet."

"Who?"

"In time."

John sank back into the leather seat, trying to ignore the throbbing pain in his back. The midday sun hung bright in the sky when the SUV turned from 10th Street N.W., into the driveway of the J. Edgar Hoover Building. The lumpy, gray concrete building represented the pinnacle of practical architectural design, lacking any charm whatsoever. In a town featuring incredible architectural masterpieces, this particular structure was the ugly stepsister of the bunch.

The truck pulled to a stop. The same man who had held the doors open earlier hopped out and held the door for Flores and John again. The General used his ID card to gain access through a door inside the garage.

The two men marched down the marble floored hallway, past a security checkpoint. The guards barely flinched, clearly demonstrating the importance of General Flores. John was impressed.

Walking past a bank of windows, they finally arrived at a non-descript wooden door. Flores once again used his ID card to open the lock, and they walked inside.

Seated at a small, oblong table was a gray-haired man, hands folded neatly across his lap. He glanced up at John and Flores as they shuffled into the room. Flores took a seat opposite the man, while John sat next to Flores.

John studied the older man. He was dressed in an

impeccable black, double-breasted overcoat, a white scarf wrapped around his neck. He sported a neatly trimmed gray beard and mustache to match his well styled hair. His ruddy face bespoke a man who had spent time outdoors, but it was his eyes that drew the most attention. Blue jewels, behind which lurked what appeared to be a deeply intelligent man. It was then that John realized that the gray-haired man was studying him just as intently.

"Dr. John Randall, Colonel Leonid Kapralov," Flores said, motioning to the gray-haired man.

"A pleasure to meet you," Kapralov said, stretching his hand out to John. Though slight, his accent conveyed his Russian heritage.

"The same colonel," John replied, sending a sideways glance to Flores.

"The Colonel arrived a short while ago. We were in the middle of a conversation when Agent Padua's call came in. Colonel, once again, my apologies for having to leave so quickly, but, as I was saying, Dr. Randall is working on an extremely important project."

"Indeed," Kapralov said. "I'm happy to see that Aminov's men failed in their attempts to apprehend you."

"Aminov? Is that the name of your associate who's behind this?" John said, eyes narrowing.

Kapralov chuckled. "I assure you, we're not associates. Not for many years."

"But you know him."

"Colonel Vasily Aminov, former Spetsnaz Commander."

"Former?" John asked.

Kapralov nodded. "A position he held through 2003, during the Second Chechen War. He was relieved of his command after destroying a civilian village in a fit of rage."

"I didn't think your government would mind having such a man in that position."

"There is much you don't know about my people, professor. We are not the violent animals many consider us to be," Kapralov said in a fatherly tone.

"You'll have to excuse me if I find that difficult to believe, given that your people kidnapped my father and Michael," John said, nodding to Flores. "Your people also weren't so gentle when they were trying to kill me, either."

Flores cleared his voice. "It wasn't the Russians who were trying to kill you, John. At least not members of the Russian military."

John furrowed his brow.

"Aminov is no longer in the employ of the Russian government. After being relieved of his command, he was forced out of military service," Kapralov explained.

"I don't understand. If he's not working for the Russian government, then who is he working for?"

"The fall of the Soviet Republic caused great chaos in my nation. The federal government lost much of its power. Some would even say it became impotent. The power vacuum created by the lack of a strong central authority allowed the rise of less scrupulous individuals to power," Kapralov replied.

John shifted in his seat. "I've read about organized crime playing a larger role in Russia. I just find it difficult to believe they would be behind something like this. General Flores, how can you be sure you can trust the Colonel? No offense."

Kapralov held up a hand. "None taken."

"Prior to Colonel Kapralov's arrival, I was contacted by his superior, General Konstantin Berezin. Berezin and I have worked together in the past and I have great admiration for him. Although we don't see eye to eye on many things, he's a man of unwavering character."

John nodded and turned to Kapralov. "I guess I owe you an apology."

Kapralov smiled. "I guess détente isn't dead." His expression turned serious. "But we still have the matter in front of us. Aminov is a dangerous man. Not to be taken lightly."

"What's our next move?" John asked.

"We have a strike team geared up and ready to fly out of Andrews. The Russian military will stand down while we hit Ivangorod and try to retrieve the device, your father and Michael," Flores explained.

"Your government is okay with this?" John asked.

"As I've said, we have a vested interest in seeing Aminov defeated. Since this will be a strike on Russian soil, our government must disavow any knowledge, of course."

"The enemy of my enemy is my friend."

Kapralov nodded. "Very good Dr. Randall. And in this case, true."

"What is Aminov trying to accomplish?" John asked.

"That is, as you Americans say, the million-dollar question. We have very little information about him and his network. As a former military intelligence officer, I'm afraid he has deep ties in the former Soviet bloc. Our assets have largely been quiet about this matter."

"Hopefully, we'll have a better idea of Aminov's goals after the raid," Flores added.

"There's one additional piece of information that you may find useful, but we're not entirely sure how it fits into Aminov's plans," Kapralov said. "Our intelligence service has obtained information on a recent raid on a Chinese weapons storage area and the nature of the items taken has created some concern."

Flores' brow furrowed. He clearly hadn't received this information before. "What items were taken?"

"Numerous uniforms, along with several crates of weapons including assault rifles, sniper rifles, explosives and…" Kapralov's voice trailed off.

"Yes?" Flores asked.

"General Flores, how familiar are you with a weapons program codenamed Medusa?" Kapralov asked.

Flores' eyes went wide.

"What's he talking about?" John asked, realizing this must be significant.

"Medusa was a prototype for a portable weapon developed for the Marine Corps in 2004. It was designed to be a non-lethal option for incapacitating enemy combatants using radio or microwaves to temporarily disable them. Our government stopped developing it because of ethical concerns about human experimentation, but there was intelligence to suggest that Russia and China were still pursuing it, but we could never confirm this," Flores answered.

Kapralov pursed his lips.

"Colonel?"

"We believe a case of these ordinances was also taken from the Chinese weapons' storage."

"And were these Chinese designed weapons?" John asked.

"Gentleman, while we share a common goal of stopping Aminov, I must remind you that our two countries still view each other as geopolitical and military enemies," Kapralov responded. He was letting them know that no additional information was coming.

"We need to move quickly on this information," Flores shifted gears. "We're operating in the dark and need to gather intelligence to get a handle on Aminov."

John nodded to Flores. "What's the next move?"

"We have a team waiting to lift off."

Chapter Twenty-Six

Ivangorod, Leningrad Oblast, Russia

May 12, Early Evening

Randall paced the floor, partially to keep warm and partially to ward off the feeling of being trapped in a small space. Frigid air seeped through the stone walls, letting him know that, wherever their captives had taken them, it was exceptionally cold. Michael sat on a worn sofa in the far corner of the room, lightly rubbing his bandaged leg, his crutches propped against the wall. If nothing else, at least their captors had provided a semblance of medical care, disinfecting and bandaging his wound, but not removing the bullet. Clean or not, the possibility of infection, sepsis and blood loss meant they were on the clock with Michael and needed to get him medical attention.

Although not a traditional cell, in the sense of metal bars secured into a concrete floor, the room was certainly secure, with only one way in or out, through a heavy wooden door with a large cylindrical lock. The walls were composed of large, irregularly shaped stones, cemented together, and the floors were an interlocking wood pattern. Above their heads, the ceiling was stained wooden beams, with long, rectangular fluorescent light fixtures. The room gave the appearance of an old castle, updated with some modern features. By the look of the structure, Randall guessed they were somewhere in Europe.

This made sense, since they had spent the better part of a day traveling from Mt. Vernon to their current location in the windowless compartment of a former commercial jetliner. This had rendered Randall's analog watch useless, but judging by the position of the sun when they arrived, it had been late afternoon. They had been in the cell for over two hours now, which meant it was likely early evening.

Despite their predicament, Randall worried about John and Liz. Had they escaped? Or had their captives found and killed them? Given their treatment of Michael, it was a definite possibility. These mercenaries were ruthless killers and the only reason they hadn't harmed Randall was that they felt he could help them. In fact, it was the only reason they hadn't killed Michael, using him as leverage to secure Randall's assistance.

Randall turned to Michael. "How are you holding up?"

"Been worse," Michael replied. "Been better, but been a lot worse." Michael smiled broadly, undoubtedly hiding how bad he felt. Movement came with grimaces of pain and his faced looked paler with each passing hour.

The sound of their cell door lock tumbler drew Randall's attention. An armed guard entered, while a second stood in the doorway.

"You, come with me," the first guard ordered through a thick accent. He pointed a finger at Randall.

"I'm not going anywhere without Michael," Randall replied.

The guards conferred. "Both, now!"

Randall walked over to Michael, who was now standing with his crutches. Randall walked by his side, ready to help if needed. Together, they were marched down the corridor of the facility, a guard in front and another in back.

Large windows framed by wood and rock revealed a deep, nearly empty courtyard, illuminated by the remnants of twilight. Randall walked closer to the windows than Michael. With the sun dropping on the horizon, the temperature was dropping significantly, the cold outside radiating through the glass.

The guards marched the men to a door held open by another black clad mercenary. As Randall stepped through the portal, he realized his guests had set up a makeshift lab with the sphere on a workbench in the center. Randall walked to the workbench while Michael hobbled to a nearby chair and the guards left them alone.

Sitting on the workbench next to the device was a pad of paper with several pages of notes. Randall picked up the pad. "Looks like someone's been busy."

"What do you mean?" Michael asked, wincing as he lowered himself onto the chair.

"They left us notes about the device," Randall scanned the information, flipping through the pages to get a handle on what Amniov's researchers had discovered.

"Anything you can use?" Michael asked.

"By the looks of it, whoever wrote these was either a geneticist or working on DNA sequencing," Randall continued to read while he explained to Michael. "There's an entire page of notes on DNA computers and the intersection between computing and biological processing. Apparently, someone recently developed a technique to embed microprocessors into living tissue."

"What's that have to do with this device?" Michael asked.

Randall's mind flashed back to the Washington room and the bone and hair samples. The purpose of the device was coming into view.

"Nick? Did you hear me?"

"I think I know what this device is for."

"Well, let's have it."

"When we found the sphere, we also found bone and hair samples nearby. Based on that and the fact they brought us here, I think this device interfaces with a living person," Randall looked over the device, rotating around it.

"What are you doing?" Michael asked.

"I'm looking for any ports or openings on it." Randall searched but didn't see any notches or even seams to suggest any sort of port existed. The device appeared to be a perfectly smooth metallic sphere. Frustrated, he went back to reading the notes.

"Any luck?" Michael stood and hopped on one foot while pulling the chair next to the workbench.

"Not yet. But the notes say that they found symbols on it and they think the symbols are some sort of control pad that operates the device."

"That makes sense. How many symbols are we talking about?"

"They counted 30."

"That's a lot, but where are they?" Michael asked, looking over the sphere.

Randall searched the device as well, looking for the

symbols the research notes referred to. Unable to find them, he picked up the device in frustration to look at the bottom, which was settled into a small recessed bowl indentation in the workbench table. Upon lifting it, multiple strange blue symbols glowed to life.

"Take a look at this," Randall said, holding the device.

"Well, I'll be," Michael commented. "How do you plan on decoding it?"

"That's a good question. It's what stumped the scientists who were studying the device, and it's clearly the reason Aminov brought us here. Even if I can't decipher all the symbols, we may still be able to operate it. The problem is, 30 symbols give us way too many combinations to try. We need to lower the odds in our favor."

"That's way above my paygrade. What do you plan to do?"

"I have an idea." Randall checked the drawers of the workstation but couldn't find what he was looking for. He walked over to the door and pounded on it, yelling for someone to come.

He continued for several minutes until he heard boots stepping up to the door. The heavy lock turned and the door slowly swung inward and two armed guards greeted Randall. They didn't look happy.

"Step back!"

Randall complied, and the guards walked in, guns trained on Randall. "You'd better have a good reason for doing this!"

"I need baby powder, a small bowl, and a small brush. Something the size of a woman's makeup brush will do," Randall replied, ignoring the threat.

The first guard was clearly confused, thrown by the odd

nature of the request. He stood there like a statue, not responding.

"Your boss expects me to figure out how this works," Randall pointed at the device. "I need a small bowl, baby powder, and a small brush to figure it out. I'm sure you don't want your boss angry with you. Right?"

The guard nodded.

"Then get me those items," Randall said.

The guards looked at each other and left the cell.

Michael wore a full-blown smile. "That professor voice gets them every time."

Randall laughed, then studied the device more, turning it over in his hands. The blue symbols winked to life each time he moved it. They covered most of the exterior of the device. Randall studied them carefully, but didn't recognize any. He checked the notes and saw the characters entered onto a sheet of paper on a table, but the translation column next to each was blank.

Several more minutes went by when the door tumbler turned again. This time, the first guard entered with his gun raised, but the second guard carried the items that Randall had requested.

"Set them on the workbench," Randall instructed.

The second guard glared for a moment, but then did as instructed. "Anything else?"

No, that'll do it.

"You'd better get to work," the second guard said.

Randall waved him off like a bothersome mosquito and checked the items the guard had brought. A moment later, the guards were gone, leaving Randall and Michael alone again. Randall emptied a small amount of powder into the bowl, then dipped the brush in, careful not to pick up too much powder. He then lightly dabbed the brush over the sphere in small, circular motions. He continued until he had covered each symbol. Placing the brush on the table, he turned to look at the sphere from different angles. A smile grew on his lips. "4 is better than 30."

"What in the world are you talking about?"

Randall motioned for Michael. "Don't touch the sphere, but take a close look."

Faint but viewable pieces of imprints were clear over 4 of the symbols on the sphere. They were little more than faint, thumbtack sized smudges, but they were there.

Michael smiled. "Who taught you that?"

Randall shrugged. "I have a friend who's an FBI investigator. She told me about this trick."

Their options narrowed. Finding the right combination now became a math exercise. They copied the symbols onto a sheet of paper and began trying different combinations. Randall pushed symbols and Michael tracked which combinations they had tried. After a couple of hours, they still had gotten nothing to happen with the device.

"No luck so far," Randall sighed.

Michael winced from the pain in his injured leg. "Don't give up. It's only a matter of time.

Buoyed by his friend's encouragement, Randall resumed entering different sequences. Another hour passed with no luck. Randall stretched his neck and looked over at Michael, who looked exhausted. Randall realized it was more than just fatigue. The injury was clearly getting to him. Without a window, it was difficult to get reading on the time, but based on how long they had been working on the device, they were well into the evening. With each passing hour, Randall's concern for Michael was growing.

"Why don't you go to the couch and get some rest," Randall said.

"I need to keep recording sequences," Michael replied, rubbing his tired eyes.

"I can do it. It'll take a little more time, but I've done this kind of work before."

Michael didn't argue. Hopping onto his crutches, he slowly hobbled to the couch, then lowered himself onto it.

Randall continued punching in different combinations, but still failed to get a response. He tried another and the symbols glowed to life and he felt a low vibration emanating from the machine. Two rectangular ports opened on either side, just large enough to fit a human hand.

Randall peered into the slotted openings, studying the inside of the sphere. "There are contoured pads inside that would fit an adult male hand."

Randall lined his hands up on each side of the sphere, ready to place them inside.

"Do you think that's a good idea?" Michael asked from the couch. His voice belied his concern.

Randall paused momentarily. Michael was right. This could be dangerous. There was no way to know what would happen if he used the device, but they had no other options. "We have to try."

He slid his hands into the ports.

Chapter Twenty-Seven

Randall was no longer in the workroom with Michael. Instead, he sat at a long, oval table with President Mercer, the Joint Chiefs of Staff, and an assortment of other serious looking women and men. They were discussing potential military responses to continued aggression by the Russians, who had expanded their push into Eastern Europe. Making matters worse, China had taken advantage of Russia's actions and had instigated military forays into India and Pakistan. The entire region balanced on the precipice of war. Segments of the group were pushing for the United States to join its allies in armed warfare in both theaters. A few even suggested that the use of tactical nuclear weapons might be necessary to contain the Russian and Chinese aggression. Mercer still sought a diplomatic solution.

The scene changed. Randall was now wedged into a small conference room with members of the Secret Service. They spoke in serious tones of an assault on President Mercer and the demands made by his captors. Randall felt a sharp, piercing pain in his chest as if someone had stabbed him. He looked down at his shirt, but there was no blood or weapon. Everything appeared to be normal.

The view shifted again. This time Randall was sitting in his living room with Sam and John. The television was on and the news commentator spoke in rapid bursts about the wars raging across Europe, Asia, and the Middle East. An emergency siren arose from the distance, a crawler beneath the newscaster announced incoming nuclear missiles targeted for multiple cities across the United States, including Washington D.C.

Randall grabbed his chest, the pain becoming unbearable. Dismembered voices called to him through the fog of pain. Was he having a heart attack and hallucinating about the voices? He turned from Sam to John, terror etched on their faces. But they weren't looking at him.

The voices. Who the hell is calling me?

Something grabbed him from behind and dragged him to the ground. Randall tumbled, hit the floor and looked up to find Michael standing over him, holding his leg, biting back the pain. "Dammit Nick, are you okay?"

"What's happening? Where are Sam and John?" Randall said, eyes darting around the room.

"You were hallucinating. I had to tackle you to unplug your hands from the machine!" Michael slumped into a chair, blood seeping through his bandaged leg.

Sanity slowly crept back into Randall's mind, and he rose to his feet. "The sphere. I had visions," he said, struggling to get the thought out. He rubbed his chest, which ached. The pain had been real, unlike the dreams produced in the hypnotic state induced by the machine.

"You were nearly white. All the blood had drained from your face and you were talking about chest pains. I thought

The Washington Prophecy

you were going to die," Michael said, puffing from the exertion.

Randall gulped air in large breaths, trying to sort out his visions from reality. The pain in his chest had subsided from a 9 to 4. It still hurt, but was getting better. "When I put my hands into the sphere, I started seeing things. I couldn't tell if they were dreams or not, but they seemed real. Like I was in the room with the people I saw."

"What did you see?" Michael rubbed his injured leg.

Randall explained his visions, drawing a concerned look from Michael.

"There have been discussions about potential military responses to the Russian invasion of Crimea, but there's no way you would have known about them. So far, American policy has been limited to economic sanctions and public reproach. I'm not sure if that would change if they invaded other countries in Eastern Europe. Thank God they haven't," Michael said.

"Yet," Randall replied, leaning against the workbench.

Michael closed his eyes. "Mercer's on his way to Europe now to speak with our allies."

"That's where they might try to kidnap him."

"What are you talking about?" Michael asked, exasperation seeping into his voice.

"In one of my visions, someone kidnapped President Mercer."

"Let's back this up for a minute. We were looking for a book of predictions from George Washington and we found it," Michael pointed at the sphere, "and we also found this."

"A book of predictions based on visions he had, from an alleged visitation. Let's not forget that," Randall said.

"You think this device was the source of Washington's visions?"

"Based on what I just experienced, yes."

"But this thing nearly killed you after using once, and it sounds like Washington used multiple times. How was he able to do it without dying?"

Randall nodded and smiled weakly. "The hair and bone. They contain Washington's DNA. Maybe this machine was designed only for his use and no one else. Maybe what happened to me was a failsafe built into the device to make sure no one else could operate it."

"That makes sense. It's entirely possible the device was designed to only interface with Washington's DNA," Michael said. He lifted himself from the couch, once again joining Randall at the workbench.

"We can't let Aminov use this device. We need to find a way out of here."

"While you were having your visions, that thing was humming," Michael nodded to the sphere. "It was getting louder as time passed. The sound reminded me of an electrical engine revving up."

Michael tapped the sphere, then pulled his hand back quickly and examined his fingers. "Damn it!"

"What's wrong?" Randall asked.

"That thing burned me!" Michael showed Randall his fingers. The tips were bright red.

Randall held his hand an inch from the top of the workstation counter. It was hot as well. "This device radiated so much heat, the top of this station could burn my hand if I touched it. What does that mean?"

"If we stick with your failsafe idea, it could be a self-destruct setting to prevent other people from using it," Michael replied.

Randall nodded in understanding, recalling his days as a Ranger. He knew that when the military developed a weapons system that utilizes new technology, they frequently include a self-destruct mechanism to prevent it from falling into enemy hands. The feature allowed a single soldier in the field to destroy the new equipment on his or her own.

"And there was no way you were going to unplug yourself from that thing without help. I had to really lay into you to knock you free. If someone used the device alone, it would stay operational until they either died or it self-destructed."

"Or both. As long as we keep the bones and hair away from these guys, they won't be able to properly operate the device. We also can't tell them what we've learned," Randall added.

"Agreed. Now we just need to find a way out of here," Michael said.

The lock on the door to their room clicked. Their captors were coming.

Chapter Twenty-Eight

Randall turned to look at the door to their cell, which opened inward. Aminov stepped in, followed by two guards. He looked angry, his eyes locked on Randall. Aminov strode directly to the workstation, stopping inches from Randall. "What have you found?"

"We've made some progress deciphering the symbols, but it's difficult. If we had some sort of key to work from, it would be much easier."

Aminov didn't blink, his eyes boring through Randall. "I brought you here to make the device work. You've done such work before. I even gave you help." Aminov nodded to the notepad.

"In the past, I've had years to research a new language, chances to search for clues and keys to help me unlock symbols. I'm working blind here. We just need more time," Randall lied.

Aminov looked at Michael, then Randall. He withdrew his Glock and pointed it at Michael's temple.

"Don't toy with me, Dr. Randall."

"Wait!" Randall yelled.

Aminov cocked the hammer.

"Don't do this. I'll figure this out," Randall pleaded.

Michael stood motionless, a look of determination set on his face.

Aminov slowly lowered his Glock. "You have one more day." He gave Michael a look of disdain, turned on his heel and marched to the door, his guard holding it open for him.

He stopped and looked back at Randall. "I suggest you get to work. Your friend's life depends on it." He exited the room.

"We have to do something. I won't let him kill you, Michael. I promise I'll figure something out," Randall said, his mind racing for a solution.

Michael exhaled.

Chapter Twenty-Nine

Senate President Gérard Babineaux guided the group from the Rue du Faubourg Saint-Honoré through the high arching entrance gate of the Elysée Palace. Completed in 1722, the Palace was used as the office of the French President since 1848. Deriving its name from Elysian Fields, the place of the blessed dead in Greek mythology, the Elysee Palace was a beautiful example of the French classical architectural style.

Babineaux paused, waiting impatiently as a member of the Republican Guard opened the door, and held it open for him and the other dignitary. Babineaux nodded, then entered the Vestibule d'Honneur. His guest, Erich Müller, Vice Chancellor of Germany, followed closely behind. He tapped his foot impatiently as Müller scanned the opulent entryway, grunting in approval of the décor. The two crossed the marble floor and waited outside the door to The Salon des Ambassadeurs, where they would wait for the meeting with the American President.

Babineaux cleared his throat, nodding his head at the door, causing a second member of the Republican Guard to open it for him. Babineaux allowed Müller to enter first, stepped into the doorway, then turned to face the guard, his right hand held up to the man's face. "We'll be meeting alone. Guard the door and notify me when the others arrive. I expect some time to prepare before they enter."

The guard nodded.

Alone in the room, the two men sat in two of the six, blue and white flower-patterned chairs around the fireplace. Babineaux watched as his German counterpart enjoyed the opulent gold leaf trim, applied liberally to decorate the walls of the room. Though not a fan of the man personally, Babineaux accepted the role that each of them shared as second in command of their respective nations…along with the other, secretive task they shared.

"Have you heard from Aminov?" Müller asked in a husky voice.

"Oui."

Müller turned his heavy gaze to Babineaux. "And?"

"The plan remains in place. We are not to act until he notifies us. For now, we are simply to listen and report back on what's discussed at the meeting."

Müller snorted. "I don't care for this waiting. The longer this goes, the better the chance that we're discovered."

"We knew what we were getting ourselves into when we accepted Aminov's offer. Now is not the time to become worried."

"Do not confuse my desire for action with concern," Müller replied, barely hiding the irritation in his voice.

"Patience. Aminov has promised that the time is growing near. Soon things will be very different, and we'll both assume a greater role in running our respective countries," Babineaux said.

"What is he waiting for, anyway?"

Babineaux shrugged. "He hasn't said."

"We need to ensure that when the time comes, there is nothing that traces these events back to us," Müller emphasized the last word.

"A simple task, in reality, since we don't know who will actually carry out Aminov's plan. We simply need to step aside when the time comes."

"Do you truly think Aminov will take the American President hostage?"

Babineaux studied Müller's face. The time for worrying about Aminov's plan had long passed. Even if the transfers to the Swiss accounts hadn't been detected by the authorities, any attempt to impede Aminov's plan would be met with severe and immediate repercussions. Aminov had made that clear and, though the Russian was many things, he wasn't one to make empty threats. The dead bodies of men who had challenged Aminov attested to this. "He's proven to be quite resourceful."

Müller grunted in approval. "So, what do we do now?"

"We wait for the President to arrive," Babineaux replied. "All the arrangements have been made. The trap has been set and we simply need for our prey to arrive and when Aminov carries out his plan, we feign our ignorance and implement our emergency measures."

"You make it sound so simple. Pray that all goes according to plan," Müller replied, turning to face Babineaux.

The sound of the door opening called Babineaux's attention. Irritated that someone was disturbing this private meeting, he cast a harsh stare toward the figure of a Republican Guard member entering the room. For some reason, the soldier seemed unperturbed. Babineaux recognized the face of a long-time member of the Guard, Albert Laurent. "What is the meaning of this interruption? I gave explicit orders not to be disturbed."

Again, Laurent was unphased by the implied threat. Clearly, the man needed to be reminded of his place in the presence of a top government official. He approached Babineaux and Müller, taking a spot directly in front of them. Instead of showing respect while addressing Babineaux, he instead stood at his full height. Imposing in stature, the six-foot two-inch tall soldier towered over both politicians. The look in his eyes was menacing. Babineaux swallowed hard, a feeling of dread sitting in the pit of his stomach.

"You would do well to hold your tongue," Laurent reprimanded. "Commander Aminov has ordered me to tell you that the kidnapping will be carried out shortly. We have the planned routes and the locations of the American Secret Service agents and Counter Sniper team members who will be stationed outside. My men are in position and ready to neutralize everyone protecting the President, but you need to be ready to do your job."

"And how exactly will you neutralize the President's detail?" Babineaux asked, all the fire gone from his voice.

"Our Chinese friends have provided us with the means to do so," Laurent offered.

"But how?" Babineaux asked again.

"That's not your concern. Just be ready," Laurent pointed a finger down at Babineaux's nose.

All the French Senate President could do was nod in understanding.

Laurent turned and walked back out the door, stopping

before opening it. "Be ready, and if you're not, I assure you there will be a steep price to pay." He opened the door and strode out, leaving the two senior politicians in a state of shocked silence.

Chapter Thirty

Randall wiped the beads of sweat forming on his temple with the back of his stained and blotchy shirtsleeve. Since Aminov had left them, he had searched for additional clues on the device for nearly two hours. There had to be something he missed. Some clue that would help him solve the riddle of the device.

"You need to take a break," Michael called out from behind him.

"Not until I figure this out."

"What if there's nothing else to figure out? What if we know as much about the device as we're going to learn?"

An icy finger traced down Randall's spine. He had banished that thought to the deepest recesses of his mind, but Michael's comment had dragged it to the light of day. If he couldn't figure out how the device worked without killing the user, Michael would be dead in less than a day. It was hard to determine what was worse, dying or having to explain to Flores how he couldn't save Michael's life. "We just have to keep trying."

"I have an idea," Michael said.

Randall turned from the workbench and looked at Michael, who was rubbing his injured leg. At least the bullet wound wasn't bleeding as badly, but Michael had grown paler, his face gaunt.

"Let's hear it."

"When you used that device, it super-heated to the point where it melted part of the workbench."

Randall nodded.

"What if we put it near the door and let it run longer? Maybe we can melt the door enough to force our way out?"

"That's an interesting idea, but that means one of us has to be hooked into it and, based on the last time, that means one of us might die."

"If we don't try, I'm dead for sure. I'm willing to take the chance."

Randall shook his head from side to side. "No way! I'm not letting you sacrifice yourself to save my hide. We'll figure something else out."

"Let's be smart about this—" Michael was interrupted by the sound of the door lock engaging.

Randall stood, moving closer to Michael, placing himself between his injured friend and the now opening door. Three guards entered, guns drawn, followed by Aminov, whose eyes were locked on Randall and Michael. The sound of their boot clicks against the stony surface was like the sound of a ticking clock counting down to an impending doom. They drew within several feet, then stopped.

Randall took one step forward. "I can figure this out, but I need more time. I guarantee I'm the only person capable of reading this language. You need us."

"Take the device," Aminov barked. One of the guards

shouldered his weapon, moved to the workbench and retrieved the sphere.

"This is a mistake. You have no idea of how that device works or what it does."

"It allows the user to see the future Dr. Randall. That's the entire reason I need it. What I didn't know was how to use it until you showed me," Aminov replied, nodding to the security cameras.

"Then you saw that it nearly killed me," Randall said. He rubbed his chest, which still badly ached. Having been so worried about Michael, he had ignored the pain. He took a deep breath and winced.

"A situation I plan to remedy by retrieving the DNA of your President Washington," Aminov said, a crooked smile forming on his lips.

"Why did you give me more time, and what are you going to do with us?" Randall asked.

"I gave you more time because I want to know as much about the device as possible. You've proven most useful Dr. Randall. There may be another task that you can assist me with. At the moment, however, I have other matters to attend to," Aminov said. He nodded for his guards to leave.

"Wait!" Randall called out.

Aminov stopped and turned to half face him.

"We need food. Michael's not going to last without it,"

"Bring them something to eat," Aminov ordered.

The lead soldier nodded in reply. The four men then walked back to the door, weapons trained on Randall and Michael to discourage any action on their part. They exited, and the door swung closed in a slow, lazy arc.

Chapter Thirty-One

The planning for the rescue of Captain Michael Flores and Dr. Randall had begun the day they had been taken hostage. The SEALs had built replica sections of the Ivangorod Fortress to practice the rescue in real time in darkness, using intelligence gathered on the structure and the composition of the forces protecting it. Imaging, provided by a network of Orion class spy satellites run by the National Reconnaissance Office (NRO) had shown that the greatest concentration of activity was focused in a small, red-tile roofed building on the North side of the compound. Further intelligence, provided by the Estonian Foreign Intelligence Service, suggested that beneath this building was a larger underground structure where it was believed the hostages were being held.

Joint Special Operations Command (JSOC) had determined the SEALs would launch the rescue from a spot Southeast of Ivangorod, across the Narva River in Estonia. The launch point had been chosen due to the terrain and cover provided by nearby vegetation, but not before some political wrangling to get approval from the upper levels of the Estonian government. Though no fan of the Russians, having suffered under the brutal former Soviet regime, Estonian leadership had little appetite for inviting a potential military response from their neighbor to the East. But, good to his word, General Berezin had delivered on his promise of support from the highest levels of the Russian government, who assured the Estonians that the Russians were eager to see this internal threat neutralized if the Americans were willing to so.

Each member of the SEAL team was outfitted in LAR V Draeger Underwater Breathing Apparatus (UBA)'s, the gear typically used by SEALs for shallow water raids. The self-contained system produced no air bubbles, providing greater stealth for the team. The plan called for the SEALs to breach the surface of the river directly at the base of the northwest section of the structure, just outside the courtyard containing the red-tiled building. They would then scale the wall and enter the grounds from that point.

Officer in Charge (OIC), Lieutenant Scott Walters requested a final sit rep from JSOC and received the all clear sign. With a flick of his fingers, he set his team in motion. The members of his squad slipped into the inky darkness of the river and began their silent crossing. The raid was underway.

Petty Officer Second Class Paul Wiśniewski was first into water, followed closely by Petty Officer Second Class Carlos Soto. Within minutes, they reached the Russian side of the river, breaching a couple of yards from shore. They scrambled from the water and into the concealed safety of the heavy tree line that started near the shore and ran within feet of the outer fortress wall. Next came Petty Officer First Class Xavier Benitez and Petty Officer Third

Class Jake Norwood, whose hulking figures emerged from the water like silent phantoms reaching from the netherworld to wreak havoc on the unsuspecting mercenaries holding Michael and Randall hostage.

Within minutes, the rest of the SEALs had completed the crossing as well, with Petty Officer Second Class Reese Morgan and Chief Petty Officer Bryce Nakamura covering their flank. Walters addressed his team in a near whisper, "Soto, you and Morgan stand guard and watch for traffic coming up or downstream. The rest of you, gear up for the wall."

Soto squatted behind a bush by the river, scanning upstream through the night vision scope of his M4 while Morgan vanished into the brush, taking up a sentry position facing downstream.

The rest of the SEALs quickly moved into position, ready to climb the wall into the fortress turned museum. Intelligence had reported minimum security on site, the enemy relying on the nature of the building to serve as a cover for their operations. The SEALs would soon learn if their intelligence was correct.

The two guards marched to the cell to carry out the orders provided by Commander Aminov. Remove the food trays left for their prisoners and then exterminate Captain Flores, who no longer served a purpose. Neither man felt remorse for the act they would soon undertake. This was combat, and they were simply following orders. Besides, being of Russian descent and having served under Aminov in active combat, there was no love lost for arrogant Americans. Although neither knew much about the Captain beyond what they had heard, it was a certainty that he was as loathsome as any American would be.

The first guard unlocked the heavy cylindrical tumbler and pushed the door inward, watching as it swung in on its hinges, creaking under the strain of the heavy slab of metal. The second guard entered, gun barrel pointing forward to dissuade either prisoner from attempting a heroic escape. They weren't expecting the sight that met their eyes.

Both men lay motionless in the cell. The captain lay on his side on the only couch in the cell, the back of his head facing out to them, his uninjured leg dangling from the sofa unnaturally, clearly unsupported by any muscular activity. The professor lay face down on the floor several feet away from the couch and he, too, was motionless.

"Get up!" the first guard demanded. Neither prisoner responded.

"On your feet or I'll shoot!" the second guard ordered, even racking the action on his weapon for effect. The captives remained motionless.

The guards shared a panicked look. The captain finally succumbing to his wound was understandable and would be met with indifference, but Commander Aminov had given them strict orders to ensure the safety of the professor. What would happen to them if he returned and discovered that the professor was dead? There was no way of knowing how their commander would respond, but it was a safe bet that he would have little qualms about holding them responsible and making examples of them, even if the situation was beyond their control.

The first guard walked toward Randall while the other moved toward Michael, each approaching their respective prisoner in a careful manner, looking for telltale signs of breathing. As the first guard drew within a few feet of

Randall, his mind flashed back to seeing the professor clutching his chest and describing the pain he had experienced as a result of using the machine. Had the device damaged his heart so badly that he had succumbed to his injuries?

He studied the professor carefully, but saw no signs of life. He prodded him with the end of his gun, but got no response. Concerned, he bent over to check for a pulse and listen for any signs of breathing. That was his mistake. Randall rolled over, fork in hand from the food brought earlier, and drove the utensil into the side of the guard's neck, hitting an artery. Blood spurted from the wound, the dazed guard reflexively reaching for the injury with both hands, trying to stay the flow of blood. His weapon clanked to the floor.

The second guard by Michael, upon hearing the commotion, spun with his weapon raised. Michael lifted his uninjured leg, landing a kick squarely on the second guard's back, knocking him forward and off balance. The guard tumbled to the ground, landing hard on his side, his weapon skittering away from him.

Randall sprang to his feet and grabbed the first guard's assault weapon and turned to cover the second guard, who scrambled for his rifle.

"Don't," Randall said evenly. His voice conveyed his dead seriousness as the guard stopped moving.

Randall stepped past the man and kicked his gun to the far side of the room. He turned to face the second guard, whose face was contorted with fear as he watched the life drain from his comrade's face. Randall felt no remorse. These men and their leader Aminov had forced him into this situation and he had simply done what was needed to protect Michael. The death of the first Russian guard was part of the cost of associating with a madman bent on wielding his influence on an unsuspecting public.

Conversely, Randall took no pleasure in taking the man's life and if there had been another way out, he would have gladly taken it. He also had no desire to kill the second guard, but that man's fate lay in his own hands. If he did as told, Randall would have no reason to further harm him. To his credit, the man seemed to sense this as he waited for Randall to give him instructions on what to do next.

"On your feet," Randall instructed.

The Russian complied, rising from the floor.

"Interlace your fingers behind your head, then turn to face me," Randall ordered.

The guard turned to face him. Fear shone in the man's eyes as he clearly hadn't expected to be bested by a professor.

"Which way to the surface once we're out the door?" Randall asked.

"To the right and up the stairs," the Russian offered no resistance.

"What's the other direction?"

"The guard station," came the morose response.

"How many are left besides you two?"

"Half a dozen inside, two more on patrol around the structure right now."

"Anything else I should know?" Randall asked.

The guard shook his head no.

Randall drew near him. "If you're lying to me, I'll come back in here and finish the job."

"That's it, I swear," the man's eyes pleaded with Randall to believe him.

"Turn around," Randall ordered.

The Russian turned to face away from Randall, who

struck the butt of the assault rifle hard onto the back of the man's head. He collapsed to the floor. Randall prodded him with his boot tip, but the man was out cold.

Randall walked to Michael's side.

"Great job Nick," Michael said. His face was white and his eyes sunken into their sockets. He didn't have much time.

Randall grasped Michael under his shoulder, lifted him from the couch, and helped him to stand. Michael wobbled like a top for a moment, trying to get his balance. "You okay?"

"Give me a minute," Michael replied. He took a deep breath and steadied himself. "I'm ready, let's go."

The two hobbled to the exit, arriving next to it. Randall slowly opened the door and peered out into the hallway, in the direction he had heard the guards travel. Seeing nothing, he pulled it open and helped Michael through. They went to the right in the direction the Russian guard had indicated only moments earlier.

The SEALs scaled the exterior wall of the fortress and entered the compound without resistance. They moved quickly, ready to engage in a manner befitting the SEAL tenant of violence of action. Wiśniewski, his night vision goggles securely in place, was the first to drop into the courtyard, followed by Walters, Benitez, and Nakamura. Griffen and the final SEAL in the squad, Petty Officer Third Class Adrian Griffen, provided cover with their silenced Walther WA2000 sniping rifles. The four SEALs in the courtyard hugged the inner wall of the fortress, winding around to a spot directly across from the small rectangular building where they believed the hostages were being held.

The building was devoid of any light, as suspected, the activity limited to the underground portion of the facility directly beneath. Shrouded in darkness, the four SEALS sprinted across the small open field between the inner wall of the larger fortress and the red-tile roofed building. Arriving by the structure, they searched for the opening that would lead them inside. Wiśniewski peered around the corner and spotted a guard walking the perimeter several feet away, his back to the SEALs. Wiśniewski sprang into action, gliding the several feet to the enemy, knife drawn. The guard had no chance. The SEAL overpowering him, his left hand clamped over his mouth, while his right forced the blade into the man's back, strategically puncturing his lungs. With a soft gurgle, the man struggled for only a moment before dropping to the earth. Wiśniewski dragged the body back around the corner. He searched the former guard, finding a security access card in his pocket. They now had a literal key into the building.

The SEALs moved furtively along the exterior wall of the stony building in the direction the guard had been walking. Arriving at a metal gate, they stopped, and Nakamura inspected the lock. Surprisingly, it appeared to be nothing more than a black antique padlock holding a chain in place that held a black slatted wrought-iron gate closed. Nakamura motioned for Benitez to remove the lock. Taking a pair of bolt cutters from his gear bag, Benitez made quick work of the ancient lock, slicing through the curved metal shackle with minimal effort. The team slipped through the gate and into the building.

Once again, Wiśniewski was tapped to lead the incursion. Donning his night vision goggles, he slid down a darkened flight of stairs, his MP10 lifted in front of him.

Randall led Michael down the hallway toward the flight of stairs the guard had indicated. With a little luck, in a few minutes, they'd be above ground again. Then Randall would have to figure out a way to get Michael and himself over the wall and out of the complex. He had seen a river just outside of the West wall and realized the county of Estonia waited just across the other side.

They closed to within ten feet of the stairs, moonlight beaming from above partially illuminated the floor. Randall took an additional step before seeing the outline of a large, armed figure hop from the stairs and into the hallway. He wasn't alone. Within seconds, three additional figures joined him. Randall spun on his heel, pulling Michael back toward the cell and away from the incoming threat.

"What are you doing, Dr. Randall?" Michael said, pulling back to the stairs. He hadn't seen the armed figures stepping onto ground level.

"We have company," Randall whispered.

"Randall," a voice called from behind, causing Randall to pause momentarily before resuming his stride back toward the cell. He was clearly hearing things now.

Accelerated footsteps rose from behind him, followed by the sound of a weapon's safety being removed.

"Randall, if that's you, you have two seconds to respond before I light you up." The voice was gruffer this time, more demanding, but clearly the individual knew his name.

With no choice, Randall turned to face the intruder, careful to leave his assault weapon pointed at the floor. "I'm

Nick Randall." He pushed Michael behind him, offering the junior Flores protection.

The lead intruder lowered his weapon. "Petty Officer Wiśniewski. We're here to get you and Captain Flores back home."

Thank God.

"How did you two get out of your cell?" Wiśniewski's voice belied his confusion at finding the two roaming the halls.

"It's a long story. Captain Flores is injured, and he's lost a lot of blood," Randall replied before sighing in relief.

"Benitez, check him out," Nakamura ordered.

A large SEAL slid past Wiśniewski, switched on a light and inspected Michael's injury. Quickly cleaning and bandaging the wound, he gave Michael a shot near the wound. "Local anesthesia for the pain. Can't give you much more because we need you to walk."

Benitez replaced Randall as Michael's assistant, helping him back up the stairs as Wiśniewski now led the group back up. The group quickly reached ground level, led by Wiśniewski, who stopped at the top step and scanned the entryway, making small arcs with his M4, his night vision goggles still in place. Finding no danger, he ascended the final step and the rest of the group filed into the entryway of the stone building.

Randall stuck close to Michael's side as Benitez continued to help him along. Michael struggled to keep his eyes open and focused, and he appeared to be fading fast. Randall could only hope that once they were out of the compound, the SEALs could administer better medical aid to his to friend, but first they needed to escape.

Wiśniewski stopped at the doorway that led into the exterior courtyard and keyed his throat mic. "We're exiting the building now with both packages in possession. I need a sitrep."

"Courtyard is clear. No bogeys in your area. You're clear to go."

"Roger that," Wiśniewski pivoted to Walters. "No bogeys in the courtyard. We're good to go."

"Wiśniewski and Nakamura, you lead, Benitez, Flores and Randall will follow. I'll cover our retreat. Let's move!" Walters ordered.

Wiśniewski and Nakamura exited the building, one covering the left and the other the right. Benitez went next, supporting Michael with one arm while holding his pistol with the other. Randall stayed close on their heels, his assault rifle ready if needed. They carefully skirted the edge of the building, following the path they had taken in. They soon reached the edge of the building and faced the same open section of courtyard they had to cross earlier. Nakamura and Wiśniewski conferred for a moment, then Wiśniewski nodded. He sprinted across the opening to the section of wall where Griffen and Norwood stood watch, while Nakamura crouched against the wall, covering Wiśniewski through his night vision scope.

Wiśniewski stopped at the wall, dropped to a crouch, and scanned the area with his MP10.

"Randall, follow Benitez and Flores to the wall. Don't stop for anything," Nakamura said, still scanning the courtyard with his weapon. Walters joined him, covering the opposite direction.

Benitez sprinted toward Wiśniewski, helping Michael with one arm, pistol at the ready if needed. Randall followed closely behind, also ready to engage the enemy if needed. They made it to the wall in short order and Norwood dropped a line to them. Benitez strapped in,

Michael and Norwood pulled him up in a matter of seconds before dropping the line for Randall. While Randall strapped in, Nakamura sprinted to their location as well, taking a position next to Wiśniewski. Walters remained as the lone sentinel still by the building, covering their retreat.

Randall gave a thumbs-up to Norwood, who pulled him up to the parapet of the wall. Once unhooked from the line, he jogged to Michael's side while Griffen tended to him. "How's he doing?" Randall asked.

Michael's head lolled to Randall. Even in the moonlight, Randall could see that most of the life had drained from his face.

"I've stopped the blood loss, but we need to get him back to camp. He needs blood and an IV drip for dehydration," Griffen answered.

"Hang in there, Michael, we're almost there," Randall said.

A moment later, Benitez was up the wall as well, adding additional cover for the remaining SEALs still on the ground. Randall peered through the escarpments and spotted Nakamura and Wiśniewski still at the base of the wall. Nakamura was strapping in for the ride up while Wiśniewski signaled for Walters to join him.

While Nakamura scaled the wall, Walters sprinted across the open courtyard to Wiśniewski's side. It was then that Randall spotted a light come on in the building, followed by the shouts of someone barking orders.

Four enemy combatants had made their way out of the building, two around the far side corner and two by the corner nearest Wiśniewski. Several shots pocked the wall above Wiśniewski's head, but the petty officer was unphased, firing a small burst toward his attackers, causing them to retreat around the corner to safety. Walters cleared the top of the wall a moment later.

"Wiśniewski, you're next!" He yelled down to his young petty officer.

The enemy heard as well, unleashing a barrage toward Wiśniewski, who could do nothing more than stay prone and hope they missed. The SEALs on the wall returned fire, forcing the enemy to seek cover once more and offering a moment for Wiśniewski to pop to his feet and strap into the line. He made it nearly to the top before the Russians all rushed into the open, half firing at him while the others aimed at the top of the wall. Two others had joined them, making six Russians against the SEAL team.

The SEALs made quick work of three Russian soldiers, killing them in the open, but not before several bullets found their mark on Wiśniewski, who tumbled back to the ground before his line caught him.

"Norwood and Nakamura, get them out of here," Walters growled.

"Randall, help me with Flores," Norwood asked as Nakamura led them along the wall back to the access point they had used to enter earlier. The ropes lay neatly curled at the top of the wall and Nakamura quickly grabbed the loose end, tossed it over the side and lowered himself to the ground on the outside of the fortress, facing the Narva River.

Someone joined Nakamura on the ground, looking up the wall toward Randall and the others. Norwood wasted no time and pulled the rope up and strapped in Michael for the trip back down. "Randall, give me a hand here."

The two men slowly lowered Michael to the ground and the new soldier below unhooked him while Walters offered cover.

"Randall you're next," Norwood announced before strapping in Randall for the trip down. A few moments later Randall was on the ground, unlatching himself while the new soldier came to his side to provide cover. Norwood soon joined them, having repelled down the wall. Shots still rang out from within the fortress as the battle raged within.

"We need to get you all across the river," Nakamura announced.

"What about the others?" Randall asked.

"Our job is to get you and Captain Flores home and we need to get moving," Nakamura barked.

He led Randall and Michael to the hidden sleds. The SEALs had brought two extra, one for Randall and one for Michael, but there was no way Michael could operate one in his current condition.

"Randall, have you ever driven one of these before, and do you know how to use a regulator?" Nakamura asked.

Randall nodded and quickly donned his gear, recalling his former special forces training. Nakamura helped fit Michael with a breathing system as well. "Come on, let's go."

The three men entered the dark waters, Nakamura helping Michael to their sled. He would have to operate the vehicle while assisting Michael, who was buckled to him. They all pushed off together and made their way through the murky water to the other side, Nakamura's sled lighting the way for the others. A few minutes later, they breached the other side near their parked vehicle.

"Give me a hand with Captain Flores," Nakamura said, barely giving Randall time to remove his equipment. Still dripping, the three men pushed their way through the brush and to the waiting truck, which was equipped with full medical supplies. They laid Michael on the gurney, and

Nakamura quickly had a blood and IV line hooked into his left arm. A small explosion arose from the distance, seeming to come from the area of the compound they had just escaped from.

Minutes later, a commotion arose from the river as angry voices emerged from the dark waters. Gunshots followed, announcing that the Russians were now fully aware of the SEAL team's presence.

Several SEALs that Randall didn't recognize dragged their equipment up from the river and began loading the truck.

"Who are they?" Randall asked Nakamura.

"Morgan and Soto, they were guarding the river while we were getting the two of you," Nakamura announced, carefully checking Michael's vitals. "The others collected computers, drives, and other materials for the techs back home to go through."

More gunfire erupted from the river.

A flurry of commotion came from the river a moment later as the gunfire drew closer to them. A steady stream of SEALs carried their gear from the riverbank, and for the first time, Randall noticed two of them carrying a lifeless body. Randall sprinted to help them out, but they waved him off. Arriving back by the truck, they set their fallen comrade's body on the ground, and Randall immediately recognized Wiśniewski's face.

"Fucking bastards got him, but we made them pay," it was Benitez, angrily throwing his regulator to the ground.

A sudden sense of sadness washed over him for the SEAL who he had barely known, but had given his life to save Michael and himself. The rest of the SEALs arrived shortly after. They loaded the rest of their gear into the truck and sped off into the darkness, away from the Fortress and deeper into the Estonian countryside.

Chapter Thirty-Two

Amari Lennubaas Military Air Base, Estonia

May 14, 7:47 a.m.

Randall sat in the back of the cavernous hold of the C130 as it taxied for takeoff. After a few minutes, the plane was aloft, heading back to the United States with Randall in tow. Michael had been stabilized at the air base hospital and would fully recover but the decision had been made to keep him on the ground until his strength returned.

Although tired, Randall was unable to sleep, his knowledge of the planned events burning in his mind. It had taken some time to convince the base commander that his knowledge of the President's impending kidnapping was legitimate, but a call to General Flores had clarified the matter. The base commander had then arranged for a secure line to be provided in the plane to avoid potential eves dropping from outside parties. Now airborne, Randall was led to a makeshift partitioned area within the plane and given access to the secure line.

Colonel Tod Augustin, the intelligence officer assigned to Randall, was surprised at the decision to allow a civilian access to a secure line, but was even more surprised when the call was placed to the Secret Service in Randall's name and was accepted. Randall could see the expression of disbelief on the Colonel's face when Deputy Director Secret Service, Roy Hallett immediately accepted the call from the civilian who was also using the plane as his personal transport back to the states.

"Randall, it's been a long time, but I'm guessing this is serious, how can I help you?" Hallett asked, true warmth and friendship in his voice, causing yet another incredulous expression to cross Augustin's face.

"Thanks for taking my call Roy. I'm sorry to bother you but I have some information that you need to know," Randall explained how he and Michael had been kidnapped and discovered the plans to abduct the President while they were being held hostage.

Hallett's voice became deadly serious. "Do you have any details about where or when?"

"Unfortunately, I don't. All I know is what I've told you, but I'm sure it'll be soon. Aminov left with the device shortly before the SEALs rescued us. I have to imagine that he'll move quickly," Randall said.

"The President is in France for a meeting with the French and Germans. Aminov could be planning something after that meeting," Hallett announced.

"You could be right, but you might want to keep an extra close eye on the President while he's in France. I'm worried that Aminov could have plants anywhere," Randall said.

Like Vogel had in Germany.

"If this was coming from anyone else, I'd call them crazy, but I know better Nick. We'll tighten the detail and make sure we're ready," Hallett said.

"Thanks Roy, I'll sleep better knowing we spoke."

"Let me know when you're in D.C. and we'll grab lunch."

Randall smiled. "Sounds good to me. I'm going to get some rest now. Take care Roy." Randall hung up and looked at Augustin who must have been convinced that Randall was a field agent. He could read the Colonel's mind. "We go way back," was all he said to the intelligence officer who just shook his head in disbelief.

Satisfied that Hallett would ensure the President's safety, Randall could finally rest, knowing that the full force of the Secret Service would be alerted to Aminov's plan and be ready to protect the President from a kidnapping attempt. Randall planned to spend the rest of the twelve-hour flight getting reacquainted with the insides of his eyelids.

Chapter Thirty-Three

Paris, France

May 14, 8:38 a.m.

President Mercer let his displeasure be known. He had flown across the Atlantic at the behest of his fellow heads of state just to be handed over to the French Senate President and the Vice Chancellor of Germany. While recognizing the importance each man played in the ruling of his respective country, Mercer couldn't help but feel a bit like a young teenager stood up by his date for the high school quarterback. While it might have been an honor for others to meet with the second most powerful people in France and Germany respectively, he was the President of the United States of America and the last time he had checked, America was still the preeminent superpower. He allowed his frustration to be tempered by the circumstances facing the western world at the moment. He looked to the two men seated across from him by the fireplace while two secret service agents watched over him. "When exactly will the Chancellor and President be available?"

"President Gaston sends his deepest regrets, but he was called away on a matter of grave national importance," Bandeaux replied.

"President Mercer, unfortunately while neither Chancellor Heisberg, nor President Gaston can be here at the moment, we promise you that we have been given complete authority to represent and act on our countries' behalf. Communicating with us is the same as speaking with them directly," Muller said.

Mercer set his jaw, his eyes burrowing through the Vice Chancellor, knowing full well the man was lying. If Mercer had sent Vice President Sanders on his behalf, while allowing him to negotiate to an extent, he would never allow him full autonomy to operate on his own. It simply wasn't how the process worked. This meant one of two things, either Muller was incompetent and completely incapable of fulfilling his duties or the man was simply dishonest. Either way, Mercer decided his interactions with the man would be extremely limited. He'd have to rely on the French Senate President. At least Babineaux hadn't insulted his intelligence.

"Both France and Germany appreciate America's efforts to create a unified response and we are anxious to discuss a plan of action," Babineaux stated.

"I understand the French Senate called an emergency session to discuss our proposal to increase sanctions on Russian businesses operating in the west. As you know, our Congress recently passed legislation to that effect in the States and the British parliament passed similar legislation in their country. But to have the desired effect we need

France and Germany to join the boycott as well. That would create the needed political pressure to force all NATO members to join us, which would send a strong message to the Russians," Mercer said.

"We're aware of your legislation but I think you fail to realize the difficult situation this places Germany into. If we join you, Russia can reduce or even cut off their supply of petroleum to our nation which would cripple our industry," Muller replied in an irritated tone.

Mercer maintained his composure. "The United States recognizes this fact and I'm prepared to open our strategic oil reserves to both of your nations as a sign of good faith if you'll support our sanctions."

Muller scoffed, "And if this situation drags on for months or even years, your strategic oil supply will be of little use to Germany."

It took every ounce of control to keep Mercer from reaching across the aisle to throttle Muller. Instead he pivoted back to Babineaux. "And what about France?"

Babineaux sighed. "Unfortunately, I have to agree with Vice Chancellor Muller. France simply cannot afford to anger Russia at this time. We have plans to develop additional nuclear power plants and wind generating capacity but until these are completed, we must find another solution."

Mercer leaned back in his chair and rubbed his eyes. This entire trip had been a waste of time. Soon the opposition back home would be calling for Mercer to take unilateral action without NATO. Worse, factions within his own party, including the Vice President, would back the notion. Mercer would be forced into a corner. Viewed as a lame duck president with only a year and a half left in his two-term presidency, he would struggle to generate any support for further diplomacy as both the opposition party and even presidential hopefuls within his own party jostled to be viewed as tough on Russia.

Without warning, the head of Mercer's presidential detail, Frank Harper, rushed to his side. "Mr. President, we need to move you immediately."

Mercer looked into the worried eyes of Harper. The man was as tough as they came with three tours of duty in Afghanistan under his belt. In his six years on the job, he has never worn this expression before. He depressed his throat mic, "Base One, this is Harp, I'm with Timberwolf and we're on the move," Harper reported, using the President's call sign, given to him as a sign of respect from his agents in reference to wolf being the largest of all canines.

"What's happening Frank?"

"It's a goddam trap, sir. They have our exits covered and they're closing in from multiple directions. I can't reach anyone over the comms. Even the Counter Sniper team is down," Harper replied. "Mr. President this is going to get nasty, I need you to stay by my side."

Mercer rose from his seat and glared at Babineaux and Muller. "Are you a part of this?"

Babineaux's eyes went wide.

Harper drew his side arm, stepping between Mercer and a Republican Guard member stationed behind Babineaux who was anxiously eyeing the President. Upon seeing Harper's weapon, the guard swung his rifle in the agent's direction. Both Harper and the guard fired simultaneously, Harper landing three shots in a close grouping in the center of the guard's chest but not before the man unleashed several rounds of his own into Harper's abdomen. Both men fell to the floor.

"Frank!" Mercer dropped to a knee by Harper who coughed blood, then stopped breathing.

The remaining Republican Guard member squared off with the two remaining Secret Service agents, who had stepped in front of Mercer to shield him. Guns were drawn on both sides, the threat of death hanging in the air. The agents began to twitch, then dropped to their knees, grasping their heads and moaning in pain. Mercer watched in confusion as they eventually fell to the ground, their bodies convulsing. It was then that he saw an additional Republican Guard member enter the room with an odd-looking device pointed at the agents.

The sleek, black weapon looked like something from a science fiction move. Having an enlarged rifle stock and pistol grip, the main body of the device bowed downward from the front, creating a long sweeping arc that leveled at the bottom where the guard member held it, a tripod fastened underneath. The end of the device where the barrel would normally be, was equipped with a large diameter lens, encapsulated in a faring that extended out and over it, creating the look of a human eye when viewed from the side.

A second guard member then entered the room and walked straight to the President. "Mr. Mercer, you have a choice. You can come along willingly or we can force you."

Mercer turned and scowled at Babineaux and Muller. "You'll both pay dearly for this when it's over."

The guard member smiled. "This is only the beginning."

"Don't count on my cooperation," Mercer growled.

"Did you really think we would have to rely on your cooperation?" the guard member withdrew an odd-looking pistol from his holster and fired at Mercer's chest.

Mercer felt pain a foot above his navel. Looking down at his shirt he noted a silver dart with a red plume lodged in his chest. He immediately recognized it as a tranquilizer dart. The world began to spin and his eyes suddenly became heavy and before he could speak, things went dark and he dropped to the floor.

"Will he be alright?" Babineaux asked.

Laurent ignored the question, speaking into his throat mic and ordering additional guards to assist them. Two soldiers jogged into the room.

"Update on the situation outside," Laurent demanded.

"The American agents have been neutralized, as well as their Counter Sniper team. The microwave weapons worked as expected. We've picked up traffic on their radios that reinforcements are on their way and will be on the scene shortly."

"Pick him up and get him into the tunnel," Laurent ordered.

The first guard pressed a small recessed panel next to the hearth of the fireplace, causing a small opening to appear. A second guard retrieved a long, metallic case, not unlike a coffin, from the compartment and laid it next to Mercer. The third man opened the case, revealing a padded compartment inside, contoured to the shape of an adult man. Also, inside were several vials, an oxygen tank and several electronic monitors. The third man went to work on Mercer, prepping him for travel.

He rolled back the president's sleeve, swabbed the inside of his arm and inserted an IV line to administer a drug to keep Mercer unconscious. Next, he hooked up the oxygen mask and set about checking the president's vital signs. "He's stable."

The other two guards lifted Mercer's unconscious body and placed him into the case, while the third ensured all of his vitals remained in safe ranges. He then switched to a small handheld tablet and compared Mercer's vitals to those on the monitors inside the case. Both matched.

"Close him up," Laurent ordered as the first two guards closed the case, locking Mercer inside.

Laurent checked his watch. It had taken less than three minutes, but the sound of growing gunfire outside warned him time was short. "Hurry, reinforcements are coming!"

Two guards lifted the case carrying Mercer and ducked into the opening as the third followed closely behind monitoring his vitals.

"What about us?" Muller asked.

Laurent looked at Muller and Babineaux in a dismissive fashion. "We need to make it look like you were unaware of the plan." He picked up the microwave weapon.

"What are you going to do with that?" Babineaux asked, trying to conceal the concern in his voice.

Laurent aimed the weapon at the two men and soon both dropped to their knees and cupped their hands around their heads.

"That's low dose. You'll both feel dizzy and nauseous until tomorrow but there'll be no long-term consequences."

Laurent entered the opening next to the mantel, then pushed a button on the inside, causing the panel to close and leaving Babineaux and Muller behind. The tunnel, a remnant of the medieval days of the facility, was an escape route leading underground in the event that marauding forces successfully overwhelmed the exterior defenses.

Laurent hit a switch embedded in the wall, causing a

string of lights strung across the ceiling of the tunnel to spring to life, illuminating the passageway. The group move quickly, the guards carrying Mercer while Laurent trailed behind. The tunnel was long and dark despite the lights and the air dank and musty as they strode along in single file. They made good time, the young guards easily bearing the weight of the American President.

Laurent marked the distance in his mind, estimating that they had traversed approximately halfway under the garden. They were well on their way to the Theatre Marigny, adjacent to the Avenue de Marigny, where an ambulance waited in the freshly constructed underground garage. The location had been carefully chosen nearly two years ago, the planning meticulously anticipating every potential situation which may have arisen.

Laurent had specifically shut down the Avenue de Marigny, staffing it with men loyal to Aminov, who had paid handsomely for their cooperation. Knowing the location of the American Secret Service they had neutralized them all, allowing them a gap in time to make a safe exit. Always planning for contingencies, a non-functioning microwave gun had been left hidden in the palace where it would later be discovered. Laurent, familiar with Secret Service tactics, knew the agents would search the area with a fine-tooth comb and would find the Russian made weapon stolen from the Chinese. Yet again, another sign that the Russian government was behind the kidnapping.

The group finally came to a juncture which turned ninety degrees to the right and straight for the theatre. Several minutes later, they exited from the tunnel and into the underground lobby of the theatre through a locked metal door. The group hustled down the long, straight crème colored hallways, lit with overhead fluorescent lights, and exited into the underground parking garage where the ambulance was waiting.

"Place him in the back and start the IV," Laurent ordered. The short acting sedative would soon wear off and Laurent needed to make sure the President slept soundly for his transport to Aminov.

Chapter Thirty-Four

Andrews Airforce Base, Maryland

May 14, 1:19 p.m.

The giant rear hatch of the C130 slowly lowered to the ground, allowing Randall and Colonel Augustin to exit the behemoth plane. They were greeted by the faces of John, Liz and General Flores. Liz threw her arms around Randall and hugged him, placing her lips close to his left ear. "Thought I'd lost you Yank." She pulled back, offering Randall a wink and a sly smile.

"I thought we had lost you dad," John said before also hugging his father.

Flores waited patiently for his turn. Once John released Randall, the general extended his hand. "It's good to see you made it back in one piece," they shook and Flores continued. "I have important information but first, I owe you my thanks for saving Michael."

"I'm glad he's safe. I was worried we were going to run out of time," Randall replied. Flores nodded, closing his eyes as he did so, clearly relieved that his son was safe. As a father, Randall could relate. The thought of losing a child is a fear that strikes terror in the heart of every parent, even hardened military men. The thought of losing John or Sam was more than he could bear and he had nearly lost both recently. Randall pushed the dark thoughts from his mind, knowing that no good would come from dwelling on them. "You mentioned you had important news?"

The question pulled Flores back to the present. "The President has been kidnapped. We received word that there was an attack at the French Presidential Palace and the President is now missing, along with the French President of the Senate and German Vice Chancellor. Vice President Sanders has assumed Presidential duties and is in a debrief with the Joint Chiefs and Secret Service Director Clancy," Flores said.

Randall frowned. He clearly hadn't reached Hallett in time to protect the President.

"You've done all you can Nick. You notified Assistant Director Hallett, but the plan was already in motion. Nothing could have stopped them."

Randall raised a brow. Once again, Flores demonstrated that his reach within the higher levels of government was significant. Was Colonel Augustin his source or someone else? It didn't really matter. Flores was clearly connected. "Has the responsible party made any demands?"

"No contact has been made at this time. We're trying to determine how an attack like this could have been orchestrated in a secure area, but our French friends have circled the wagons and largely gone silent. We're trying to get a forensics team to enter the palace and search for clues, but the French are stonewalling. Seems their pride has been injured and they want to be the ones to set thing right," Flores replied.

"There might be something we can do," Randall said.

Flores cocked his head to one side, a look of confusion on his face. "What do you mean?"

"Before we were captured by Aminov and his team, we retrieved a book from Washington's tomb that was written by Ben Franklin. I haven't had a chance to read it but there may be some clues about the device that might shed some light on who this group might be and what their goal is."

"Liz and John brought it with them. They thought you might want to read it, and if there's something that could help us find the President, we better get started right away," Flores said.

Liz grabbed Randall's arm and led him to the waiting Black SUV, where John was already waiting. "I started to look through it but there were parts that simply didn't make sense to me. Talk of ghosts and such. To be honest Nick, it makes me wonder a bit about you Yanks."

Randall covered his mouth, stifling a laugh. They entered the Black SUV and started their ride back to the Pentagon, with Liz in the middle, flanked by the Randall boys on either side. Liz removed the book from her handbag and handed it to Randall, who held it gingerly in his hands. The weathered, brown calf skin cover was cracked, especially near the back spine where the cover hinged. I single leather strap was looped around the midsection of the book, halfway up its vertical length. Randall immediately recognized it was a typical journal from Franklin's time. He carefully unwrapped the leather strap and drew the cover back. The deckle edge paper inside the cover identified the journal as belonging to Franklin.

Randall carefully turned the first page and began to study the book, while Liz read over his shoulder. The ride back to the Pentagon afforded Randall a rare reading opportunity and Franklin's book didn't disappoint. "This is amazing. Franklin goes into detail about the way Washington came into possession of the device and how it helped the colonies plan their strategy to beat the British."

"You sound quite excited about that last part," Liz joked.

Randall grinned sheepishly. "Sorry about that. Just a fan of Washington and amazed that he was able to take a ragtag bunch of militias and form them into a fighting force capable of beating the most disciplined and experienced army in the world at the time."

"Clearly not our finest hour," Liz commented.

"According to Franklin, General Washington was paid a visit by a spirit who inspired him when he was in great despair," Randall said.

Liz nodded her head, clearly having already read this part. "I hadn't realized this was going to be a ghost story."

"Well apparently, Washington's ghost, as you put it, had an interest in seeing the young nation survive and wanted to provide Washington with some assistance to help the cause."

"Hence the device we found under Washington's tomb," John added.

"Right."

"Don't you find it a bit odd that a ghost would be in possession of a piece of advanced electronic machinery?" Liz pointed out.

"I think it's safe to assume that Washington's ghost wasn't a ghost at all but something else entirely," Randall replied.

Liz closed her eyes. "Please don't tell me what I think you're going to tell me."

Randall bit his tongue. No sense heading back down that road again. "Apparently, the device gave Washington the ability to see the future, or at least potential outcomes, which explains what I experienced when I was being held captive."

"You were able to see the future?" Liz asked, straining to hide the doubt in her voice.

Randall understood her suspicion. Before his experiences with the device, if someone had told him there was a machine that allowed the user to view potential future events, he would have been highly skeptical. It was the nature of scientists to doubt such outlandish claims until some type of research confirmed the assertion. "Maybe seeing the future isn't the right way to frame my experience. It was more of seeing possible outcomes of future events. I'm not sure why I witnessed the scenario with the President, but based on what happened, I clearly saw events that came to pass."

Liz studied Randall carefully. She was still clearly trying to determine if she could accept what she was hearing, and Randall could see the doubt melting away. He had to give Liz credit because most scientists and people in general would never had accepted the things she had heard and seen, but Liz clearly had an open mind and was willing to at least entertain such theories.

"Keep reading," Liz urged.

Randall turned the page and was shocked at what he read next. He glanced up at Liz who was grinning ear to ear. "There's another book." Liz nodded slowly, her face morphing to one of full acceptance. Randall read quickly, fully entranced by the material disclosed by Franklin. He finished the final pages of the book, set it on his lap and removed his glasses. He pinched nose between thumb and forefinger, closing his eyes to fully digest the contents.

"What do you think?" Liz asked, urging him out of his deep thoughts.

The final pages of the Franklin notes disclosed the existence of a book, authored by then General Washington, explaining how the device operated and how he used it. The disclosure that the man, considered by many to be the Father of Our County, had written a secret book, which, if Franklin's notes were to be believed, could verify that he had received a device from a non-human entity that gave him the ability to foresee future events was monumental. Just as stunning was the possibility that Washington's notes might describe the device in detail and explain how to use it. He leaned over and whispered in Liz's ear. "Does Jim Flores know about this?"

"The General was very respectful of your discovery. He allowed me to keep the book at all times, wanting you to be the one who read it and devise a plan of action. He thinks very highly of you Nick," Liz whispered back.

Randall looked up to the front passenger seat where Flores sat, engrossed with some task on his phone. "Jim," Randall tapped Flores' shoulder.

Flores finished his task, then set his phone on his lap. He turned to face Randall and Liz. "Did you find something?"

"Yes, but I'd rather not discuss this until we're back in your office. How long until we get there," Randall asked.

Flores frowned. "Nick, this vehicle is fully secure and Agent Vicenti can be trusted with any information."

"I believe I know what we need to do next," Nick replied, relenting on his request to wait.

Flores sat attentively while Randall explained what he

had read, beginning with the explanation of how Washington came into possession of the device, and information he had relayed to Franklin, who dutifully recorded these facts in his book. Flores sat stone faced, nodding occasionally as he absorbed the information. Randall finally arrived at the part of the explanation that served as his call to action. "At the end of his book, Franklin referenced a book written by Washington. He alleges that this book explains, in detail, how Washington operated the device."

Flores nodded slowly, urging Randall to finish his explanation.

"I believe if we find the Washington book, we'll have a better understanding of why the kidnappers want the device and possibly use the book as leverage to negotiate for the President's release," Randall said.

"Did the book explain where to find the book?" Flores asked.

"It didn't, but I think I have a good idea of where to look."

"How?" Flores said, furrowing his brow.

"The link between Washington, Franklin, and this device is no coincidence. Washington needed someone with a scientific mind, who he could trust, to help him figure out how to work the device, while keeping its existence a secret. The two communicated in a type of written cypher, referring to things that only the two of them understood. References to location of Franklin's book in Washington's tomb is an example. If we accept the fact that these two were the only ones who knew about the device, that they both favored cryptic messages that relied upon knowledge that they both possessed, and consider that the Franklin book was hidden at Washington's tomb, there's only one place the Washington book could be."

"Where?"
Randall smiled. "Franklin's tomb."

Chapter Thirty-Five

Christ Church Burial Ground, Philadelphia, PA

May 14, 5:47 p.m.

It had taken some convincing, but Randall had finally and successfully convinced Flores that they would find Washington's book at Franklin's tomb. Despite their experiences together, Flores had still struggled to believe that Randall could deduce something as specific as the location of the book through a series of seemingly unrelated facts as he had recounted in the car ride from Andrews to Christ Church Burial Ground, where Franklin was entombed. Fortunately for Randall, his persistence and one additional fact, proven through a simple internet search on his phone, had sealed the deal.

Randall had read aloud the second to last paragraph from Franklin's book which had read:

... *books, much like people, prefer the company of others. Search where one might find the Cover of an old Book, Its Contents torn out, And stript of its Lettering and Gilding, waiting to appear once more, In a new & more perfect Edition, Corrected and Amended By the Author.*

Unsure of the meaning, Flores had pointed out that, despite his acclaimed writing ability, Franklin's grammar had failed him spectacularly. It wasn't until Randall had shown Flores the words that Franklin had planned to use on his tombstone that he had accepted Randall's assertion. The passage from Franklin's book from Washington's tomb nearly matched his planned epitaph. Once again, the master of ciphers and codes had used wordplay to provide the location of the Washington book. Flores was once again impressed with Randall's ability to find meaning, but then again, it was becoming fairly commonplace.

The issue now would be how to search the tomb, when it sat exposed to any passerby who cared to look through the copper fence on Arch Street to see it. As if to emphasize the point, Randall marveled at well over two dozen pennies resting on the tombstone covering the grave, a testament to Franklin's adage "a penny saved in a penny earned." Unfortunately, this access to the people posed a serious difficulty to Randall, Liz and John. The solution, as John had proposed was simple. They would dress like caretakers of the grounds and place sheets over the fence and surrounding areas under the guise of maintenance of Franklin's grave.

Aiding them was the fact that the grounds had closed at 4:00 p.m., leaving the area vacant. A well-placed call from a member of Flores team would ensure that no staff of the facility would question the presence of the heretofore caretakers.

John set to hanging several large, off-white drop cloths

to cover the fence facing Arch Street to provide privacy from passersby. Using zip ties, he threaded them through the grommets on the ends of the cloths and secured them to the fence posts, creating a formidable barrier that even someone with keen eyesight would have difficulty penetrating. Fighting a stiff breeze at times, John succeeded at covering the opening from top to bottom, using a few heavy stones to hold the base of the cloths to cover the small gap under the fence.

As John worked on covering the fence, Randall and Liz stood shoulder to shoulder examining rough drawings of the construction of the tomb as it existed below ground level. The side-view sketches provided a description of the different layers and materials involved in the composition of Franklin's final resting place. Randall wrinkled his nose at the thought of once again damaging a historical landmark in the hopes of solving a problem. The last time had involved breaking into the Vatican grottos and opening the ancient crypt of a deceased pope. As a lifelong Catholic, that experience hadn't set well, but had been necessary to save his daughter's life. At least this time, it was only the grave of one of the Founding Fathers of the county. Randall closed his eyes and sighed.

"Rob the graves of important historical figures much?" Liz joked, bumping Randall's shoulder with her own, jarring him back to his present task.

"Only twice," Randall replied, eyeing the hulking presence of Agent Vicenti, who leaned on the handle of a shovel, clearly irritated at being assigned to this task.

"Are we ready to do this?" Vicenti asked, shifting his considerable weight as he leaned on the garden tool.

Randall turned to survey the graveyard, taking in the view of the multitude of tombstones of many shapes and sizes. Along with the traditional arched stones were crosses, obelisks, and several structures that resembled colonial style houses. Some were intricately carved and ornately decorated, while others were broken and weathered. He marveled at the history on display before him in the Colonial and Revolution-era graveyard. The online description he had read on the car ride from Andrews had stated that the grounds contained 1,400 markers on two beautiful acres right in the heart of historic Philadelphia and served as the final resting place of not only Benjamin Franklin but four other signers of the Declaration of Independence.

"Well?" groused an impatient Vicenti.

"Before we start digging, we need to remove the tomb cover, but we need to be careful not to damage it," Randall said. "According to the plans, it's a three-inch marble slab, but there's no way to tell how it's been affected by weathering."

"Don't worry doc, we'll be careful with it," assured Agent Ticzon, one of the other three agents assigned to the detail, along with Agents Hartfield and Serrano.

Ticzon hefted a five-foot crowbar, wedging it into a seam between the marble tomb cover and the concrete edge, which formed the outer shell of the grave. He nodded for Hartfield to do the same with his crowbar. "Once we get it up high enough, you two grab it," he said to Vicenti and Serrano who stood ready with gloved hands. "On three. One, two three."

The two agents leaned onto their respective crowbars, but initially the slab resisted movement. It finally relented under the constant pressure applied by the two men and began to move. Randall grimaced at the loud popping sound that resulted from the stone's movement, fearing they had broken the marble slab.

"It's okay dad, that was just the sound of the marble separating from the ground beneath it. After all of these years, the force of gravity probably made them stick together," John said, clearly sensing his dad's concern.

Randall sighed in relief, then turned his focus back to the task at hand. He watched as the four agents hefted the marble slab and gently set it aside. Small bits had in fact broken off on two of the four corners of the slab, and several areas had chipped away on some of the edges, but most of the damage was a result of normal wear and could be easily repaired. Now came the actual hard work of digging through the earth that covered the tomb, which, according to the diagrams and past custom was six feet under the surface. Since Franklin had been buried in 1790, his grave would have been buried six feet deep to keep grave robbers from trying to exhume the remains. There was a macabre irony to the situation, given that historians had discovered many skeletal remains at Franklin's house on Craven Street in England, the result of an illegal anatomy school run by Benjamin Franklin's young friend and protégé, William Hewson. Franklin had indeed led an interesting life.

Once again, it was the agents who bore the burden of the physical labor needed to exhume the grave as they took turns digging. Randall's mind ran wild with thoughts of what they would find buried with Franklin in his coffin and he couldn't wait to find out. As it turned out, he wouldn't have to wait long as the blade from Agent Serrano's shovel struck something solid about four feet down.

"Whatever it is, it's not the coffin. It's too small for that," Serrano reported, digging around the edges of whatever he had found. He continued to clear the dirt from around the rectangular object, jabbing the edge of his shovel into the earth around the object to clear away the dirt.

Randall moved closer, ever the Archeologist, trying to ensure that whatever they had found be preserved as best as possible. He judged the object to be approximately two feet long by two feet wide. It was impossible to tell the depth of the object until they freed it from the dirt. "Let me take it from here," he climbed into the hole and held out his hand for the shovel, never breaking eye contact with the chest they had found. He had decided it was a metal chest, based on the size and exposed surfaces he could see.

Serrano handed over the shovel without protest, clambering out of the shallow, grave sized opening. Randall knelt by the chest, running his hand over the surface, then along the edge to try to clear away the dirt without damaging the chest. The earth was too tightly packed and required use of the shovel. He sighed, realizing that he didn't have time to use the proper careful technique to uncover the object and keep from damaging it. This wasn't an archeological dig, it was a hurried attempt to retrieve an item needed to save the life of the president and prevent some sort of horrific plan from a still unknown adversary.

He dug as carefully as he could around the object, slowly removing the hardened earth around it. Upon closer inspection, the chest was wooden, likely oak or walnut, the dark earth around it staining it a deep brown color. Randall continued to dig carefully, not certain of how sturdy the wood remained.

"We've got to get a move on," Vicenti urged.

"There's no way of telling if the chest is rotted through or not," Randall explained, not stopping his deliberate removal process. "If I go too fast, the chest could collapse and we could irreparably damage whatever's inside." His message must have found its mark because Vicenti no longer protested.

Several minutes later, Randall had excavated to the base of the chest. Satisfied that he had sufficiently freed the object, he set the shovel down and hefted the box up. It came free with relative ease, undamaged. "Here, take this, but be careful," he handed the box up to Serrano who handled the chest with the delicateness of a new father holding his child for the first time.

Randall scrambled out of the hole. "Set it down here," he patted on a flat spot next to Franklin's grave. Serrano complied.

Randall wiped his hands on his pant legs, cleaning off the dirt as best as he could. He removed a pair of reading glasses from his pocket and kneeled by the chest, carefully examining it. The wood was partially rotted, but not as badly as he would have imagined for a wooden chest buried for over two hundred years. The front of the chest was adorned with a heavy, metal padlock, dating back to Franklin's era. Randall studied it, considering whether to cut the lock off or try to remove it without damaging the relic. Sadly, they didn't have time to take the subtle approach, he needed to know if Washington's book was in the chest or if they needed to keep digging. He glanced over to Franklin's grave, clearly preferring not to play the role of graverobber and leaving Mr. Franklin's remains undisturbed.

"Can you bring me the bolt cutters?" Randall asked, glad that they had stopped at a hardware store along the way to pick them up.

Serrano jogged to back to the Black Suburban, retrieved the cutters, along with a rag, and brought them back to Randall.

"Thanks," Randall took the rag and wet it with water

from a bottle he had brought to the site. He cleaned his hands thoroughly, then dried them on the clean end of the towel. His hands now clean, he hefted the bolt cutters and carefully lined up the blades on the padlock loop and squeezed. After a moment, the metal gave way to the pressure of the blades and snapped apart. Randall set the bolt cutters down. By now, both Liz and John had joined him, eager to see what was inside.

"Here we go," Randall flipped the lid open, revealing straw filled to the brim of the container.

"Padding for whatever's inside," Liz observed.

She was right. Packing peanuts and air-filled pouches weren't in existence during Franklin's time, hay serving as the preferred method of cushioning the contents of such containers. Randall reached through the straw, feeling his way around the contents until his hand struck something solid. He grasped the object and plucked it from the chest.

Whatever lay inside was wrapped in cloth, held in place by a tied piece of leather string. Randall untied the knot and removed the string then folded back the cloth cover, revealing a leather clad book. He flipped it open and scanned the cover page, which featured President Washington's signature prominently at the bottom center of the page. Randall quickly read the first paragraph. "Washington entrusted Franklin with this book to hide it so that no one else could find it," he announced proudly before looking up at Liz, then John, their faces beaming. "We found it!"

"Congratulations dad! You figured out Franklin's riddle!" John patted his father's shoulder. Randall smiled and nodded, then continued reading the book, scanning pages as he flipped through it.

"We need to get back to Jim's office and study this,"

Randall announced. "Let's take the chest as well. We'll want to check it more carefully to see if there's anything else inside and to carbon date it."

Serrano understood. "Let's fill the hole back in and replace the lid of the grave."

The four agents shoveling in tandem made short work of refiling the hole and restoring Franklin's grave to the state they had found it. Within an hour, they were on the road back to the Pentagon, their mission successfully completed without incident.

Chapter Thirty-Six

Pentagon, Washington D. C.

May 14, 10:02 p.m.

Randall sat across the desk from Flores, trying to wrap his head around the information he received. John and Liz sat to his left and right, respectively. Having arrived thirty minutes earlier, he had thought that their discovery of the Washington book and information he had gleaned so far from would be the big news of the evening. He was dead wrong. Flores had his lead technician, Angela Fowlkes present the information to them so that she could answer any questions they had, but to this point, they had all sat quietly and listened as Fowlkes explained what had been gathered from the hard drives captured at Ivangorod Fortress.

"You're saying Aminov is trying to set off WW 3 to topple the governments of the United States, Russia and

China and install a new seat of power in the European Union, with France and Germany as the head. And if he succeeds, he'll impose martial law under the guise of rebuilding from the war?" Randall asked, finally breaking his silence.

"That's correct. He's already in the advanced stages of enacting his plan, but wanted the device you discovered to help plan tactics," Fowlkes responded. "With the device he'll be able to know the outcome of each potential scenario so that he can enact the strategies that ensure a victory."

"And in the process be able to counteract any measures we take in response," Flores added.

"That's correct General. If this device operates as explained, Aminov would utilize it the way we currently use AI algorithms for war planning, except this device would provide actual outcomes and not high probability outcomes as our current supercomputers produce," Fowlkes replied.

"What other information were you able to gather from the seized equipment?" John asked.

"Unfortunately, there was a security feature installed on most of the drives that converted the files to unreadable coding once we tried to access them. Aminov hired some very sharp computer programmers to protect his systems. This is unlike anything we've seen," Fowlkes said.

"So, everything else is lost?" Randall asked.

"Not necessarily. Our programmers are working to decrypt the files and see if we can recover any additional information. The problem is, without the key that created the encryption, it's a very tedious process. It could take days, weeks or even longer to recover these files. It's also possible that we may lose some of them entirely. It's too early to tell." Fowlkes explained.

"Thank you, Agent Fowlkes," Flores said, dismissing the technician. Fowlkes nodded and left the group.

"Nick, I don't need to tell you the gravity of this situation. We're on a very tight timeline to stop Aminov."

"Have you notified the Vice President?" Liz asked.

Flores stiffened, his features hardening and his eyes narrowing. He forced his lips closed as if forcing back the words he truly wanted to say. "Dawn Franklin notified me that Vice President Sanders has limited access due to the current circumstances involving the President. I tried to explain that we have critical information regarding the nature of the group that kidnapped the President, but she directed me to the Office of the White House Liaison."

Randall slowly nodded his head in recognition of the underlying meaning of Flores message. Rumors of a serious rift in the White House had surfaced in the news shortly after the election. Apparently, the choice of Ron Sanders on the ticket as Mercer's running mate had been entirely a political decision to woo voters in the Northwest. Apparently, the two men had barely spoken outside of required meetings of State since arriving at the Whitehouse. The rumor mill painted pictures of Sanders as a narcissist whose only reason for running for office was to acquire power. His choice of Dawn Franklin, a person whose personality was so abrasive she had been excluded from social events planned by other staff in the Mercer administration, only served to confirm the rumors.

"What's our next move?" Randall asked.

"We have to wait. At this time, we need to see what the Vice President plans to do. He's currently meeting with the Joint Chiefs to determine a course of action. Once that's decided, we'll have a better idea of what our next move should be."

Randall furrowed his brow. "How will you know the Vice President's plans if he won't involve you in the planning?"

"I have contacts on the Joint Chiefs. When a decision is made, I'll find out immediately," Flores replied.

The three sat in stunned silence, unsure of how to respond. Finally, Flores broke the silence. "You must all be exhausted. We have quarters you can use to get some rest. There's nothing else we can do at this time."

"I'd like to go home and get some rest. Would it be possible to have someone drive me?" Liz asked.

"Of course. I'll have one of my staff drive you. How about you gentlemen?" Flores asked, ever the generous host.

"I'll take you up on your offer. I'd like to be here in case something happens," Randall replied.

"I'd like to stay too," John added.

"Very good. Give us a few minutes and we'll make arrangements," Flores stood and walked out of the room.

"Liz, I'm sorry you were dragged into this and I understand if you've had enough and are ready to go back to just being a guest professor," Randall said, feeling genuinely sorry for the stress she had suffered.

Liz cracked a weary smile. "And miss out on all the fun? I wouldn't dream of it! I just need my beauty rest and then I'll be back bright and early."

Randall smiled for the first time since arriving at the Pentagon. If Liz could still manage a joke under the current circumstances, maybe things weren't as bad as they seemed.

Chapter Thirty-Seven

Training Camp, Pakistan

May 15, 7:17 a.m.

The soldier stood at attention, his body like a solid iron rod, his gaze fixed on the bare, pockmarked stone wall in front of him. This pleased Aminov who relished the respect demonstrated by his younger report. The stoicism took him back to a better place and time, when younger soldiers respected and feared their superiors. Years ago, this fear and respect allowed the Russian military to accomplish incredible feats. Feats that today's corrupted army could never dream to achieve. The corruption reached the highest levels, where senior officers prostituted themselves to the highest bidder, frequently selling arms to members of the Russian mafia or Bratva. Their lack of loyalty to the motherland and singular focus on making themselves rich disgusted Aminov.

No matter. When his plan came to fruition, he would rectify this sad state of affairs and he was close. So very close. While the raid on the compound and release of his prisoners displeased him, the impact on his plan was negligible. He had the device and a better understanding of how it worked. Now he just needed Washington's DNA and he would be unstoppable. For all of their posturing and military might, the Americans would be unable to stop him, their impotence on display for all to see. He would know the outcome of any battle, any strategy at his disposal before his enemies even realized what had happened.

The thought of victory so close was intoxicating, but to assume he would win was folly. Years of planning and combat had taught him that victory was never guaranteed until the enemy surrendered and if there was one thing he knew about the American's they would never surrender. Their arrogance wouldn't permit it. He would have to destroy them to gain their submission and he would be only too happy to oblige them. Years of facing the Americans in a military chess game had made him grow to despise them and he was ready to bring them to their knees.

Aminov's eyes flicked upward to the soldier still standing at attention. The man still hadn't moved. "Dismissed."

The soldier snapped his arm up to salute his commander, spun on his heel and marched out of Aminov's office. Aminov waited until the door had closed and latched before opening his laptop and enabling a secure, scrambled channel for his next order of business.

"Monsieur Aminov, good to see you," Babineaux cooed. "I trust you're pleased with the progress we've made on our project."

The Frenchman wore a sickening sweet smile that reeked of insincerity. Aminov had to force down the bile rising in his stomach. "Have the accounts been created and linked back to the Prime Minister and Chancellor?"

Babineaux's face morphed to a frown, the mirth in his eyes vanishing with Aminov's snub. "Yes. The Swiss account has been created and tied back to both men. We were able to gather both of their signatures, personal banking information, identification numbers and other necessary information to associate the accounts with both Prime Minister Laurent and Chancellor Fuchs."

"And you've identified someone to serve as the source of the link who can't be traced back to any of us?" Aminov asked.

"Yes," Babineaux nodded, face still glum.

When Aminov had groomed Babineaux for this assignment, he had done so knowing that he had sufficient damaging information on the man to guarantee his compliance. To say that Babineaux was dirty was like calling Tchaikovsky a mediocre composer. The man had his fingers in so many schemes that Aminov's bigger concern was being linked to the man. But Babineaux had proven himself to be useful, even resourceful at times. As much as he hated to admit it, the French President of the Senate had proven to be a good choice for this part of his plan.

"Contact your source and tell him or her to release the information," Aminov ordered.

Babineaux nodded in reply.

"Babineaux," Aminov said, his voice firm. The Frenchman lifted his eyes to face Aminov on the screen. "Well done."

"Thank you, Mr. Aminov. I'll speak to my contact at once!"

Aminov nodded and severed the connection. When the press learned of this, the French and German governments would have no choice but to relieve the Prime Minister and Chancellor of their duties, positioning Babineaux and Müller to assume the leadership roles of their respective countries. His plan was truly taking shape and soon, the rest of Europe and America wouldn't know what hit them.

Chapter Thirty-Eight

White House Situation Room, Washington D. C.

May 14, 11:37 p.m.

A flurry of activity filled the White House situation room, most of it directed by Chief of Staff Dawn Franklin, clearly enjoying her newfound powers and lording it over such a powerful group. Director of Secret Service Bill Clancy sat on one side of the table, joining FBI Director David Friedman, CIA Director Frank Tarkington and a host of others. Missing from the group was General Frank Murphy, commander of the Joint Special Operations Command (JSOC) and Vice President Sanders.

Murphy had been delayed in route to the White House, but Clancy and he had spent the early part of the day discussing the intelligence gathered by the recent raid on the Ivangorod Fortress by the Seal Team which had freed Captain Flores and Professor Randall. The data gathered thus far had stunned both men and when they had ended their meeting, Murphy had said his next call would be to Sanders to update him on the intel. During the early hours of the morning, the Cabinet had gathered to invoke the Twenty-fifth amendment to appoint Sanders with presidential powers.

Clancy had just made it back to his office when he had been called back for a meeting with Murphy and Sanders, at the White House. What transpired next had shocked him as much as the intel from Ivangorod. As if the kidnapping of the President and subsequent discovery of the plan by Aminov to start a conflict hadn't been bad enough, now came news that a secret source had leaked damaging evidence of the involvement of both French Prime Minister Laurent and German Chancellor Fuchs involvement in the President's kidnapping. The leak had led to the discovery of a $50 million-dollar transaction into a Swiss bank account with ties to a shell corporation linked to both men. The wire transfer had happened minutes before the President had been taken. Worse, the transaction had originated from an account tied to the Russian republic of Georgia, indicating that the Russians may have also played a role in the kidnapping.

Making matters worse, Chief of Staff Franklin had made it clear that Vice President Sanders was deeply disturbed that he was not consulted regarding the raid to free Randall and Captain Flores. She had taken a full three minutes to make it clear to Clancy and everyone else in the room that the Vice President would make all further decisions regarding covert operations and that any further rogue actions on the part of agency heads or Joint Chief members would result in their immediate dismissal. Clancy had tried to point out that the raid had netted them valuable intel which could shed light into the motive behind the President's kidnapping, but he had been almost immediately cut off by Franklin, whose ego had swollen so large, it was surprising she could still fit in the room.

A voice arose from the door, causing Clancy to look up just as Murphy entered and was greeted by one of his staffers. Catching a glimpse of Clancy, Murphy made a beeline for the Director, removing his hat and setting it on the table as he took the seat directly to his right. He had barely settled in when Franklin started into him.

"General Murphy, have you reviewed the information my assistant sent to you?"

"Chief of Staff Franklin, I barely had time to get into the car to make this meeting—."

"General, I would remind you that Vice President Sanders is furious that you failed to consult him regarding the raid and I would strongly urge you to immediately take action whenever any information is sent from this office."

"And I would remind you that the Cabinet had not yet invoked the twenty-fifth amendment when we ordered the raid and, therefore, presidential powers had not yet been passed to Vice President Sanders."

Franklin dropped her hands onto the polished wood surface of the table, jutting her chin out at Murphy, her eyes wide with fury. "You serve at the pleasure of the Vice President and I recommend that you strongly consider your choice of words when addressing him... or me."

Murphy's eyes narrowed, but to his credit, he bit back his words, demonstrating great discipline borne of years of service. He formulated an appropriate response, but before he could speak, the assembled crowd rose to their feet as Vice President Sanders entered the room. The man strutted like the peacock he thought he was into the room, before taking his seat and motioning for others to sit as well.

"General Murphy, did you review the information my Chief of Staff provided you?" Sanders asked, eliciting a crooked grin from Franklin.

"Mr. Vice President, I explained to Chief of Staff Franklin that I had just started to review it in the car ride over," Murphy replied.

"I see, but you had time to authorize a raid without consulting me," Sanders quipped. The Vice President turned to face his FBI Director before Murphy could respond. "No matter, we have more important issues to attend to. Director Friedman, please update us on the investigation into Prime Minister Laurent and Chancellor Fuchs."

Friedman, a tall, balding man with thin wired glasses nodded to his assistant who typed at a keyboard and brought up a report on one of the wall mounted monitors in the front of the room, as well as onto the recessed monitors in front of each individual sitting at the table. "As I'm sure you've all heard by now, an unidentified tip led to the discovery of a Swiss bank account with ties back to both the Prime Minister and Chancellor. A large wire transfer occurred shortly before the President was kidnapped while visiting with the French President of the Senate and the German Vice Chancellor in Paris. The timing of the transfer and the other information we've collected to this point support the notion that the Prime Minister and Chancellor may have been involved with the kidnapping."

"Has your team made any additional discoveries?" Sanders asked.

"Not yet, this information is still quite new and our counterparts in both France and Germany were caught off guard as much as we were. We have a forensics team reviewing the materials and have requested the assistance of the Swiss authorities in the matter, but are awaiting a response."

Clancy flinched at the news, his heart going out to his French and German counterparts. His experience working with both The General Directorate for External Security in France and the German Bundesnachrichtendienst had led him to respect their professionalism and partnership. While bound by strict secrecy, his interactions with his French and German counterparts on joint operations had mostly been very positive. There had been negative exchanges at times, but he had made several friends along the way as well. Both agencies had to be reeling at this discovery, his French counterparts having the double dagger for the failure to head off the kidnapping of the President. Though the public posturing was that the French had closed ranks after the kidnapping, Clancy and his team had been working closely with the French through back channels.

"What about ties back to the Russian government?" Sanders asked, catching Clancy off guard. By the look on Murphy's face, the General was as shocked as he was.

"Our initial investigation has identified the wire transfer as having been routed through a server located in Chechnya. However, we still haven't confirmed the source. We really need the help of our Swiss friends to track this down," Friedman reported.

Murphy looked like a boxer who had the wind knocked out of him. His head hung low and his eyes closed as if in deep thought. Clancy understood his reaction. Murphy had helped to arrange a covert meeting between the Russians and General James Flores, the latter having developed an appreciation for General Konstantin Berezin through many years of military service. Now it appeared that the Russians may have had a hand in the kidnapping of the President and if they had, Murphy bore a great deal of the responsibility.

"Sounds like proof that the Russians were behind the President's kidnapping and the Prime Minister and Chancellor were paid to arrange his capture," Franklin snorted.

"Director Friedman, do you concur?" Sanders asked.

Friedman hesitated, curling his lip. "We need more time to verify this information."

"We've verified the wire transfer and bank routing information to both Prime Minister Laurent and Chancellor Fuchs and we've traced the funding of the payment through a server located on Russian soil. What more proof do we need!" Franklin demanded.

"That's the problem," Friedman continued, his voice even. "This was too easy. An anonymous tip leading to this much information in such a short time period is unheard of. Normally it'd take days or even weeks or longer to uncover this much information. Something doesn't feel right."

"Something doesn't feel right? What are you talking about?" Franklin's eyes were wide. Sanders waved off his Chief of Staff.

"Do you have any other leads Mr. Friedman?" Sanders asked.

"No sir we don't."

Sanders turned to face Director Tarkington. "Does the CIA have any information about the kidnapping?"

"We have operatives in the field working sources, but nothing at this time," Tarkington replied.

"Director Clancy, does the Secret Service have any leads into the President's disappearance?"

Clancy realized what Sanders was doing. He was

familiar with the man's aspirations to become President and he was going to play the situation for all it was worth. The anonymous lead and the information generated, coupled with the fact that the Secret Service had made little headway provided Sanders with the cover he needed to act. "At this time, we have very little information, but we're working with Interpol and other resources and following up on possible scenarios."

"In other words, the Secret Service has no leads," Sanders responded, shutting down Clancy.

"Gentlemen, the facts seem clear to me. The best information we have points to the Russians as the culprits behind the President's kidnapping. Simply put, this is an act of war and the only thing the Russians understand is force. General Murphy, I want you prepare scenarios for possible military action against the Russians. We need to send a clear message to our adversaries that the United States of America will not tolerate the kidnapping of our President and allow the responsible party to go unpunished," Sanders said, pounding his fist on the polished maple table for effect.

"Mr. Vice President, with all due respect, we don't have sufficient information to support the claim that the Russians kidnapped the President. Director Friedman has stated such. In my opinion we need more time for agencies to do their job. We have excellent people at work and if you —"

"General Murphy, our President is being held hostage somewhere and the longer we wait, the less chance we have of finding him. We need to pressure the Russians into admitting what they've done and letting them know we won't stand for it," Sanders fumed.

"Mr. Vice President, you raise a good point. No one has claimed responsibility for the act and there's been no ransom demand. None of this makes sense," Friedman weighed in.

Sanders nearly lost it. "Your jobs," he now pointed his finger around the table. "Are to provide me with information and options and the only information we have came from an anonymous source! General Murphy, you will prepare possible military responses to this heinous act or I'll find someone who will."

Sanders rose to his feet and stomped out of the Situation Room with Franklin in tow, leaving the others in a state of near shock.

Chapter Thirty-Nine

Galwan Valley, Disputed Border Region between China and India

May 15, 8:22 a.m.

Colonel Bai surveyed the Galwan River, which carved its way through the narrow valley bearing its name. Flowing through the Karakoram mountains, the area had been a flash point between China and India in their border dispute. The root source of the territorial dispute, an ill-defined 2,100-mile-long border, changed as rivers shifted courses, and lakes filled and drained as a result of melting snowcaps in the region. The ever-shifting line resulted in bringing soldiers from each army face to face at many points, sparking confrontation.

Colonel Bai, ever a student of history, was well aware of the violent nature of the border dispute. He was equally aware of the 1996 agreement prohibiting the use of guns and explosives near the border, but had no intent of following its dictate. His assignment had been clear. Cross into disputed territory, engage Indian forces, cause as many casualties and fatalities as possible, and leave plenty of evidence that the PLA was behind the raid. Bai had every intent of fulfilling his duties and inflicting as much death on the unsuspecting Indian army as possible. Although Aminov had been silent on the matter, Bai was certain his commander wouldn't be squeamish about the use of excessive violence. His troops were well armed, sporting Chinese made QBZ-95 assault rifles, QCW05 submachine guns, and QBU88 sniper rifles equipped with bipods and 4x telescopic sight, offering a longer kill range.

Bai would rely on the element of surprise to catch his enemy off guard, allowing his men to create as much mayhem as possible in close quarter combat. His snipers had been directed to shoot all enemy combatants attempting to flee the skirmish—preferably in the back—to ensure an enraged Indian leadership. As he surveyed the gray dirt valley, dotted by islands of green vegetation fed by the Galwan River and its tributaries, he simply awaited an update from his scouts to ensure his fire teams were properly situated for maximum damage. He didn't have to wait long.

"Bravo team to base. Enemy unit confirmed and currently stationary. Awaiting further orders."

"Bravo team, hold position," Bai said into his radio. His scout had confirmed what his drone had visualized earlier. Thirty-two Indian soldiers were stationed near a small tributary from the river, likely preparing for patrol. He had brought a full company for this assignment, inserted by stealth choppers under the cover of darkness and deposited to a ridgeline just outside the valley. His one hundred soldiers had hiked the remaining way over the course of the evening, taking their current position until ready to attack. They would divide into two units and perform a pincer movement, a military attack by the two coordinated forces to close in on the enemy from two different directions. Anyone who tried to escape over the river tributary would be gunned down by the snipers. They would kill them all except for one or two who they would allow to escape to notify their superiors.

"Snipers ready. All squads, move out," Bai hissed into his radio. The incursion had begun.

In a short time, his men were in position on both sides of the Indian platoon and opened fire, creating a kill zone between the two opposing pincer forces. The Indian soldiers didn't know what hit them as automatic gunfire littered the area, their comrades dropping in a hailstorm of lead. The remaining Indian soldiers formed a defensive ring and finally returned fire, initially wavering on whether to engage, mindful of the 1996 agreement. Their hesitation cost them additional lives and Bai's forces showed no mercy. Of the original thirty-two soldiers, less than half remained.

What happened next was precisely what Bai had planned for. The Indian soldiers dispersed, running from the merciless onslaught. Those who headed to the river were gunned down by the snipers. Two soldiers fled toward the safety of the deeper valley, leaving five men pinned down and fully surrounded by Bai's soldiers. Bai ordered his men to stay in position and continue to draw the Indian's soldier's fire, slowing draining them of their remaining ammunition. Once spent, the Indian soldiers raised their hands above their heads to surrender. Aminov's orders were specific, they were to make a scene not likely to be forgotten. Bai happily complied, having his men filet the remaining five soldiers like fish caught on a deep-sea boat. He was sure to leave sufficient spent rounds, weapons, and gear to be sure the Indian government knew that the PLA was responsible for this massacre.

Chapter Forty

Pentagon, Washington D. C.

May 15, 5:47 a.m.

Randall woke from a dream about a trip to Boston where his family had tickets to a Red Sox game. Sam and John were teenagers, and the family had taken a trip to Massachusetts to see family and had decided to catch a game. Growing up in the Carolinas, Randall had become a fan of the Sox from watching their affiliate team play in the Carolina leagues and the affection had stuck and he had passed that love of baseball onto both of his kids. It had been a wonderful family vacation, and he had slept deeply and enjoyed the mental respite from the pressure cooker of events that he found himself mired in. He hoped that this was a sign that things had improved overnight.

Randall took a quick shower and shaved in the quarters Flores had provided, then headed over to Flores office, wondering if John had already joined the General. When he arrived, he found Flores, and another soldier huddled over the table, half empty cups of coffee in front of them. Randall didn't recognize the other man, but immediately recognized from the three stars running across the shoulders of his uniform that this man was a general who outranked Flores. Judging by his red eyes, stubble-covered chin, wrinkled shirt and generally haggard appearance, this general hadn't slept the previous night and possibly longer.

The General's eyes lifted from Flores, coming to rest squarely on Randall's face. "Is this the gentleman you've been telling me about James?"

"Dr. Nick Randall, meet General Frank Murphy Joint Special Operations Commander," Flores announced.

"Good to meet you General Murphy," Randall offered his hand and the two men shook.

"Please sit down, Dr. Randall," Murphy gestured to the empty black chair next to him. "Jim has told me about your exploits and it's a pleasure to meet you."

Randall was stunned to discover that Flores had spoken about him to other high-ranking officials. If the JSOC Commander knew about him, who else had Flores spoken to about him? Randall quickly pushed the thought aside. "The pleasure's mine General Murphy."

"Frank's fine Nick. Do you mind if I call you by your first name?" Murphy asked immediately conveying that his ego was in check and that the title of JSOC Commander hadn't gone to his head. Randall nodded in reply.

"What's happened overnight," Randall asked, taking a seat next to Murphy.

"There's been some new developments," Flores started in, "The President's Cabinet has invoked the twenty-fifth amendment and Vice President Sanders has been given full presidential authority."

Randall's face belied his feelings for the Vice President causing Murphy to chuckle.

"Not a fan of the Vice President I see," Murphy commented. "It's okay, neither am I. Unfortunately, he's in control of the government and therefore is my Commander-in-Chief."

"Tell him what the Vice President is asking for," Flores urged.

Murphy's expression turned dead serious. "Nick, what I'm about to tell you cannot leave this room. Do you understand?"

Randall nodded for Murphy to continue.

"Vice President Sanders has asked us to create military scenarios against the Russians for their possible involvement in kidnapping President Mercer," Murphy said.

"He can't be serious about this. Does he know that Aminov isn't working for the Russians and that it was General Berezin who notified us that the Russians had disassociated themselves from Aminov and provided information to help us?" Randall asked.

"He doesn't believe that. In fact, he's quite unhappy with the fact that I sent a SEAL team in to rescue you and Captain Flores without asking his permission," Murphy replied.

"Based on the timing, the twenty-fifth amendment hadn't been invoked yet, so it shouldn't make a difference," Randall said, his voice rising in frustration.

Once again Murphy grinned. "I agree, but that doesn't matter, he feels slighted and has ordered me to provide him with operational plans and I have no choice but to comply."

Randall was amazed. Vice President Sanders' feelings

were hurt, so he was considering an act of war against the Russians because of it.

"There's more Nick," Flores said. Randall shifted his gaze. "A company of PLA regulars engaged a platoon of Indian soldiers in the Galawan Valley and killed them all. The Indian government has expelled all Chinese diplomats and is recalling all of their personnel from their embassy in China. There's talk of war between the two nations."

This was a nightmare. Not only was the Vice President of the United States considering war against the Russians, now the Indians were considering an armed conflict with the Chinese. Randall was all too familiar with the fact that all four nations possessed nuclear weapons, including tactical nukes for regional use. The theory being that the use of such weapons might contain and prevent all out nuclear war. Unfortunately, the theory relied on the concept of cooler heads prevailing, but if tactical nukes were released, there was little chance that the country on the receiving end would be anything but enraged.

"This is insanity! What was the Chinese government thinking!" Randall growled.

"They're claiming it wasn't their soldiers who engaged the Indian army. They're denying everything and have expelled all Indian diplomats from China for making the accusation," Murphy answered.

"Do we have any intel to suggest they're right?" Randall asked.

Murphy shifted his gaze to Flores who nodded.

"The PLA has become much more aggressive but we wouldn't have expected them to pull a stunt like that given the border issue with India, Pakistan and, the recent issues with the militarization of the Spratly Islands. It doesn't make sense that they'd want to anger the Indian government," Murphy said.

"But?" Randall asked.

"We have drone footage of the incident and the attacking force were wearing PLA uniforms. We also have several still images of this man, who appears to be a PLA officer," Murphy replied, removing several images of an Asian soldier from a folder. The man's face was hard and unforgiving and his uniform showed the rank of Colonel in the Chinese army. Randall memorized his face. Whoever committed the acts described by Murphy was a monster and one Randall hoped never to face.

"What are we going to do?" Randall asked.

"I'm delaying the release of military plans to Vice President Sanders as long as I can and we've dispatched our diplomats to both India and China to try to cool things down over there. We're trying to buy some time, but we need concrete proof that Aminov is behind both issues. That's the only way we can prevent war in Europe and Asia," Murphy said.

"Nick, you said that the device that Aminov possesses requires the use of Washington's DNA to properly operate, correct?" Flores asked.

"Yes, otherwise it works on a limited basis but then becomes a ticking time-bomb," Randall answered.

"Our only chance is to attempt an exchange with Aminov for Washington's DNA and conduct a covert raid to capture the device and free President Mercer," Flores said.

"But how do we find Aminov?" Randall asked.

"You provided the answer yourself a short time ago," Murphy said. "We'll have to rely on Jim's old friend General Konstantin Berezin. He or one of his men must have a way to contact him or at least have some idea of how we can contact him," Murphy replied.

"Nick, you're the only one who's used this device and understands how it works. I know it's a lot to ask but we need you to join the raid. Will you do it?" Flores asked.

"Of course. I can't stand on the sidelines when the world's about to burn," Randall answered. "What are our next steps?"

"Jim will reach out to Berezin while I put together the team and ops. We won't have the time for the usual training because we have no idea where we're going. It'll have to be on the fly," Murphy said.

Randall nodded in understanding.

"Don't worry Nick, these boys are the best in the business. They're ready for any challenge we put in front of them," Murphy said.

Before Randall could respond, Flores responded for him. "Nick is former Special Forces. He was an excellent marksman and was involved in several classified raids."

Murphy raised a brow and nodded, clearly impressed with this bit of information. Randall was once again amazed at how thorough Flores researched his history. The General was clearly a man who did his homework.

Chapter Forty-One

Pentagon, Washington D. C.

May 15, 12:51 p.m.

John and Randall sat in a break room, having lunch. Although the Pentagon had the latest and greatest of technology in place, the cafeteria served the same standard fare provided in any public building. Randall had updated John on all that had transpired while he was asleep and John, in his typical positive way had pointed out that it was always darkest before the dawn. It was a wonderful trait, one he had picked up from his mom. Randall on the other hand wasn't so sure. While John poked at his grilled chicken dish, Randall stared at the white tile floor, lost in thought. "I'm sure it's just going to take time to get the message to Aminov through General Berezin," John said, washing down the chicken with some iced tea.

"I'm sure you're right," Randall replied, absentmindedly nudging a discarded sugar packet on the floor with the tip of his boot. He looked down at his wrinkled tan cotton pants, realizing for the first time that he hadn't changed clothes in two days. His wife Anne and the kids had always said that he could get lost in his work and this was no different. "You know, once this is over, we need to—" Randall's cell phone buzzed. At first, he didn't realize what was happening.

"Are you going to pick up?" John asked, motioning to the phone with his cup.

Randall looked down and realized what was happening. It was Flores. He slid the green bar to the right to answer. "Did he contact us?"

"I need the two of you to come back immediately," Flores said in an even but serious tone.

"We're on our way," Randall clicked the phone off. "We need to go back to his office."

John set down his cup and left a tip for the serving staff. "Let's go."

Moments later, they were back in the same conference room as before, but Flores wasn't present yet.

"Where's the General?" John asked, taking a seat.

"I'm sure he'll be along in a minute."

As if on cue, Flores hurried into the room, shut the door behind him and took a seat opposite the Randalls.

"Berezin was able to reach Aminov through back-channels and he's supposed to contact us at any moment." Flores announced.

"Did Berezin give us an idea of what Aminov wants?" Randall asked.

Flores shook his head. "Berezin didn't speak directly with Aminov and had no feedback from him. He simply contacted an Aminov associate who passed our message along to him."

It was now a waiting game and Randall hoped it wouldn't be a long wait. An hour and a half later, his hope had diminished. Flores had taken the time to respond to emails, but Randall and John could only tap their fingers on the desk to pass the time, having to surrender their phones once in the secure office space.

"Maybe this contact was wrong or lied to Berezin," John wondered aloud.

Randall had contemplated the same thought, but before he could respond, Flores' encrypted desk phone rang. Flores hit the answer button, placing the phone in speaker mode. "Flores," he said to the caller.

"I'm quite sure you're tracing this call General Flores, but I can assure you your trace will fail," a voice on the other end announced.

"Who am I speaking with," Flores asked.

"You asked for the call General, please don't waste my time with games," Aminov replied.

"I just needed to confirm it was you Mr. Aminov," Flores said, in an even tone.

"What did you want to discuss?"

"You've kidnapped our president and we're trying to make arrangements to get him back."

"Shouldn't your Vice President Sanders be on this call? I understand the Cabinet has already invoked the twenty-fifth amendment. I'm sure he would be unhappy to know that someone is negotiating for the President's return without his knowledge. He seemed quite unhappy that no one sought his approval for the raid on my compound."

"I assure you Vice President Sanders is fully aware of my actions," Flores lied.

"What do you have to offer me in return for your president's release?"

"We have something that your device needs to properly work."

"My device is functioning quite well."

"You saw what happened when we tried to use it without the DNA, it nearly cost me my life," Randall jumped in.

"Dr. Randall, so good of you to join our conversation. How is Captain Flores?" Aminov asked.

"You need the DNA Aminov and we have it. You're too close to completing your plan to risk it all now," Randall replied, ignoring the jab.

The line went silent. Randall wondered if he had pushed too hard.

"Mr. Aminov, are you still there?" Flores asked, concern creeping into his voice.

Nothing. If he had ruined the only chance they had of connecting with Aminov and finding the President, it would haunt him. Still, something stirred inside him. Anger, bordering on rage against the man who had nearly killed Michael in cold blood. He wasn't about to let this bastard win again, even in this game of intimidation. Screw him. Flores turned to face Randall.

"Hang up," Randall said as Flores looked at him incredulously.

"Aminov?" Flores said.

"Hang up on him. If he's too stupid to realize we hold the key to his plans, then let him fail," Randall said, doubling down.

Flores face spoke of a cross between bewilderment and awe. Clearly, he hadn't expected Randall to react this way. He looked at John who carried the same look of confusion.

"I'll hang up for you," Randall rose violently knocking his chair against the wall, causing a loud crash. He mumbled under his breath, swearing at the former Spetsnaz agent.

"What are you doing?" Flores said, sticking his hand out to block Randall.

"Hang up on the son of a bitch! If he doesn't want to talk to us, screw him!" Randall reached for the phone and the two men tussled for a moment, while John watched, his mouth hanging open, too dumbfounded to speak.

"Flores!" Aminov yelled from the phone. Flores eyes were wide and he once again looked at Randall who was still snarling. "I'll speak to you about terms but first, get Randall out of the room."

Randall didn't have to be told, he nodded at Flores and walked out of the room leaving three stunned men in his wake. He headed back to the quarters where he slept but was too wired from the experience to sit down and wait. Instead, he chose to walk the corridors of the Pentagon, or at least the very limited part he had access to. He bounded down the hallway toward the cafeteria where he and John had lunch, reached it, then turned right back around, adrenaline still coursing through his veins. After several minutes of back and forth, his nerves finally began to settle.

It occurred to him that neither Flores nor John had come out of the office yet, so he decided to go back to the cafeteria and get some coffee. Decaf. He found an empty table in the corner away from a group having a late lunch, eschewing company for the solitude of a corner table. His body, having returned to a normal state, relaxed at the table and his mind was curiously quiet.

After a short time, he picked up the sound of someone walking from the direction of Flores office and immediately recognized the face of his son. John was grinning like a school boy who finally had enough nerve to ask out a cheerleader and got a yes. He walked up to his father and stood a moment, smiling, but not talking.

"Well? What happened?"

"Aminov agreed to a time and place to meet. General Flores wants to talk to you about it," John said, still grinning.

"What's so funny?" Randall asked, knowing full well the answer.

"I don't think I've seen you like that in a long time. You don't usually lose your cool, but this time it worked. I think you surprised General Flores too."

Chapter Forty-Two

Bela, Pakistan

May 16, 3:37 p.m.

The feeling of déjà vu was unavoidable as the three Sikorsky SH-60B Seahawk helicopters swooped down the valley toward the arranged meeting place with Aminov. Randall stared out the window of the lead chopper, lost in a world of his own thoughts, his headphones blocking much of the noise from the big helicopter's engine whine and thrumming blades. Nearly a year ago, Randall had ridden the army's version of the same chopper on another mission that cost the lives of several soldiers and saw his daughter kidnapped by a madman. Randall hoped for a better outcome this time. At least John and Liz would be safe. Randall had convinced Flores to arrange for the pair to watch the exchange from the safety of a secure room at the

Pentagon and the General had explained that only Nick could go.

Flores had explained to that, although Aminov had demanded that Randall leave the room while they discussed the exchange, the Russian had wanted him to be part of the exchange team since he was the only person who had actually understood how the device worked. Aminov had demanded that Randall be present in case he had questions and Flores had to agree to the provision, ensuring that the professor would answer all questions asked. After all, there was a price to be paid for returning the President.

Flores had not been happy with the proposed exchange location and timeframe, his team needing to fly half way around the world and not having sufficient time to prepare for various contingencies. Though the insertion and extraction methods had been reviewed, the quick turnaround had meant very little time to gather sufficient satellite data and conduct proper surveillance on the area specified by Aminov. In other words, the team was going in blind. They had no idea of the size and composition of the enemy force. Flores explained that it was exactly the strategy he would have used to gain a tactical advantage on his enemy. He had also made it clear to Randall, that although he had promised Aminov that the professor would be there, Randall had the right to decline and no one would think less of him. Of course, there was no way Randall would allow that. He would see this through to the end and ensure the President was returned safely.

Randall certainly couldn't claim that Flores was trying to gloss over the potential dangers of the mission, code named Handoff, but he had pushed aside his concerns. Besides, this was a simple exchange, the President for Washington's DNA. Watching over the operation and serving as

Randall's personal body guards was a Special Forces Operational Detachment of 12 men. Waiting on standby, another two Special Forces Detachments would be transported to the same landing zone to support the mission if needed. His previous service had taught him that the men he'd be joining on the ground were true professionals, committed to the mission and his safety.

Although Flores hadn't been able to assess the area, Israeli intelligence had provided some eyes on the ground around the neighborhood. The building where the exchange would take place was in a small neighborhood on the outskirts of the southern town of Bela. A small city approximately 124 miles west of Karachi and the Arabian Sea, the area held an important place in the history for its role in Alexander the Great's Asian Campaign in the year 325 B.C. Now it would play another major role in history, the exchange of a living American President for the skeletal remains of the country's first leader.

Curiously, the building stood adjacent to a hillside, prompting Flores to re-task an NSA spy satellite to scour the area for telltale signs of structures or fortifications constructed by Aminov around the building or potentially into the hillside. Using ground penetrating radar, the satellite would, theoretically, provide evidence of any structure buried beneath both areas. However, when the satellite passed over the area, its instruments failed to penetrate to any depth, prompting Flores to theorize that Aminov had built a base or some other structure either into the hillside or under the exchange site.

The main body of the force would enter the swap area first, ensuring it was safe for Randall to enter with Washington's DNA. They would then make initial contact with Aminov's men. Two snipers would be strategically placed, one to cover the entrance to the building and the other to cover the adjacent hillside. Once secure, they would radio for Randall to bring the DNA with him. The two sides would meet, the exchange would take place and both President Mercer and Randall would be whisked away in the Blackhawk and taken out to the USS Lake Champlain (CG 57), a Ticonderoga-class cruiser waiting off the coast.

A tap on his shoulder called Randall back to the present. It was Captain Moore. "We're three and half minutes out," Moore said, alerting Randall to prepare to disembark. "Alpha, recon the area and surrounding neighborhoods. I want potential threats and the locations of enemy combatants identified. No surprises here." Moore turned his attention to Randall and his protective detail. "Thomas, Vázquez you stay back with Dr. Randall. Once the all clear is announced, bring him and the package into the meeting location. Once we get eyes on the President, Delgado will provide cover on him at all times. Anyone breathes funny near him, take him down. Remember, our top priority is the safe return of President Mercer, and Dr. Randall in that order. No offense Randall."

"None taken."

"Everyone, memorize your maps. ETA to LZ is two minutes. Look sharp!" Moore was referring to satellite reconnaissance photos that showed the location of their objective, extraction point and potential alternatives should they be needed. For the operation, Flores had worked with JSOC to arrange for the use of the NSA spy satellite network to loiter over the objective to allow for real time reconnaissance and communications.

The lead Seahawk buzzed over a hillside and swooped into a green valley located just outside of the town. The ground rushed up quickly towards the descending chopper as the pilot identified a small, clear patch of earth to land. With a soft thud, the chopper hit the patch and the side hatch opened. The team exited the chopper, Randall exiting last, with the box containing Washington's hair and bone sample in a padded gear bag strapped on his back.

One of the lab technicians had also provided Randall with a small tube of an off-white powdery substance. The tech had explained that they had taken a small piece of Washington's bone and ground it into a fine powder in the hopes of extracting a DNA sample. Upon hearing that the machine required the first president's DNA to operate properly, the technician had provided the sample to Randall in the event he needed to use the device. Randall simply had to cover his hands with the powder and the device should operate as if Washington himself was using it.

Nearby, the other choppers also touched down and dispatched their respective crews. All thirteen members of the operation were now on the ground. The exchange was on.

Alpha team led the campaign, fanning out to provide a protective perimeter. Each soldier wore a fiber-optic wide-angle camera that relayed anything in their field of view back to Flores and the others in the command center. Randall hunkered down with Thomas and Vázquez until the all clear message was given and they began their hike into Bela. Flores had arranged for the team to pick up an all-terrain vehicle from a prearranged safe-house, left by the Israeli intelligence at the edge of town. The truck would be used to extract President Mercer and Randall to the landing zone once the trade happened. The goal was to evacuate them as quickly as possible.

The team threaded a tree lined gorge, Alpha team taking point and Randall in the back. Randall was surprised by the amount of greenery as they approached the outskirts of the town. They made the remaining half-mile hike in short order, spotting the safe-house. A low slung, white cement, rectangular structure sitting along a road made of interlocking stones, it sat at the edge of a small grouping of buildings marking the beginning of the town.

Prior to exposing the location of the team, Moore checked with Command to ensure Israeli intelligence had checked with their assets on the ground to ensure they weren't walking into a trap. The word came back all clear.

Moore motioned with his hand sending White and Hernandez into action. The two soldiers entered the building, sweeping the single-story home. Moments later, Hernandez reported back. "All clear."

The remaining team members entered the home, Randall and his protective detail the last to enter. The safe-house was a traditional cement and block wall home, the walls painted and off-white color. Mismatched pieces of furniture and traditional Pakistani rugs adorned the otherwise spartanly decorated house. Moore wasted little time, moving from the main room into the adjacent courtyard, while White maintained the watch by the front door. Randall peered out the back door, spotting a black Mercedes Benz sports utility vehicle parked in the courtyard. Looked like the President would be riding in style.

Randall moved to the side as he eyed Captain Moore returning from the courtyard. "Tran, keep an eye on that thing," Moore pointed to the Mercedes, "And be ready to roll if we radio you."

"Affirmative, sir," Tran replied, jogging over to the Mercedes. He checked under the seat of the vehicle and fished out a small keyring and proceeded to unlock the gate directly in front of the Mercedes. If called, he'd slide it open and be on his way.

"Hernandez, do you have eyes on transfer site?" Moore asked his first sniper, talking into his throat mic.

"Affirmative, no activity at this time," came the reply.

"White, are you in position?" Moore asked his second sniper, tasked with keeping an eye on the hillside adjacent to the building where the swap would happen.

"Affirmative," came the reply.

"Any signs of activity?"

"Negative. No signs of ingress or egress."

"Report back if you see something."

"Affirmative."

"Nest, this is Eagle, any news on the view inside?"

"Negative. May be related to the composition of the ceiling. Can you get eyes on it?"

The fact that the satellite couldn't penetrate the structure clearly worried Moore.

"Hernandez, I need an assessment of the ceiling."

"Roger." A moment passed. "Looks like typical construction."

"Nest. Can you give us a sitrep? Over," Moore asked, wanting confirmation from Flores.

"Roger, Eagle. You're all clear."

"Roger."

Moore turned to Randall. "Our target is approximately eight blocks from here. Our snipers are in position and the exchange is in ten minutes. Are you ready?" Randall nodded in reply. "Good." Moore keyed his throat mic. "Alpha team, move out for exchange."

His men exited the safehouse, advancing cautiously, freezing at the sounds of activity in the neighborhood. Once again Randall took up the rear with Thomas and

Vázquez flanking him. He adjusted the strap for the DNA box and palmed the tube the technician had given him. He decided to put it into the zipper pocket of the uniform Flores had provided.

The team split into two groups, Randall's group hugging the buildings on the side of the street they were on. The other group had scooted a block over so that they could converge on the exchange site from both sides, ensuring they weren't walking into a trap. Residents stared from windows across the street at the Americans making their way down the block, a mix of concern and wonder in their eyes at the sight of the heavily armed soldiers.

They closed the distance to the exchange site in remarkably short order. When they were one block away, Moore held up his hand for the group to stop, his free hand going to his throat mic. From his own time in the service, Randall understood what the Captain was doing.

"Nest, we're ready to enter the den, requesting final sitrep. Over."

"Roger. All clear."

"Roger that. Entering the den. Eagle out."

"Godspeed."

The team moved quickly. A minute later, they had covered the last block and stopped just short of the final turn. Moore motioned for two soldiers to make the turn onto the street where their final destination lay. He signaled for Randall, Thomas and Vázquez to join him.

"Wait here. Once we recon the building, we'll give you the all clear to bring Randall," Moore's instructions were clearly for his men. Both men nodded their understanding. Although this was meant to be a simple exchange, Moore was clearly treating this as a potential ambush situation. Moore led the remainder of the group around the final turn to the exchange site, Thomas peered around the corner to watch his squad as they moved in on the location.

An enormous shock wave tore through the surrounding air, lifting Thomas from the ground and tossing him backwards at least six feet before slamming him to the ground as a plume of bright light brightened the fading twilight. Next came a wall of super heated air, which funneled past the front of the building, the hot vapor curling around the corner, heating the space where Randall and Vázquez stood.

"Vázquez, are you there?" White called out over both men's earpieces.

"White is that you?" Vázquez replied, pulling Randall away from the corner. Then sprinting over to check on Thomas. "What the hell happened?"

"They must have set off a trip wire. They're all gone."

"Hernandez?"

"Fried. There was a huge fireball from the building. What about Thomas?"

"He's dead," Vázquez replied.

"Get Randall back to the safehouse," Flores commanded, having watched the entire situation unfold through each soldier's camera.

"Roger that. Tran, bring the fucking truck around!" Vázquez yelled, leading Randall away from the explosion and back down the street toward the safehouse. Another large blast echoed from the distance in the direction they were sprinting.

"Tran, come in!" Vázquez shouted. Tran didn't reply.

"White, can you get eyes on the safehouse?"

Rustling came through the line before White came back on the radio. "The blast was right near the safehouse. Take another route."

Vázquez pivoted around the corner, Randall sticking as close to him as he could.

"Eagle, we're sending in another detachment, rendezvous at the extraction site," Flores ordered over the radio.

Another series of blasts echoed further away—in the direction of their landing zone.

"Nest, can you reach the other detachment?" Vázquez asked, zigzagging around another corner, fearing now that they were being followed.

"Negative, we're unable to reach them.

"Fuck! Come on Randall, move your ass!" Vázquez demanded.

Another sound arose in the distance, the unmistakable sound of large vehicle engines, the pitch rising and getting louder. Randall instantly recognized the Doppler effect as multiple vehicles appeared to be approaching them from different directions. They'd soon be trapped. Vázquez hustled into a recessed doorway and Randall followed him in.

"It's like they know everything we're going to do before we do it!" Vázquez exclaimed.

Ice flowed through Randall's veins as a horrible realization set in. "They do know."

"What the in hell are you talking about!" an exasperated Vázquez asked.

"The device Aminov has, the one that we're exchanging the DNA for, he's using it against us," Randall replied.

Vázquez' look of bewilderment spoke volumes.

"We found a device hidden in a room under Mt. Vernon that allows the user to predict the future. Aminov ambushed us and took the device, but it requires DNA from President Washington to operate properly. That's why we're trying to exchange it for President Mercer," Randall calmly explained.

"If it needs Washington's DNA to function properly, how are they using it?" Vázquez asked calmly, not firing off the myriad of questions that must be on his mind. To his credit, he remained focused on the task at hand, his training clearly working.

"It can still work without the DNA, but it'll kill the user and then turn into a lethal device that superheats and explodes if it's not stopped."

Randall could see the wheels turning in Vasquez mind. "If we act in an irrational manner, would that help?"

Randall had to think for a moment. If Aminov role played various scenarios and the machine provided potential outcomes, it was likely based on standard tactical behavior. It was possible that the machine wouldn't foresee the outcome of an action completely outside of standard strategic behavior. Randall had to give Vázquez' credit for his thoughtful approach in such a stressful situation. "It might."

"Then that's what we'll do." Vázquez handed Randall his pistol. "You know how to use it?"

"I do," Randall replied, deciding to forgo the explanation of his previous military experience.

"Someday, we'll have to have a long talk about this," Vázquez said.

"I'll buy the drinks," Randall replied.

"You're on. Follow me," Vázquez peered around the corner of the alcove, then began walking back toward the initial exchange area, his weapon in front of him. Randall's understood role was to cover their flank, offer cover fire if needed and keep an eye out for trouble.

The sound of multiple vehicles continued to roar in the

back ground, the engine sound bouncing off of the neighborhood buildings, making it difficult to tell exactly where they were.

"What's the plan once we get there?" Randall asked.

"We look for a way into the facility. They won't be thinking we'd do that."

Randall silently shook his head. He wasn't sure it was the best plan, but if he were being honest, he couldn't think of anything better.

"White, you there?" Vázquez asked.

"I thought I'd lost you guys," White replied.

"Have you been able to reach Nest?"

"Negative."

"You need to find somewhere to hide."

"No way! I'm staying put to provide you with cover and intel."

"You need to get your ass down from there and find cover! These guys have a device that knows what we're going to do before we do it!"

"What are you talking about?"

"I don't have time to explain, just find cover!"

The faint buzzing sound arose from the west, growing in intensity. It sounded like a swarm of large insects getting closer. The two men ducked around another corner, now on the side street they originally traversed to get to the exchange site.

"Shit!" Vázquez cursed.

"The buzzing? What it is?" Randall asked.

"Drones." Vázquez keyed his throat mic. "White get to cover. Now!"

"I—"

White's microphone cut off the moment they heard another explosion, this time from a rooftop. A black plume of smoke rose from the perch where White had positioned himself for the mission.

John and Liz stared at the snowy monitor, both in a state of shock. Flores had permitted both to watch the exchange happen from a secure room in the Pentagon as part of the deal he had made with Randall. John was stunned at how quickly the situation had deteriorated from the initial insertion to the strike on White from the rooftop. There was only one way that Aminov could have pulled off such a lopsided victory. "He's using the device."

Still in shock, it took Liz's brain a moment to register that John had spoken. "I'm sorry, what did you say?"

"Aminov is using the device against us. It's the only thing that makes sense. He's outmaneuvered the strike force at every turn, seemingly knowing where every soldier was at any moment. Worse, he knew what we were going to do before we even did it. It's the only solution that makes sense," John said, not allowing his mind to go down the road of what would happen to his father.

"Comm, I need the satellite feed. We still have two assets on the ground," Flores said tersely into the communications microphone on the table.

"Sir, something's jamming our signal. The technicians are working on it now," the communications officer responded.

"Tell them to get the signal up A.S.A.P," Flores growled.

"He can't use it consistently though," John continued.

"John, I'm sorry, but I don't understand what you're talking about," Liz said, an edge appearing in her voice.

"My dad explained that he used the device we found at

Mt. Vernon and was able to see the kidnapping of President Mercer before it happened. That's what the device allows the user to do, but he also said that it would have killed him if Michael hadn't separated him from it. He said that he felt like he was going into cardiac arrest," John explained.

"How does that help in this situation?" Liz asked.

"When we found the device, we also found the bone and hair from Washington stored nearby. We had theorized that the device was designed to be used by George Washington only and that a user requires Washington's DNA to operate it. My dad proved that the device can be used without Washington's DNA, but not without the device killing him," John watched as Liz struggled to accept all of this. Who could blame her? If he hadn't been with his father and witnessed some of the things he had seen, he would feel the same way.

Liz nodded for John to continue.

"Based on this, if Dad and Vázquez can hold out for a while longer, the device will stop working and I'm going to wager that Aminov will have a hard time getting one of his men to use the machine again if they all see it kill one of their comrades," John said.

"We need to get a message to your father," Liz understood and walked to Flores who was on the far side of the room engaged in a heated discussion on another secure line. "General, we need to get a message to Nick."

Flores held up his hand while he finished the call. "We can't get them a message, something is jamming our communications links."

By this time, John had joined them.

"You need to keep trying. Whatever is jamming the signal will eventually stop, or at least stop for a short time," Liz pressed.

Reading the confusion on Flores' face, John explained the situation as he had with Liz.

"How long did your dad say he used the device before it almost killed him?" Flores asked.

"Several minutes at most. That leaves Aminov with two choices. Have one soldier use it until he's dead or have someone use it for a few minutes, take a break and then use it again. He can't use it continually until he has the DNA," John explained.

Flores nodded, then punched the microphone on the desktop speaker phone. "This is Flores, send this message out every minute, regardless of whether you feel the signal is jammed." He then nodded to John who provided the message for his father.

Randall and Vázquez entered the charred remnants of the building where the exchange was initially to take place. Vázquez had tried contacting home base multiple times but had received only static. They had to assume they were on their own and working against an enemy that could predict their actions. The only solution they could formulate was to behave counter to standard tactics in an attempt to throw off Aminov and coming here fit the bill.

Vázquez led the way, with Randall covering their flank. Randall had decided to explain his past service and had been rewarded with Thomas' assault weapon picked up on their way back. The sounds of approaching vehicles had subsided, casting them into an eerie silence.

The inside of the building was otherworldly, marked with black charred walls and melted and twisted exposed metal. Heat still radiated from the blast, although far less than when the initial fireball had ravaged the area. The pair moved slowly and silently through the gutted, darkened building. The lack of windows meant that the deeper they entered, the darker their world became. The air was thick and musty making breathing difficult, but the pair pushed on. There had to be an entrance into Aminov's facility and they hoped to find it, but when they did, then what? It wasn't the first time Randall had been in this situation, but experience made it no less concerning.

They had reached the end of the first room, finding a door dead center in the middle of the back wall. Darkness filled the doorway, leaving them unable to see what lay beyond. Vázquez pulled to the side of the doorway making sure to keep his weapon trained on the opening. Randall fell in line behind him. The two made eye contact and Vázquez pointed at the tip of Randall's gun then held up three fingers. Randall understood they would enter on the count of three and he turned on his gun mounted light. Vázquez started the countdown, three, two, one—they entered the doorway, Vázquez' gun mounted light leading the way.

It was a hallway running perpendicular to the path followed in the first room, both ends leading once again into complete darkness. Vázquez turned right and Randall turned left, both illuminating the hallway several feet in each direction. Randall's side was a normal hallway, like you would find in any typical home. He felt a tap on his shoulder, spun around to see Vázquez pointing at his eyes, then down right hallway. Randall looked past him and saw the hallway terminate in a dead-end.

Vázquez must have sensed his confusion, then pointed his light directly at the ground at the end of the hallway, tracing a square pattern. It was then that Randall saw the faint outline on the floor. It was a trap door, undoubtedly leading to an area beneath the building. Vázquez walked slowly down the hallway, clearly checking for booby-traps and other false panels in the passage. Both men arrived at the trap door, which filled the final four feet of the hallway.

Recessed within the door was a finger hold to lift the door to gain access. Randall's heart beat faster, but he controlled his breathing, slowing it and taking deep breaths to remain calm. Vázquez pointed at him and motioned for him to open the door. Randall understood and Vázquez took at position, facing the opening, his gun pointed downward to cover anyone who might come out. Randall threaded his finger into the hold and slowly pealed the door upward revealing a stair case leading underground. Once again, Vázquez led the way, moving carefully down one step at a time, sweeping the path with the beam of his gun mounted light.

The staircase was long, too long for them to see where it led to or what awaited them at the bottom. Randall kept several paces back from Vázquez, allowing space in case they needed to evacuate quickly and covering their flank. They moved slowly, carefully, each step measured in anticipation of danger. They reached a landing and Vázquez pivoted, now facing down the stairs with Randall still covering their six. The landing marked the midpoint of the stairs, Vázquez light now illuminating the floor below.

A slamming sound rose from above. At the same moment, a flood of lights washed both men in brightness, causing both to recoil, closing their eyes against the sudden brightness.

"We've been waiting for you," a voice called out from the lower level in an accent Randall recognized as Russian.

Squinting against the brightness, Randall struggled to see what they were up against. He was greeted by the uneasy site of nearly a dozen armed mercenaries. Worst, the sudden brightness had caught Vázquez off guard as well as he shielded eyes trying to visualize what they were up against.

"Sergeant, point your weapon at the ground, move to the bottom of the steps, then slide it to me," Aminov ordered confidently. "Dr. Randall, do the same. Quickly, both of you."

Outgunned and outnumbered, first Vázquez complied, then Randall.

"I have to give you credit Sergeant Vázquez. Your strategy caused me to sacrifice a second good man to adjust to your strategy. Of course, with the help of Dr. Randall, further sacrifices of my men won't be necessary. Isn't that right professor?

"Don't help him Doc. Let them try to figure out themselves," Vázquez growled.

"Sergeant Vázquez, I'm disappointed by your stance, but not altogether surprised," Aminov nodded to one of his men, who stowed his assault weapon, withdrew a pistol and walked over to Vázquez, executing him at point-blank range. A spray of pink and grey brain matter splattered back onto the floor, some catching Randall on his pant leg.

"You son of a bitch! That wasn't necessary!" Randall yelled, taking a step toward Aminov.

"Enough!" Aminov ordered, causing several of his men to train their weapons on Randall. "You're in no position to comment on any of this. You've caused me a great deal of problems with your escape, but now you're going to help me understand how this device works."

"What makes you think I'll help you? I'm not afraid to die," Randall replied.

"I think I'll be able to change your mind."

Chapter Forty-Three

Randall was led at gunpoint to another level of Aminov's facility which ran deeper than he could have imagined. The bright lights were nearly blinding as he shuffled down the long corridor, an assault weapon muzzle pressed into his back as a reminder to keep moving. Still in shock at the execution of Private Vázquez, Randall contemplated what came next. His mind was set that he wouldn't assist Aminov further, choosing to die at the hands of the manic rather than help him to murder millions of innocent people. Still, Aminov's last comment rang in his mind. What did he mean by feeling he could change Randall's mind? Torture? Not a pleasant prospect, but he would have to steel himself against the possibility. If nothing else, his time in the Special Forces had prepared him for that possibility.

The guards stopped by a sturdy looking metal door inset into the hallway. The lead guard unlocked the door, while the guard behind Randall pushed him in, the door locking behind him. Seated on a cot at the end of the, gray, concrete walled cell was a man in wrinkled suit pants and white shirt, caked with blood stains. It took Randall a moment, but when the man looked up, his haggard, bloodied face was immediately recognizable.

"Mr. President, are you okay?"

President Mercer rubbed his bloodshot eyes and let out a long, loud sigh. "Nick Randall?"

Randall was flattered that Mercer recognized him, having only met him once in Germany, preventing an attempt on his life and the lives of all G7 Conference members. "Yes sir, it's me. I'm glad to see you're still alive."

"What are you doing here? Did Vice President Sanders send a team?

"No Mr. President. General Flores sent a team to try to arrange an exchange for you. Vice President Sanders wasn't a part of the decision."

Mercer nodded slowly, a thin grin spreading across his lips. "I wouldn't expect him to unless it benefitted him somehow."

Randall was impressed at Mercer's ability to still find humor after having been through what appeared to be repeated beatings.

"What happened? Is the rest of the extraction team working on getting us out of here?" Mercer asked.

"Unfortunately, I'm all that's left."

Mercer's thin grin evaporated, replaced by a look of confusion. Randall went on to explain the finding of the device and the discovery of Aminov's plan to use it to incite multiple wars between world powers to allow a new world order to arise. He also touched on how the device was used to defeat the team sent to rescue him.

"All those soldiers losing their lives. They never had a chance." Mercer shook his head. "Sanders isn't up to this.

He's going to get sucked into a conflict with the Russians to feed his ego. Has anyone pushed back?"

"General Murphy, FBI Director Friedman, CIA Director Tarkington are all trying to reason with him, but he's ordered Murphy to draw up war plans with Russia. Including the use of tactical nukes."

"The son of a bitch is crazy. We can't go to war with the Russians and certainly can't use nukes. Once that genie is out of the bottle, we'll never put it back in."

"I agree, and General Murphy is trying to stall him, but I don't know how successful he's been."

"If we can't get out of here, tens of millions of people could die if we go to war with the Russians, not to mention if war breaks out between China and India. This is insanity."

Mercer sat up straighter and looked Randall in the eye. "You said you found a book by President Washington that explained how the device works along with his DNA. Does Aminov have everything?"

"No. He doesn't have the book, but he's threatened me and said he'd make me tell him how to use the device."

"Will you?"

Randall shook his head. "I'd rather die than help him."

Mercer shook his head and closed his eyes. "It could get rough for you. I've dealt with men like Aminov before. He's ruthless and won't stop until he gets what he wants."

Randall nodded in agreement. All he could do was resist as best as possible.

The tumbler to the door lock turned. Their captors were coming for him.

Chapter Forty-Four

Murphy led Flores and John down the staircase to the Situation Room beneath the White House. Despite the gravity of the situation, John couldn't help but be awed to be in an area off limits to anyone except the rarest of individuals involved in the operation of government in its darkest hours. All he could think about was talking to his dad about this. Then reality set in. His father was in grave danger, and so was the entire free world. He needed to be at his best at this moment.

He was still amazed that General Murphy had somehow arranged for him to be present to speak with Vice President Sanders. Considering that less than two hours ago, he was at the Pentagon watching the Presidential exchange go horribly wrong and he was now here was nothing short of surreal. The last memory he held of his father was sharing his idea that Aminov must be using the device to know what they were doing before they even did it. There was no way of knowing if his father and Sergeant Vázquez were even alive. He couldn't allow his

The Washington Prophecy

mind to go there. He had to focus on the task at hand. For his dad.

As they funneled into the Situation Room, John was immediately taken by the size of the room, which was much smaller than he had anticipated. The dark Cherrywood table filled a great portion of the room, leaving just enough room for a dozen black chairs arranged around it and another half dozen lining the walls adjacent to the table on each side.

At the front of the room were a series of carefully placed monitors to allow any seat in the house a view of the critical information being shared with the group. Those with a seat at the table were provided with their own monitors, recessed into the table in front of them.

John was led to a corner chair to the left of the table, against the wall. He had never seen so many highly decorated soldiers in his life. Joining them were several men and women in suits. Two he immediately recognized as the Directors of the FBI and CIA, but others he didn't. Flores took a seat next to him, while Murphy took a seat at the table. The only one missing now was Sanders.

John searched the faces of the men and women in the room. None looked like they had slept in days. An air of despair filled the room which was nearly silent except for a few murmured conversations. An impeccably dressed woman entered the room, immediately drawing all eyes of everyone in the room. She was followed by Vice President Sanders. Everyone stood, nearly in unison.

Sanders took a seat at the head of the table, causing everyone else in the room to sit as well.

"General Murphy, do you have the plans I asked for?" Sanders asked, rubbing his eyes. He looked haggard, the gravity of the situation clearly weighing on him.

"Mr. Vice President, before we get to those plans, I'd like to have some guests present some information you may find relevant," Murphy replied.

The impeccably dressed woman rolled her eyes, allowing an exasperated breath to escape her lips. "General Murphy, Vice President Sanders asked for war plans. You can't even deliver on a simple order from our Commander-in-Chief!"

Sanders waived to her to stop, clearly irritated. "Who exactly are your guests and what information do they have?"

"Mr. Vice President, I'd like to introduce General James Flores and Dr. Jonathan Randall," Murphy said.

Sanders set his jaw. "You brought these two into this meeting? What were you thinking?"

"Mr. Vice President, we have information that we don't believe has been presented to you, but that's critical to the situation," Flores said, jumping in.

"Exactly what information do you have? Have you launched an unauthorized military action like before?" Sanders goaded.

If he only knew.

"Mr. Vice President, we have information on Mr. Aminov's plan and the device he now possesses. We believe he's behind both the kidnapping of President Mercer and the attack in India," Flores continued.

"Go on," Sanders prodded.

"We have information that supports this theory. Mr. Aminov is deliberately trying to start wars in multiple theaters of operation, both between NATO and Russia and between China and India. His goal is to provoke each side to inflict enough damage to the other to render their remaining military forces and government structures inoperable," Flores explained.

"And how did you come across this information?" Sanders asked, disdain dripping from his voice.

"We acquired it when we rescued Dr. Randall and Captain Flores."

"Your son?"

"Yes sir."

Sanders sat back in the chair, closed his eyes and shook his head. "You expect me to buy this?"

"Mr. Vice President," John rose from his seat. "I've seen the device that Mr. Aminov possesses."

"Are you Randall?" Sanders wrinkled his nose as he spoke.

John could feel the weight of every eye in the room upon him. "Yes sir, I am. I was there when the device was discovered. It's unlike anything I've ever seen. The technology is far beyond anything we possess."

"What are you inferring?" Sanders asked.

"Whoever built this device understands properties of quantum processing that even our top minds in the field can't grasp."

"Who built this fantastical device?" Sanders eyes bored through John.

"I don't know Mr. Vice President, but what General Flores had told you is entirely true. We can't fall into Aminov's trap. He's betting that we will."

"Mr. Vice President, I strongly recommend that you listen to Dr. Randall. He's an expert in the field and is entirely correct about the device and Aminov's plan," Flores said.

"What proof do you have besides Randall's testimony?"

Flores looked to Murphy who nodded. "We have

computer drives recovered from the raid on Aminov's compound."

Sanders seethed. "I've heard enough. General Murphy, where are the plans?"

"Don't you get it? People have given their lives to stop Aminov! He's a madman and you're playing right into his hands!" John snarled.

"Get him out of here!" Sanders pounded the table then pointed a finger at John.

Flores stood. "You're making the gravest mistake in the history of this country."

Sanders eyes bulged from his head, a large vein popping from his temple.

"You've just committed professional suicide!" Sanders stammered.

John pushed his chair against the wall and marched down the narrow isle between the row of seats against the wall and the main table and Flores followed right behind him. A serious looking uniformed man marched toward them, clearly meant to make sure both men left. They met near the end of the table, adjacent to Sanders. John stopped. "My dad was right about you. All you care about is your political career."

"Get the hell out of here!" Sanders was apoplectic.

As John walked out, he turned to glance back and caught General Murphy covering his mouth trying to suppress a smile.

Chapter Forty-Five

John and Flores re-entered the planning room at the Pentagon, causing Liz to look up from the table.

"What happened?" She asked, her voice rising.

"John told Vice President Sanders the truth," Flores replied, dropping his hat on the table.

"And?" Liz asked, her eyes pleading for information.

"I'll likely be dishonorably discharged," Flores dropped into his seat.

Liz's eyes shot to John.

"We told Sanders about the device and Aminov's plans and he basically told us to hit the road," John said, taking a seat next to Liz.

"That bloody idiot!" Liz yelled, not even attempting to hide the disdain in her voice.

John smiled for the first time in days.

"You shouldn't have let him go James," Liz said, eyes looking down at her hands. "He's a professor, not a damn soldier."

Flores drew his lips into a tight bow.

John looked at Liz, her eyes were glassy, she was fighting back tears. She was the first woman to show this kind of affection for his dad and she was clearly in pain.

"Liz, I know you care about my dad just like I do, but it's not General Flores fault. My dad's a very stubborn man. Once he gets something in his mind, there's no convincing him otherwise. Believe me, he's been like that since I was small," John placed a hand on Liz's arm.

"I know, it's one of the things about him that I like," Liz sniffled. "James, I'm sorry for what I said. I'm just worried about Nick."

"Me too, but if there's anyone out there that can find a way out of this, it's my dad. I don't know how he does it, but I've seen him do it time and again," John assured.

Flores picked up the secure line in front of him.

"What are you going to do?" John asked.

"Going down fighting," Flores replied. John heard a muffled voice on the other end of the line. "Activate plan imminent redemption," Flores said into the phone before hanging up.

"I don't understand." John said.

"If I'm going to be discharged, my last act is going to be to try to rescue your father. I owe it to him for all he's done." Flores looked directly at John, determination shining in his eyes.

"Thank you General."

Chapter Forty-Six

The door to the cell swung open revealing two guards, assault rifles in hand. "Get up!" The first growled.

Randall and Mercer shared a glance before Randall rose to his feet.

"Both of you," the guard snarled.

"Where are you taking us?" Randall asked.

"No questions! Move!"

The guard meant business, but why was Mercer coming? Randall wasn't sure what Aminov had in mind, but whatever it was, it wasn't good. Randall felt a heavy weight in the pit of his stomach.

The guards marched Randall and Mercer into a small, barren room. Every surface was concrete. The walls, the floor, even the ceiling, except for the single bank of fluorescent lights. In the center of the floor were two folding chairs centered on a large, square piece of plastic drop cloth. Aminov leaned against a table on the far wall, watching them with the dispassionate appearance of a lion watching its prey unknowingly entering its domain. On the table behind him was the device Randall had found at Mt. Vernon and the bag containing Washington's DNA.

"Sit," the guard ordered.

Randall scanned the room, watching Mercer take a seat before sitting himself. Aminov nodded to his men, indicating that they should leave. Randall watched in surprise as the two guards left the three men alone in the drab, gray room. If Amniov felt uncomfortable being outnumbered two to one, he wasn't showing it. Then again, he was a special operations soldier and also a man who didn't mind sentencing millions of people to death to achieve his twisted goal. He stood motionless, staring through Randall and Mercer. Randall turned to watch Mercer. Surprisingly, the President didn't seem phased by Aminov's presence. Though clearly fatigued and injured, he returned an equally dead stare.

"Are you going to tell us why we're here?" Mercer asked in an even tone, finally ending the silence.

A small grin snaked across Aminov's face. "Dr. Randall, are you ready to show me how the device works?"

"No," Randall replied, folding his arms across his chest.

"Typical American. So proud, so righteous," Aminov shook his head while he spoke.

"Mr. Aminov, I have no intention of helping you, regardless of what you do to me. I can't be a part of helping you to kill millions of innocent people, even if it means suffering at your hands," Randall said earnestly.

"I believe you Dr. Randall. I've read your file. Former Special Operations before leaving to become a college professor. Quite impressive. I could have used a man with your skills," Aminov eyed Randall as he spoke, again there was no emotion behind his eyes.

"So, what do you want?" Mercer asked.

Aminov, rose to his full height. He easily crested six feet by several inches, his body hard and lean, his face scarred and disfigured. "I want Dr. Randall to tell me how to use the device without having to expend my people."

"I can't," Randall said as Aminov drew closer, hovering over the two seated Americans.

"I know Dr. Randall. That's why he's here," Aminov drew a gun from his waistband, racked a round into the chamber and placed the tip against Mercer's temple. "You've demonstrated that you aren't afraid to die, but you've also demonstrated that you can't allow someone else to die when you can prevent it." Aminov cocked the hammer of the gun. "You now have a choice. Tell me how to use the device, using your President Washington's DNA, or I will kill President Mercer."

"You can't do that," Randall protested.

"But I can," Aminov pressed the barrel into Mercer's head harder, causing him to pull his head back against the pressure, grimacing from the pain of the gun barrel pressing into his skin.

"Don't tell him anything Randall," Mercer said.

"You're running out of time Dr. Randall," there was no feeling in Aminov's voice, just cold hard truth.

"Mr. President, I can't let him kill you," Randall said.

"Don't do it!" Mercer demanded.

"Five, four, three, two—"

"Stop! I'll help you," Randall said.

Aminov pushed the gun harder into Mercer's head. "Show me."

Randall stood and walked over to the table and removed the small vial from the bag he had brought. "The technicians at the Pentagon ground some of the Washington's bone to a fine powder. They believed it would be enough to operate the device."

"There's very little DNA in that small amount of bone," Aminov observed.

"You have to understand. Whoever built this device possessed far greater technology than anything we can imagine. We theorize that the device is exceptionally sensitive, only requiring a small amount of DNA from President Washington to recognize him," Randall explained.

"Randall, stop!" Mercer yelled, drawing a backhanded slap from Aminov.

"Continue Professor."

Randall poured the white powdery substance all over his hands, but the tube was only half used. He rubbed vigorously, covering his entire hand, knocking the vial from the table in his earnest hand wringing. The vial tumbled to the floor, shattering on contact the concrete floor. "Damit!" Randall said, stepping back from the table, stepping all over the now spilled powder on the floor.

"Leave it," Aminov hissed.

Randall turned his attention to the device, remembering the last time he used it. "You have to enter these symbols in this sequence then place your hands in here," he tapped the glowing symbols, which caused the device to glow to life. After finishing, the two ports on the side opened, revealing the palm pads.

"Very good professor. Now you can show me how to properly use it," Aminov smiled, then fished a radio from his pocket with a free hand. "Come and get our guest."

The doors swung open and the two guards entered the room again.

"Randall, you shouldn't have helped him. He's a

murderer!" Mercer protested, while he was hauled to his feet by the guards. They pushed him toward the door. "You're a traitor Randall! A goddam traitor!"

The guards forced him out of the door, which latched closed, leaving Randall alone with Aminov.

Chapter Forty-Seven

Randall walked the march of the damned, retracing the steps that had initially led him to the concrete room with Aminov hours ago. He knew what awaited him when he returned to the cell and Mercer. The President had made his feelings perfectly clear and Randall was still somewhat jarred by being called a traitor. But he couldn't let that psychopath kill Mercer, even it meant getting his hands dirty by working with him.

The walk seemed interminable as they marched down the fluorescent lit hallway, the clicking of their shoes the only sound joining them. They finally arrived at the same metal door Randall had been taken to earlier in the day. One guard motioned for Randall to back away from the door, while the other opened it. The rear guard shoved Randall in the back roughly, propelling him into the tiny room.

Randall immediately spied Mercer seated on his cot, working his jaw back and forth. He looked up at Randall, watching every step he took. The metal door slammed shut behind him, leaving the two men alone.

"The blood of millions of people is on your hands Randall. May God have mercy on your soul," Mercer looked back down at the ground.

"Mr. President—"

Mercer held up a hand, shaking his head. "Save it."

"It won't work," Randall leaned against the wall.

Mercer's head swiveled toward Randall, his eyes narrowing. "What do you mean?"

"Aminov won't be able to use the device without turning it into a bomb. I made sure of that," Randall replied, a full-blown grin spreading across his face.

"What are you talking about?"

Randall strode to the cot opposite Mercer and took a seat on the edge. "They don't have Washington's DNA. I had the tech at the Pentagon swap out Washington's femur for another one. They found one at the local morgue and doctored it to make it look old."

"But you used it and got the device to work?" Mercer was confused.

"The powder in the vial was Washington's ground up bone. I knew I had to make the device work to make Aminov believe it."

"But they gave you too much, and you had to make sure you didn't leave any for Aminov so you knocked the vial on the ground and then stepped on the DNA to contaminate it," the grin on Mercer's face stretched from ear to ear. "You deserve an Oscar for that performance! Well done."

"Aminov's going to use the device, thinking he has the key to the system but it will detonate and kill all of them. And probably us too."

"Small price to pay to save millions of people."

"I agree, but I'm not giving up yet. There's a chance we could survive if they leave us here when Aminov uses the device. I'd still like to see if we can protect you Mr. President. If we can find a way out of here, you could stop Vice President Sanders from starting a war with Russia."

Mercer nodded his head. "I'm sorry for how I treated you."

"No need to apologize. Your reaction sold it better than anything I could have done."

"How do you know Aminov won't figure it out and stop before it explodes?"

Randall's expression turned dead serious. "I was hooked up to that device back in Aminov's base in Russia. I was able to see your kidnapping so I know it works. But then, things started to go wrong. I felt like I was having a heart attack and my mind started to jump from scene to scene. If Michael hadn't separated me from the device, it would have killed me. As it was, it still melted part of the workstation we had it on. Aminov plans to use it himself. He doesn't want anyone else to have the glory and that'll be what kills him."

Mercer nodded in understanding. "Good job Nick, let's hope you're right."

Chapter Forty-Eight

Time passed as the two men talked, Mercer eschewing the normal formality of being President. They were just two men, fathers and husbands, swapping stories about their families and upbringing. Mercer seemed especially interested in Randall's description of growing up in North Carolina, fascinated with Randall's description of his father's boat business and his understanding of hydrodynamics, despite never having earned a college degree in the subject. Their reverie was cut short when the familiar sound of their cell door lock opening called their attention back to reality.

The same two guards who had come to get them earlier were once again standing in the doorway, the same threat of violence emanating from their weapons. "Up, the General wants to see both of you," the lead guard announced.

Wearily, Randall rose to his feet and Mercer did the same. They took a step forward but one of the guards stopped them.

"Put your hands out," the guard ordered.

Randall and Mercer complied. What choice did they have?

The guard placed handcuffs on Randall first and then on Mercer. They then shuffled out the door and into the brightness of the hallway. This time instead of the path they took to the concrete room, the guards led them to an elevator at the far-left side of the corridor, where two additional guards waited. The car was huge, easily fitting Mercer, Randall and their four escorts, weapons included. The lead guard punched a code into the control panel and the elevator car doors slid closed and they went down.

They dropped several floors, then the doors parted, revealing a large, octagonal command center staffed with over twenty people, seated at terminals facing huge ceiling and wall mounted monitors, forming a one-hundred-and-eighty-degree arc. Randall scanned them quickly, noting maps and multiple views of several geographic areas including Beijing, New Delhi, Paris, Berlin, Moscow and Washington D. C. A shiver ran down his spine as he realized several of the views were from the inside of buildings, including the Capitol Building. Aminov had people on the inside of each government, his access was unfettered.

Located at the center of the back of the arc was a raised seat, occupied by Aminov. Directly in front of him, at chest level was a metallic pedestal with a concave opening on top. Randall immediately recognized its purpose—to hold the device while in use. Aminov spotted Randall and Mercer.

"Bring them here," Aminov ordered his guards, who followed his directions. "Mr. President, I wanted to you have a front-row seat to this historic moment where I ascend to power and end American dominance on the world stage." Though he tried to hide it, for the first time, Randall heard the emotion in his voice.

The guards led Mercer and Randall to Aminov's side, stopping several feet back.

"Dr. Randall, I must thank you for helping to make this possible. Without you, I would never have been able to access the full power of the device," Aminov said.

"What do you plan to do with us?" Randall asked.

Aminov closed his eyes. "President Mercer will remain my prisoner here until he's no longer of use. He could still prove to be a useful bargaining chip if the Americans are able to still provide any fight. As for you Professor, you've served your purpose and are of no further use to me."

"You can't just kill him!" Mercer protested.

"My dear President Mercer, I can do whatever I want," Aminov replied.

"Bring me the device," Aminov told a single guard who nodded and walked to a tall metal cabinet to the left of Aminov's perch.

The guard punched a sequence into the keypad and was rewarded with a heavy clicking sound. He pulled on the handle, swinging the heavy, four-inch-thick doors open. Inside, on the ground was the device, which the soldier hefted and carried to Aminov, leaving the cabinet open.

Randall studied the interior. He gauged it to be three feet wide, about two feet deep and eight feet tall. Just large enough for a man to fit into. It would have to be where Mercer rode out the explosion, but first they would have to figure out how to get him in. He cocked his head within inches of Mercer's ear and whispered. "When the time's right, get inside there and pull the doors shut."

Mercer shot Randall a side glance. "What about you?"

"I'll figure something out," Randall answered, still surveying the room. Aminov had clearly spared no expense. Randall's eyes stopped when they landed on a soldier dressed differently from anyone else in the command center. Green and gray digital camouflage fatigues with a red flag and a semi-circle of yellow stars encircling a single larger yellow star emblazoned on the patch sewn on the sleeve. Randall immediately recognized the uniform of the People's Liberation Army of China.

More shocking than seeing the uniform was the man wearing it. Randall recalled the conversation in Flores' office at the Pentagon about the attack on the Indian army. The man standing to Aminov's side was the man he had seen from the still pictures taken from the drone footage. He now had the proof that Aminov was behind the attack that was spurring a potential war between China and India. The problem was, he had no way to get the information into the hands of the people who could prevent the conflict.

The guard with the device lowered it onto the pedestal and secured it in place, then backed away, leaving Aminov with full control.

"I've waited many years for this and have borne the scars of warfare and the deeper scars of betrayal of our former leaders. Today begins a new chapter in the history of the world," Aminov opened a small compartment on the armrest of his chair and removed a small container with a white powdery substance. He carefully spread it on his hands, just as Randall had done. "Colonel Bai, escort Dr. Randall back to his cell. I'll deal with him later."

"Yes sir! You," Bai pointed his index finger at Randall. "Come with me and please give me a reason to hurt you."

Aminov smiled and shook his head.

Randall stood his ground, watching Aminov, waiting to make sure he laid his hands on the device. He did, then closed his eyes. Randall felt a sharp blow to the back of his head.

"I told you to come with me!" Bai demanded.

"You also told me to give you a reason to hurt me. Just following orders," Randall replied staring down Bai, before turning to walk back to the elevator. He was rewarded with a boot to the backside.

"Keep it up funny man and I'll show you what pain really means," Bai growled.

Randall turned one last time to see Aminov. His eyes were twitching, he was fully engaged with the machine.

Chapter Forty-Nine

Randall walked quickly into the hallway, eager to get on the elevator and back near his cell before the device detonated. He stopped by the elevator and waited for Bai.

"What's your hurry? All you have to look forward to is a slow painful death. If I were you, I would try to enjoy the short time you have left," Bai goaded, finally arriving by the elevator and punching the code into the keypad.

Randall bit his tongue, knowing the timing had to be perfect to have a chance to live. He stared straight ahead as they waited for the elevator.

"Hey old man, I'm talking to you!" Bai grabbed his shoulder and forced him to face him. "When I talk to you, you better damn well pay attention!"

He punched Randall in the gut, causing him to double over. Randall stumbled backwards a few steps, trying to catch his breath. He steeled himself, then looked Bai straight in the eyes.

"Easy to be a tough guy when the man you're fighting is handcuffed," Randall prodded.

Bai's eyes went wide with rage. "Is that right," he fished the keys from his pocket and tossed them to Randall. "Unlock them." He licked his lips. "Then we'll see how tough you really are."

The elevator doors slid open. "After you," Bai hissed.

Randall removed the handcuffs, then rubbed his wrists before entering the car. This was going to be a long, hard ride. He stepped into the car, standing right in the center.

Bai shook his head. "For a professor, you sure are stupid." He stepped into the car, and drove his shoulder right into Randall's chest, sending him crashing into the back of the elevator car. Randall hit the back hard and tumbled to the floor as the doors closed. He looked up a Bai who was clearly pleased with himself. The elevator car started its journey up.

The hell with it. If this was how he was going down, he might as well go out fighting. It had been over two decades since active duty, but he recalled his training like it was yesterday. Assess your opponent and use his weakness against him. Bai was four inches taller, about twenty years younger and lot stronger. He undoubtedly viewed Randall as no threat and he would use that against him.

Randall picked himself up off the floor and took a fighting stance. "Is that the best you've got?"

Again, fury filled Bai's eyes, "You sonofabitch, I'll kill—"

Randall didn't let him finish his sentence, landing a jab and a right cross to Bai's chin, causing him to stagger backwards.

Bai wiped the blood from his lip and stared through Randall. "You're a dead man."

He took a fighting stance, and the men circled each other in the large elevator car. Bai moved with the speed of a panther, landing a combination to Randall's head before sweeping his feet with leg. Randall went down hard, bouncing off the floor of the moving elevator.

"Get up!" Bai raged. The elevator came to a stop, and the doors opened. Bai pushed the closed button. "You're not getting off this elevator alive."

Randall rolled on the ground, grunting in pain, partially real but also trying to lure Bai in for an attack. He bit, kicking Randall with his booted foot. The surprise in his eyes was real as Randall grabbed his leg and rolled onto it, pulling Bai to the floor of the car. He landed a couple of quick elbow strikes to Bai's head, clearly shaking the younger man. The two men grappled on the floor, punching and kicking at each other. Bai jammed Randall against the side, repeatedly punching first his face and then his stomach. Randall's ribs ached with pain at the beating. Bai rose to his feet, towering over Randall, clearly thinking the fight was nearly over.

Randall lunged directly at Bai, catching him off guard. He used the larger man's size against him, striking low and catching him under the chin and driving him backwards. Bai's head struck the closed front door of the elevator car hard, denting the metal with the force of the impact. He fell to the ground unconscious.

Randall steadied himself, then opened the elevator door and dragged Bai out. As he did, an explosion rose from above, shaking the suspended ceiling lights above and jarring the entire structure. Randall had to brace himself to keep from falling. He had to move quickly, hoping Mercer had been able to get to the safety of the cabinet.

Randall dragged Bai to the cell where they had been held earlier and locked him inside. He needed to keep the soldier safe so that he could prove Aminov was behind the faked Chinese attack.

He walked back to the elevator and grabbed Bai's gun, placing it in the waistband of his pants. He then realized there was no way of knowing if it had been damaged. It was entirely possible that he could end up trapped inside it or worse, the cable may have sustained enough damage that it could collapse, taking the car and him with it on a one-way trip to certain death. He'd need to find another way up to the command center. He began checking every door in the hallway until he reached the end and found a stairwell. He entered and started on his way down. It didn't take him long to get to the command center level.

Knowing a fire could be raging he pressed his hand against the door to feel for heat. It was cool to the touch. He pushed on the door and it opened slightly before jamming. The explosion must have knocked debris behind the door that was now blocking it. Randall leaned into the door with all of his weight and pushed. It slowly began to move before finally opening with great resistance. With just enough room to move through the door, Randall squeezed through and was shocked by the sight before him.

The part of the command center behind the device pedestal, while severely charred and damaged, was mostly intact. The rest of the center was vaporized, a ring carved deep into the earth with its edge starting at the pedestal. An observer not knowing what had happened would have thought a large boring device had carved out the ring. The device had also vanished, taking with it Aminov's arms up to his elbows. A still smoldering husk of his body the only thing remaining.

President Mercer!

Randall stepped over charred and twisted debris and made his way to the cabinet. Discovering the doors ajar, he pushed them aside and found the cabinet empty. The ceiling above began to moan and creak under the load of supporting the structure over the huge cavity hollowed out by the device.

Based on the lack of any other bodies on the level, it was unlikely that the President had survived. Randall felt a pang of guilt at being unable to save Mercer, but as the structure above his head continued to creak, he now had another choice to make. Would he go down a level and save Bai, risking his own life to a potential collapse? He had no choice. He needed Bai to prove that Aminov was responsible for the attack on the Indian army. Besides, he couldn't leave him to die. Randall would bring him back and have him stand trial for his crimes.

Randall made his way back to the stairs, hustling up to the cell block level. He quickly traversed the hallway and arrived at the door. Before opening it, he checked the gun magazine and opened the action to make sure a round was chambered. He wanted to avoid any surprises should Bai choose to challenge him. Opening the lock, he pushed the door open with this foot, holding the gun in front of him.

Bai was seated on the cot, rubbing the back of his head. Upon seeing Randall, he stood and took a step towards the door. Randall wasted no time, cocking the hammer. His expression conveyed his seriousness.

Bai froze in place, the realization that Randall wasn't just a professor finally settling upon him. "What happens next?"

"Depends on how well you behave," Randall replied.

The facility settled again, the structure straining to fight against the force of gravity. As it did, Bai's eyes went wide and darted around.

"Walk to the door slowly, fingers interlaced behind your head," Randall ordered.

Bai begrudgingly complied. His eyes belying his feelings at being bested. He slowly made his way to the door, while Randall held it open. As he got within several feet, Randall ordered him to turn around and face the inside of the cell.

"Now back up slowly," Randall instructed.

Bai complied, and both men were soon out of the cell.

"You first," Randall said as Bai walked down the hallway towards the stairs and reached the door.

"I can't really open the door with my hands like this," Bai complained.

"Slowly move one hand down and turn the knob, then push and hold it open with your boot. Then interlace your fingers again," Randall instructed, clearly demonstrating he knew what he was doing.

Once again Bai did as told, standing in the doorway, holding the door open. Randall followed him closely, the gun pointed at his back. "Walk"

The two made it half way up the staircase when the building shifted. Bits of concrete and paint fell like a dusting of snow. Bai glanced back for a moment and tensed.

"Don't even think about it," Randall warned.

They continued climbing the stairs, reaching the next level where they would exit. They were several steps from the top when the building shifted more severely this time. Randall lost his balance for a moment, having to grab at the railing with both hands, losing cover on Bai. It was all he needed. Bai covered the two steps between them in an instant, knocking Randall down the flight of stairs. Randall tumbled down a dozen stairs, finally coming to a stop on a landing, face up.

"So long old man!" Bai yelled from the top of the stairs, making his way out the doors.

Randall's body ached, but he still held his gun. He

moved each limb carefully, finally determining that nothing was broken. He rolled onto his stomach and pushed himself up. His head hurt like hell and he had to steady himself by placing a hand on the wall. The building shifted again, this time, the far wall settled a couple of inches lower. It was the side over the hollowed out opening carved by the device. The building could collapse at any time. This was no longer about proving Aminov was responsible for the attack in India, it was simply survival.

Randall grabbed the handrail and pulled himself up the stairs, one step at a time, finally making it back up to the door and walked through. He was now in the underground level where Vazquez was murdered. He crossed the floor, and the building settled again, sloping away from the last staircase he had to climb to reach ground level. The ground beneath him moaned from the strain. He had to hurry.

He made the staircase and started to climb, finally reaching the trapdoor that would take him to ground level. He grabbed the handle and pushed, but it was locked. He leaned into it but it wouldn't budge.

Bai.

The bastard had locked it, knowing Randall would be trailing by several minutes and it was the only way out. He had saved Bai, just to have him block his only way out of this deathtrap. He shot out the locking mechanism, then rammed the door with his shoulder, doing nothing more than injuring himself. He pounded on the door and yelled. No response. He'd be dead soon.

He started down the stairs, frantic to find a way out, when the trap door opened and a solider, clad in black came down several steps, assault rifle in hand.

Somehow things had now gotten worse. Randall scrambled back the way he came.

"Professor Nick Randall?" the soldier called, crouched on the steps, his gun at the ready.

Randall stopped. "Yes, that's me."

"Frank Rice, I'm with the FBI HURT Team We'd better get you out of here before this place collapses," the soldier said, shouldering his weapon.

Thank God.

Randall climbed the stairs, following Rice out of the lower level, into the hallway and then sprinted out of the building back into the daylight. There he found Mercer, several additional members of the HURT Team and Colonel Bai, lying face down on the ground, his hands zip tied behind him.

Mercer jogged to his side. "Good to see you Nick. I thought we'd lost you."

"Glad you stuck around," Randall replied, shaking his hand. The sound of a helicopter rose from the distance and he watched it land in the open space adjacent to the building.

"Let's go home," Mercer said.

Randall couldn't agree more.

Chapter Fifty

USS Lake Champlain, Arabian Sea

May 17, 5:42 a.m.

The group sat in the Sikorsky Seahawk, heading for the USS Lake Champlain. Although the HURT Team had notified the ship's commander that Mercer had been rescued, he had communicated back to Mercer that they were unable to reach Vice President Sanders and the situation had grown worse. Sanders had relieved Murphy of his duty after he refused to produce the plans for an attack against the Russians. He had replaced him with a more aggressive officer, General Michael Morningside, a man that many said suffered from a Napoleonic complex who had repeatedly taken a harder line against Russia. A political animal much more than a soldier, he had a reputation for rising through the ranks by means of deception and alignment with politicians who would exchange promotions for political favors. He was more than happy to order the deployment of an armored brigade to the border of the Crimean Peninsula to send a message to the Russians.

Worse, the Indian Government had reportedly moved missile batteries into place, near the disputed border with China and was sailing the INS Vikramaditya, a modified Kiev-class aircraft carrier and the flagship of the Indian Navy, towards the Spratly Islands. A disputed archipelago in the South China Sea composed of islands lying off the coasts of the Philippines, Malaysia, and southern Vietnam, India's actions were seen as little more than an attempt at retribution to the People's Liberation Army and to let them know that India would not be intimidated by China's military might.

If calmer heads didn't prevail, the possibility of an all-out war in Europe and Asia was very likely. Despite Aminov's death, his plan was coming to fruition. Mercer was furious at the lack of response from the White House, but until they reached the Champlain and he was able to contact the Pentagon and Congress from a secure line, he was powerless to stop the madness. After an interminable hour in flight, the Seahawk finally landed on the deck of the Champlain. Mercer, eschewing safety and the normal décor of a President, was the first person off the helicopter and made a beeline for the bridge. Randall, having just saved his life, was allowed to accompany Mercer.

"Mr. President," Captain Steven M. Foley said, saluting the Commander-in-Chief. "We have a secure satellite line ready for you."

Mercer saluted back. "Thank you, please take me there immediately."

Foley ended his salute and led Mercer to the Combat Information Center (CIC) the nerve center of the Champlain. Randall followed closely behind. "Sir, you'll have to wait here," Foley said to Randall.

"He's with me Captain," Mercer said.

"Yes sir Mr. President," Foley replied, and, to his credit didn't seem to take issue with a civilian joining the President in a secure communications environment.

Arriving in the CIC, Mercer and Randall found the communications officer waiting. "Mr. President, who would like us to contact?"

"Put me in touch with the White House immediately," Mercer ordered.

The communications officer went to work and sheepishly reported that the White House would not allow the call to go through, claiming Sanders was in the Situation Room and could not be disturbed.

Mercer was furious. "That power hungry bastard. Put me through to FBI Director Friedman."

All Randall could do was sit and listen and hope that Mercer could stop this madness.

Unlike the White House, Friedman picked up immediately. "Mr. President, I'm relieved to hear you're safe."

"Thank you, David. I appreciate you sending your team in. I realize that you were placing your career in jeopardy, and won't forget this," Mercer replied.

"Yes sir. What can I do for you now?" Friedman asked.

"Are you with Sanders in the Situation Room?"

"Negative Mr. President. Vice President Sanders has things locked down tightly and wouldn't allow me to attend," Friedman explained.

"I need you to contact Chief of Staff Nate Jarrett and

The Washington Prophecy

have him notify the Cabinet that I'm safe and that, on my authority, all further military action against Russia is to cease. I'm revoking the temporary transfer of power to Vice President Sanders and I want a link established to the Situation Room and my Secret Service detail reinstated. Can you do that David?" Mercer asked.

"Yes sir, I'll get to work on it right away," Friedman.

"Have Nate contact me A.S.A.P." Mercer ordered.

"Will do Mr. President. I'm glad you're safe," Friedman said.

"Thanks David," Mercer hung up the line.

"How long do think it will take your Chief of Staff to carry out your orders?" Randall asked.

"Not long and once I get ahold of Sanders, he's going to wish he was never granted authority," Mercer said through gritted teeth.

Randall was glad he wasn't in the President's crosshairs but Sanders had earned the wrath. As if answering the question he had just posed to Mercer, the phone rang.

"Yes, I'll put you through," the communications officer said. "Mr. President, it's for you." He handed the phone to Mercer.

"Nate, did David give you my instructions?" Mercer asked? "Good. Am I patched through to the Situation Room? This is President Mercer, I'm ordering a halt to all military actions against Russia and the reinstatement of General Murphy as JSOC Commander. Is that understood? Good. Vice President Sanders, I'm removing your temporary authority under the Twenty-fifth amendment. I'll need Airforce One and Secret Service dispatched to Ramstein Air Base immediately," Mercer said.

Randall couldn't hear the conversation on the other end

of the line, but it was clear from watching Mercer that the man was a true leader. Though he never raised his voice, it was understood that he was the Commander-in-Chief and knew what he was doing. Randall could practically hear the relief from the others in the Situation Room at not having to move forward with plans to attack Russia. Finally, some sanity had been restored.

"I'll also need Ambassador Khatri to contact me immediately. We need to request a meeting with President Laghari and Prime Minister Bakshi to explain that the Chinese were not behind the attack on Indian troops in the Galwan Valley," Mercer said, pausing to hear a response from his team. "I understand they're meeting with their Cabinet discussing military action against China. That's the whole point. I need to be there to present what we've discovered to explain they could be initiating war based on a false premise."

Randall could hear a commotion on the other end of the line, but couldn't hear what was actually being said. Mercer would soon answer the question.

"That's right, I plan to go to India to address the President, Prime Minister and Cabinet directly. This situation demands my direct involvement. I don't care about what I've been through, this is my job and I plan to do it!" Mercer was leaving no doubt about what would be done and who would be doing it. As he spoke, a seaman brought him a fresh change of clothes, setting it on the chair next to him. Mercer nodded in thanks.

The rest of the conversation was short and Mercer soon hung up the phone.

"Sounds like you're planning a trip Mr. President. It also sounds like the Joint Chiefs aren't too happy with your decision," Randall mused.

"Sometimes being the boss means having to do something unpopular," Mercer grabbed the change of clothes. "Excuse me," Mercer left for a private stateroom to change and Randall decided it was time to get some rest. While his adventure was over, President Mercer still had work to do.

Chapter Fifty-One

Pentagon, Washington D. C.

May 18, 7:36 a.m.

After arriving at Ramstein Airbase with the President, Mercer thanked Randall a final time for all he had done, extending an invitation to dinner at the White House once things had calmed down. The two men had shaken hands and Mercer, Secret Service entourage in tow, was whisked away to Air Force One. Randall had one final satisfying view of Colonel Bai marched in leg and arm irons, to a second Air Force jet for the trip to India to face the music. The size of the contingency charged with watching over the disgraced henchman ensured that no funny business would transpire.

For his part, Randall was happy to be heading back home and slept for the entire flight. He was awakened by an aircrewman who announced they would be touching down at Andrews Air Force base shortly. Randall rubbed the sleep from his eyes, a bit disoriented by the long, deep sleep he had experienced following his ordeal in Pakistan. He emerged from the plane to the bright sun, having to squint to see where he was going since he had no sunglasses. He walked onto the tarmac and was greeted by two familiar faces.

"It's good to see you dad. I was worried we had lost you for a while," John hugged his father hard before releasing him.

"Is this typical Yankee academic behavior?" Liz said smiling. "If it is, I'll happily return to my safe little school across the pond." She too hugged Randall, deep and long.

"I can't tell you both how happy I am to be home," Randall said.

The three walked astride and into a waiting Chevy Suburban that took them on the now familiar trip to the Pentagon where they were waved through the security checkpoint. Flores was clearly waiting to debrief his occasional field agent. A few minutes later, they were walking down the corridor to Flores' conference room.

"If you'll both excuse me, I need to use the restroom. I'll be back in a minute," John said, veering off down a different corridor.

It seemed odd to Randall that his son was now so familiar with this section of the Pentagon. He had clearly been spending too much time here. Liz grabbed his hand and walked closer as they entered the conference room. They took a seat next to each other, alone for the moment.

"I was very worried about you Nick. I thought I had lost you," Liz said, looking directly into Randall's eyes, her look conveying her concern.

"I'm sorry about that. I don't think anyone expected things to go the way they did," Randall said.

Liz squeezed his hand harder. "You mean a lot to me and I've found myself having deeper feelings for you."

Randall felt a pang of guilt. He had sensed it too and cared about Liz in a way that he hadn't felt since his wife Anne had passed away. Unfortunately, he wasn't sure if he was ready to take the next step. He squeezed Liz's hand back. "Liz, you're a very special person and I've come to have feelings about you too, but I'm just not sure I'm ready to move on from Anne. I know it probably seems silly after all these years, and I certainly have strong feelings for you, but I just can't let go. At least not yet."

Liz looked deeply into Randall's eyes, not speaking for a moment, still holding his hands. Her lips flickered a bit, but she still smiled. "It's not silly at all. Your loyalty is one of things I like most about you. I can see it from the way you act with John. You're a very caring man." Liz sighed. "I guess our timing just isn't right."

Before Randall could respond, Flores walked in the room and took a seat opposite Liz and Randall. "I hope I'm not interrupting anything."

"I'm just telling Nick how glad I am that he made it back," Liz beamed, squeezing Randall's hand again before releasing. "I don't think I've ever experienced anything like that before."

"To be honest, neither have I," Flores replied. "You certainly had us worried Nick."

Randall shifted gears, still wanting to share more with Liz, but realizing the moment had passed. "I'm just sorry that none of the others made it. You should be proud of your men. They did their best to protect me and I wouldn't be here today if not for their sacrifices."

"Each man will receive honors and each of their families will be taken care of. It's always the worst part of these missions," Flores said.

John entered the room and took a seat next to Flores. "What did I miss?"

"We were just telling your dad how grateful we are for his service and how worried we were," Liz replied.

"That's for sure. Please don't do anything like that again," John said, shooting his dad a look, followed by a tired smile.

"I'll do my best," Randall replied. "Was President Mercer able to convince the Indian government that the Chinese weren't responsible for the attack on their troops?"

"I'm happy to report that he was. Both countries have agreed to reestablish diplomatic ties and reopen embassies in each other's countries. Fortunately, your efforts to save Colonel Bai paid off. His presence with the President, along with drone footage convinced the Indians and helped the Chinese to understand why the Indian government reacted the way they did. If you hadn't saved him, there's no telling how things would have played out," Flores said, nodding his head for effect.

"Looks like you prevented a war dad," John said proudly.

"Don't let it go to your head Yank," Liz joked, grabbing Randall's arm.

Everyone laughed, the sense of relief overwhelming.

"Liz, do you plan to stay on in your teaching post?" Flores asked.

She nodded. "My assignment runs through December and I must say, I'll certainly have a different outlook on things now."

"You realize that you cannot share anything about what happened here," Flores said, his tone turning serious.

"Of course, James," Liz replied.

Flores smile returned. "I must thank all of you for your help. You all risked your lives and our country owes you all our gratitude."

"Happy to help," John said, sharing a sympathy shared by all three.

"I guess it's time to call it a day then. I'm ready for a light dinner and bed," Liz smiled.

"Agreed," John said.

"I'll arrange for transportation for all of you," Flores said.

All three got up to leave.

"Nick, would you mind sticking around for a moment?" Flores asked.

Randall furrowed his brow. "I'll catch up with you two in a minute."

"Ok dad," John looked from his dad then to Flores. He looked like he was going to say something but turned to walk out with Liz.

Randall lowered himself back into his seat. "Is there something I can help you with?"

"Nick, we've known each other for three years now and you've helped us through some difficult situations. I wish I could say those were the only operations I've overseen during that time but they're not," Flores said. "President Mercer and I have spoken about this and I'd like you to consider formally joining my department. We need your expertise on a daily basis and not solely in a field capacity. To put it bluntly, we're fighting a daily battle and losing."

Randall nodded for Flores to continue.

"You've been introduced to only a small part of my

command. There's a great deal more we're doing for the country."

"What exactly is under your direction?" Randall asked.

"I oversee the Department of Anomalous Phenomenon Response, DAPR for short. My agency is charged with rapid response to uncommon events worldwide and it's my team's job to contain any situation that arises to prevent the loss of life. We're also the lead agency when a previously unknown phenomenon is discovered and are tasked with conducting research to determine the best path forward. We have access to cutting edge technology and weapons systems developed by the brightest minds in the world," Flores responded.

"And how do you see me fitting into the picture? To be honest, I'm not sure I'm cut out for any more experiences like the one I just survived," Randall said.

"I appreciate your honesty Nick, but you have a unique skill-set. You're not only a top academic researcher, you have military training that's come in handy. You're also open to concepts that, quite frankly, most scientists aren't willing to accept."

"I've heard that before," Randall smiled. "But I'm not sure I'm your man."

Flores opened a drawer in front of him and took out a small locked briefcase and set it on the desk in front of him. He slid the briefcase to Randall who eyed it suspiciously.

"What's in that?" Randall asked.

"Something for you to ponder when you're ready. You've been through a lot Nick and you've served your country well. I don't have the right to ask more of you, but I am anyway. But for now, I know John and Liz are waiting for you. If you have an interest, call my department and we'll give you the code. Open that, check it out and get back to me," Flores said.

"I can do that James."

"Good!" Flores rose to his feet. "Thanks for all you've done Nick." He extended his hand and the two men shook. "I'll walk you out to your ride."

The two men walked down through the hallway without saying a word, finally arriving at a door guarded by two armed soldiers. John and Liz were standing outside chatting.

"Take care Nick and I look forward to hearing back from you," Flores said.

"You too James," one of the soldiers held the door open for Randall who stepped out into bright sunshine.

"So glad you could join us," Liz commented, smiling.

"The pleasure is mine," Randall replied.

"What's that?" John asked.

"To be honest, I'm not sure. James asked me to take a look and give him a call afterwards," Randall said.

The three entered the black Suburban and Randall set the briefcase down on the seat next to him.

"Sounds mysterious," Liz offered.

"I hope it's not another situation like the one we just finished," John observed soberly.

"It's not," Randall lied. "He just wants my opinion on something."

The Suburban drove down the winding entryway of the Pentagon, and for the moment, Randall was satisfied to simply be home.

More by Robert Rapoza

  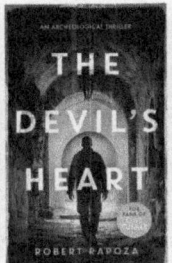 

vinci-books.com/nickrandallseries

Follow the link to stay up to date with Robert Rapoza's new releases

About the Author

Robert Rapoza is the award-winning author of *The Lost Tribe*, *The Bermuda Connection*, and *The Devil's Heart*. His action-packed thrillers have been described as a cross between the works of Dan Brown and Indiana Jones, keeping readers riveted from beginning to end. Tommy Howell from *Readers' Favorite* calls protagonist Nick Randall "A statesman and action hero worthy of Pierce Brosnan or Liam Neeson." A member of the Southern California Writers Association, Robert Rapoza resides in the Los Angeles area.